UNPROTECTED

Sophie Jonas-Hill

ISBN paperback: 978-1-9160693-0-5
ISBN eBook: 978-1-9160693-1-2

Retreat West Books
retreatwestbooks.com

For all those who have suffered loss and miscarriage,
and keep on fighting

CONTENTS

CHAPTER ONE

It's not you

MY GLASS EXPLODES against the wall. Max ducks, though I don't throw it anywhere near him, the *nice* drink he made me before we had a *nice* chat about everything. 'Don't I deserve a better line than that?'

'But it's really not you, it really is me, it's—'

'For fuck's sake Max!'

Please, babes, it's not like that, it's just...us, you know, us—'

'Oh, so it's us? It's not me, then, it's us? Because that's so much better.' Thanks Max, thanks for that. My laugh is glass sharp inside me, brutal, it hurts all the way down.

He's keeping his distance, all hunched up, hands out. A lion taming stance.

'Look, babe, I just can't see you go through it again, and I know you want to. I know you will, and I just can't—'

'But that's it, Max, innit? You don't have to, do you? I'll do it, I'll do all of it, you know, just like when we redecorated?' Ouch, low blow—it's not like I let him do any decorating, do I?

'Don't. Don't do that, don't try and make it be funny.'

'Laugh or cry, Max, laugh or cry.'

And I'm so sick of crying, so maybe let's give laughing a go instead? Ha ha, Max, ha ha—why are you doing this to me now? Is it some kind of joke, Max? Are you kidding me?

The drink on the wall has made a huge, dark, satisfying splat. A blood splatter splat. There's glass on the floor, a huge shard sticking up against the skirting. *You're so sharp, girl, you'll cut yourself one day.* I really want to pick it up and wrap it in paper, make it safe. But I don't.

'You're so strong,' Max stays. So much stronger than I am, so much more.'

I'm not strong. I'm the glass on the floor, all smashed up.

'You're so much stronger than I am,' he says again, as if saying it twice will make it real, will mean what he's doing is okay. 'And I know you'd do it all again in a heartbeat, I know you'd put yourself through it all again—'

'Yes, I would, and that's my choice, Max, my bloody choice—don't tell me what you think I can do.' Oh shit, and that comes out all jagged sounding, like I'm swallowing a sob, which I am. 'Don't tell me what I can do.

Because I *know* what I can do, right?

'But I can't, don't you see? I just can't watch you go through it again, it's not fair on you, you know it isn't, and you won't stop if I'm here—'

'So, you're fucking off and leaving me? Jesus, Max, I might not even get pregnant again.' Yeah, because that would be a whole lot better. Weeks and weeks of it, of taking my temperature and pissing on sticks and joyless sex. Just what we need.

'That's the point though,' Max says, reading my mind.

Who could stand it, really? Months of me wanting to be pregnant again, and him wanting me to be pregnant again, and then me being pregnant again, and then? Stop making sense please, Max.

'I just need some time out, you know?' He's not looking at me. Big old rockabilly Max, is looking at his feet, picking at the seam on his jeans. 'I know what you want, but I … I don't think, I don't …'

I'm going to agree with him in a second, I'm going to see his point of view, in case that might work for now, give me time, a chance to change his mind again later, but then he starts using words that aren't his, words like "perspective" and "contemplation" and "taking time to reconnect" and I hear the words and stop listening to how he's stringing them together, because there's something else going on here, I can feel it. Which is good, because that means maybe this isn't all his own idea.

'Who you've been talking to?' I ask.

'What?'

'Who have you been talking to, Max? Come on, you don't use words like closure, unless you're talking about a door.'

'Christ, you don't think there's someone else, do—'

'No, I don't.'

Of course I don't, not that. You can lay plenty at Max's door but he's not cheating on me. Not like that, anyway. Not the usual, quick fuck long lie kind of a way, anyway. Maybe worse than that. Should have seen it coming. There were signs. The text messages, his phone set to silent but him unable to resist having a look, not able to leave it long enough for me to be out of the room. Then, 'Want something from the shop?'

He's got friends, Max. Female friends; the sort who've known him for years, the tomboy sort who've always had him on their reserve bench. Lovely Max who's always there when they've been dumped, when they need to talk, when they need a boyfriend without all the hassle and shit that goes with it. Their big brother, their best friend, their "Oh, you know, Max and me go back ages. We always used to do that thing, you know, the thing you do with friends? That if we're both still single when we're old, I dunno, forty, we'll get married and, like, adopt fifty kids!"

Only then I'd come along, and it was all, "It's so great

to meet you. Max has told me so much about you." Me, spiky, rubber-faced. Older than him. Not by much, not enough to matter, but enough for them to mention it all the time. "Are you really? God, you don't look it, you'd never know. You look amazing. Really." And then they'd tell me about his last girlfriend, or the one before that, who they really liked, and ask if I know her.

He's been talking to one of them, because these are their words. Or his sisters' words, who treat him just the same. Dear old Max, always there to move stuff, to punch cheating husbands—yes, that's right—Max hates cheaters, see, so I know he's not doing that. Always there to take the kids out because he's so good with them, and they need a good man in their lives, a good man like Max.

'It's not like that,' he says. He's standing there, waiting to see if I believe him. I imagine what they've said to him, all the friends and the sisters—imagine them saying how, really, he's being the good guy, doing the right thing. And of course, he doesn't want to do it, of course it's really hard, but then doing the right thing is hard. The easy thing would be to stay, but that would be "enabling"—yes, he's just used that word now too, and I imagine they used it when he'd said something like, *"I just can't talk to her about it, y'know? Not anymore. She's in so much pain, and I just don't know what to say to make it better."*

Then they'd have been, *"But you can't make it better*

Max, love/pet/sweetheart (delete as appropriate) that's it, right? The two of you have been through so much over the last three years, it's not surprising you can't think straight anymore. I mean, don't get me wrong, she's a lovely girl, she's brilliant, you know I think the world of her, but she needs help, really she does, and you're just too close to help anymore, you know?" Or some shit like that.

I watch the words coming out of his mouth, then I watch him stop saying them.

'Well. You've got to do what you think's for the best then, haven't you?' I say. Lovely Max, my big, soft man, with his great big arms and his sweet, stupid, lovely face. 'Go on then, fuck off.'

Because if he's going to do this to me, I'm going to pretend like I'm the one pushing him away. I deserve some dignity, I deserve the last fucking line.

Ha-ha, Max, Ha ha.

I'm so sharp, I'm going to cut myself.

HE GOES INTO the bedroom. My bedroom now I suppose. I sit on the sofa. My sofa. I hear him move about, taking down the holdall from the top of wardrobe. He goes into the bathroom, gets his toothbrush. I should be crying. But all the tears I might have used for Max leaving me, have already been wrung out, squeezed out, by the last three years of being pregnant, then not. I was so sure that we were forever, I've cried it all out with him over what we've lost because I thought I'd never have to cry about losing him.

I look sideways at the window and see my reflection. Sitting on the sofa, alone. My face all hard and bony, white and stretched tight, as if my thoughts are shrinking down to nothing so fast they're pulling on my skin. Knees up, forearms on knees, hands balled into fists. I look down at the intricate patterns tattooed on the backs of my hands, and it's as if they're crawling, moving. My skin itching with them.

He's taking his time. Maybe he's having second thoughts?

No, don't think that—look at your reflection, focus on that. I look down at the street, at the yellow glow of the taxi rank just up from the flat. There's a figure coming down towards it, their shadow thrown long behind them and so I make myself focus on them. I'm almost surprised when I recognise them, not someone I know but someone I've seen around—a girl, all mouth and trousers, as Max would say, as Max did say about her. He'll bump into her again, if he leaves now; I focus back on him. He's still in the bedroom, getting his stuff. He's taking ages, and the girl's gone now, into the taxi office.

Maybe he hadn't planned all this for today, maybe he just blurted it out, so that's why he's not packed or anything? Maybe there isn't anyone behind all this, but him, then? I go to the window, watch as the city becomes all night sky. I want the wings on my back to unfurl, want them to be real, to rip free from under my skin and stretch out, bloodied and newborn; want my toes to be claws. I am a thing of feathers and knives, with hunched wings on my back and Max is the prince in a fairy story, tricked into being with me, and now the scales have fallen from his eyes. That's how he looks at me anyway, when he comes back into the room, bag packed, jacket on; as if he can't quite believe he'd ever fallen for the lie of me in the first place and is sorry about it. Not for himself but me; sorry for me, sorry that I'd had to pretend all this time not to be made of feathers and knives, but be an actual woman, which of course I'm not.

Because a real woman, would be able to have a baby, wouldn't she?

'Where are you going?'

'Matt and Steve's. They've got a spare room.'

'Well that's good then, isn't it?'

He puts the bag down, shuffles his feet, comes over. I really want not to cry. I want to be as cold and hard and unbreakable as granite. But I'm holding him and he's holding me, and I'm crying like I want him to be sorry for me, trying to make him change his mind.

'Shit, babe, are you gonna be alright? Oh, shit, babe, please, don't—' Max hates crying women. That's what makes him such a good friend, such a good man, such a good big brother; because he'd do anything in the world to make you better, to fix you, so you won't cry. But he can't, can he, Max? He can't fix me. And that's it, really. That's why he's going. I'm unfixable.

The flat rattles from his great big feet as he goes down the stairs. The holdall scrapes on the wall, then the street door rattles. I pick up my phone, there's a missed called from my sister—wow, great timing Lauren—sniff, try to get control of myself, and when I can't, scroll and stab my finger on Cassie's name.

'Hi,' her answer phone says. 'I'm busy having fun. Leave me a message and who knows? I might have fun with you next.'

So, now what am I meant to do?

CHAPTER TWO

Does it hurt?

I WAKE UP at five in the afternoon, because I couldn't sleep last night. The drrr, drrr of my phone on vibrate drills into my brain, and I know without looking it's Cassie, and that now, three weeks after it wasn't me but him, she's not going to give up.

'No.' I say, when I answer.

'There's no, no,' she says. 'There's you getting up, getting your arse in gear, and you coming out. Alright?'

'No.' I say again and then three more times after that. Because then that's a yes. Or so I've been led to believe.

I fall out of bed. I pee, I shower, I tell myself I'll ring her back and say no.

But I don't. I look at my face in the mirror and bare my teeth in something that could be called a smile.

In the kitchen the blind is still drawn. I stare at the inside of my fridge, bathed in its blue glow, the hum gnawing at the base of my skull. I eat cheese, then go back to the bedroom. I won't go. I'll wait until ten, or eleven, and then text and say I'm staying at home, as the last thing I need is to go and get shit-faced in a fetish club.

But I find myself inching into latex jeans, clipping on braces and buckling on my Westwood heels. I don't bother with much else, a t-shirt to cover my modesty when I'm about to leave. Keys-phone-cash, keys, phone, cash, hat. I tumble out into a cracked black, split black, yellow black night.

Round to Cassie's, rehearsing the "yeah babe, hi, babe, how's it going babes?" as I go. Building a suit of armour from them.

'Hey babe, how you doing?' Cassie asks when she opens the door.

'I'm good, you know? Good, yeah, babes.'

'No—how are you really doing, after, you know, everything?'

'No. But hey, you know?' And as Cassie knows everything, she knows that's enough for now.

'Cool babes, cool. Wanna drink?'

Fuck yeah.

And another, and another, and another.

People arrive.

'Hi babes, hi babes, how's you?'

'You know, cool,' I say, in the voice I use to lie to people I know, and people I half know, and the people they half know. The crowd, the crew, the usual suspects; all asking how I am and hoping I'm not really going to tell them. Crick, crack, crick, crack—walking on egg shells, until we all have another drink, and another—and here comes Mary-Mary, bringing all the stuff I said I wouldn't do again, chopping up in the kitchen on Cassie's barely used worktops.

'You want, babes?' Cassie's holding a rolled note over a black glass plate.

Broken glass smashes between my eyes—hard, sharp, glitter bright. I'm laughing, clutching the bridge of my nose as the insides of my eye-balls peel clean.

Option one—chemical management.

'Been an age, babes, how you doin'?'

'I'm good, you know?'

'Hell, you are now.'

Down the stairs, piling into the taxi next to that bloke who used to go out with that girl—him anyway, making a joke, telling a story.

'Heart FM, are you serious? Kiss, mate, Kiss FM.' Because I can't think of any other station, apart from Radio Four.

'How's work going?' The bloke next to me asks.

'Oh, I'm kind of, you know, taking some time out? I got some savings, so I thought I'd kick back.'

'Sure. I heard what happened, I mean with Max, I mean with—'

'Thanks, dude.'

He's looking at me like I'm something edible and he's

very hungry.

'Hey, that one, turn it up, mate, turn it up!'

'Want another little bomb?'

'Fuck, yeah.'

I KNOW THE people on the door and they know me, and we all make a point of saying hello so that everybody else knows that we know each other. They might be the nicest people in the place. I'm quite sure they're nicer than I am.

Boom! Wall of sound hits me. Wet heat and light; complicated girls held together with glitter and attitude, chewing gum skin, tight over sharp bones; stocky bald men in leather sniffing at their heels. It's gay boys and fey boys, and Jack-The-Lads, heterosexual, homosexual, bisexual, bi-curious or just plain confused; transexual, asexual, animal, vegetable or fucking mineral—take your pick.

I'm not sure when or where, because it's a night of six hours in five minutes and five minutes in six hours, but I hear them talking about me. They're saying how they don't know what to say, don't know how Max could do it, not after *everything*. Then they notice I'm there, or I notice they're there and they're still saying they can't imagine how I do it, can't believe how strong I am.

'It is what it is,' I tell them.

In the toilet cubical I snort as much MDMA as I can, because I am not strong. I screw my eyes up tight so that none of it, not a hint of it shows. It is what it is, it is what it is, it is—

And ... breathe.

I dance and dance. Every tune they play is the best fucking tune there's ever been, or ever will be, until the next one, which is even better.

At the bar someone's forced against me in the crush, laughs, turns and makes a joke about it, the two of us shipwrecked and holding on together. The joke means he's allowed to run his index finger along the waist band of my latex jeans, and I laugh because it's funny. But I don't stay because I love this song.

'Catch you later,' he threatens, his grin the last thing of him to vanish. Oh, why, we're all mad here.

I scramble into the chill with Mary-Mary, into the smoke heavy blast of outside for the cigarette I stopped smoking years ago. I talk shit with a girl in a red corset who's doing a PHD and working as a nanny, and two jittery Italians who can't look me in the eye. Hands shake, lips chatter; my fingers rest in the satin tight curve of the girl's waist and it feels good. I kiss her, and that feels even better, but then I lose her in the smoke.

Then the pain hits me so fucking hard, that I think this time I might break in half. I close my eyes and breath in all the powder I've got left but it's not enough. It doesn't hurt enough to help.

If I own the pain, I can control the pain, if I own the

pain, I can control the pain. I need somebody to hurt me, because I'm so out of control, it's going to take everything in the world to bring me down again.

In five minutes, I've done five hours. In five minutes it's lights up, sound down, all the debris of a dark night swept into corners. It's not time yet, it can't be time yet; not with the memory of red satin under my fingertips and the pulse of the best song ever in my veins.

'Where we going?'

'You going somewhere?'

'After-party, you going after-party?'

WET BRIGHT DAWN light, street pitted and rain dripping, clustered with goodbyes. The sky is soft grey to blush, pearled with orange lights drifting to sleep against the dawn. It's so empty. Like the rain's swept everything away and softened the world to just cloud. In that moment, I'm at peace, so far away from the person I am, from the person whose fault it isn't, I'm almost back inside myself again, almost home.

Only this isn't home. This a flat somewhere that belongs to someone I know just well enough for them to give me a hug and ask how I am, though not well enough that they really care.

There's an idiot in the kitchen holding court, telling me and everyone else how it is. 'It's, like, all this shit about consent an' that?'

'Who's this wanker?' Someone sniggers in my ear, someone who's lips chatter with suppressed laughter, their fingers holding an unlit cigarette.

'I mean, this girl was saying, like, you can't sleep with a drunk woman anymore, and I'm like, dude, this is London? If I had to wait until every girl I went home with was sober, I'd, like, never sleep with anyone, am I right? I mean, there's not a sober woman in London right now, like, right now, so what the fuck you supposed to—'

'Ask her,' I tell the arsehole. 'Yeah, why don't you fucking ask first?' Heat burns through me, my finger jabbing in his face. 'And guess what, if she's too drunk to answer, then she's too fucking drunk to say yes, which is the same as saying no, right?'

'Jesus, I was only saying, it's not like—'

'Yeah, so what is it like?' I should back off, but why should I back off? They're all looking at me, these strangers in this strange kitchen, and the fire of it is searing through me. 'You look me in the fucking eye and tell me what it's like.'

And he scuttles away, because he can't.

'You go girl, fuck me. You want a cigarette?' It's the man with the chattering lips, the one who left his smile with me earlier.

Then we're together against the soft grey sky, leaning our elbows on a balcony railing, looking out over someone else's Sunday. I feel the heat of the flame as he lights the cigarette I'm not meant to be smoking, the heat in his fingers as he cups them round my face, the two of us washed up at the edge of the party together.

'Hey babe, we're gonna head. You coming?' Cassie says.

'You're not going, are you?' he asks, his grin wider than the smile of the sky above London.

'Think I'm gonna hang, you know?'

'You sure, babe?' And she holds me, Cassie, all the beauty that she is around me, and for a second she's bigger than the city, and I feel the beat of her heart in her chest, and hearing it makes me want to cry, because she's so warm and alive and real, and too good for me, too good and kind for me.

'Text me when you get in, yeah?'

The sensation of her lingers on my skin after she's gone, as if it's trying to hold onto the memory of her. As if it's trying to warn me to behave.

'You're okay, right?' he asks me.

'I'm cool.'

'Good, because there's something I wanna ask you, yeah?'

CHAPTER THREE

Not cool

WAKING UP, FOUR things hit me in quick succession.

One—despite a whole three hours of sleep, I'm still in the itchy, twitchy, half-high brain space that does not make a solid foundation for rational thought.

Two—I stink.

Three—I'm naked in bed with the boy from the after-party. Shit, shit, shit! I am naked, in bed, with the boy from the after-party!

And four, which is the one that prompts me into action, it's coming up to eleven o'clock, which means the radio beside my bed is about to click into life, and as it's Sunday, that means *The Archers* omnibus. And boy, that really ain't cool, now is it? Not when you're trying to pretend like you're not a middle class, forty-two-year-old, white woman.

There's the click, then the discrete digital hum of twenty-first century technology warming up. In its blue glow I make the lunge but the bloody theme tune trills out into the room.

'Shit.' And just in case the boy from the after party is not woken up yet, in trying to hit the snooze button, I slip and thump my elbow into his chest.

'Whoa!'

'Shit, sorry—'

'What're you doing?'

'The radio, it was just, the radio came on, and I was just....'

'Trying not to wake me up?'

'Yeah, something like that.'

'Thanks.' He folds his arms behind his head and grins up at me from the pillow, making himself at home, all elbows and collar bones.

Oh shit, he's here in my bed, and there aren't enough drugs in the whole world to make me even begin to pretend I don't remember what we did last night, because I do, in pinpoint, Technicolor, three-dee fucking surround sound detail. Fucking being the operative word.

He gets up out of the bed and stretches. He's stark, bollock naked. He seems even more naked than the way everyone else in the world does because there's a hell of a lot of him to be bare. I mean, I'm five-ten in my bare feet, and Max is six-two, which is tall enough, but this boy? He's got to be what... six-six, six-eight? And all six foot eight of him is standing in my bedroom stretching and being so bloody naked, I have to look away before my eyes hurt.

Nice arse, though.

'Need a slash,' he announces.

Shit. What have I done?

I know Max left me, so it should serve him bloody right, right? But that's bullshit, and I feel as guilty as hell. And to my shame, my utter chagrin, guilty though I am, the thing I'm most worried about is whether anyone saw us, and if they'll tell Max? Because I was feeling very comfortable on the moral high ground, which was cold and lonely but still the moral high ground. Now I can feel it slipping away from me.

I get up, keeping low as if I'm under observation. Consider putting last night's knickers on, like some muscle memory of past one-night stands and as if this isn't my place and they're all I've got. But I go to my underwear drawer and pull out a pair of serviceable, skin tone, boy-leg shorts.

Who is he, anyway? I can't even remember his bloody name, and I can't remember who he knows. Was he at the club, was that it? The after party? Who's after party was it anyway? That friend of Cassie's lovely boyfriend? Who's always her "lovely" boyfriend because he's just so bloody lovely and nice, just like I thought Max was, before he fucked off. Anyway, it was his friend's flat, that friend who does something in film. Is that who the boy knows?

Or is he that friend of Mary-Mary's? Must stop calling her that because that's Cassie and mine's nickname for her, because she's a bit, you know, contrary—says black's white just because. Not her friend but her flat mate's friend, her flat mate who's younger and we're sure Mary Mary sleeps with from time to time, but when Mary Mary lets her off the leash, she goes off with a guy, a tall guy— and yes, I think this is him. Yes, this boy is Mary-Mary's part-time lesbian lover's part-time lover. So that's nice and easy, then.

I look at my pants, my serviceable skin tone briefs and go for Wonder Woman stars and stripes pants instead. Oh yes, and from what I can see/remember, he's about twenty-eight, at a pinch, at a stretch, if I'm being really generous and looking at things in the best possible light. Twenty-eight, or six or five, even, which makes him fourteen years younger than me.

Shit.

Oh, come on. I pull on a t-shirt, one of my gym ones, one of my newer, nicer gym ones with the flattering neckline. That's no age, not these days. You're still shit-hot, despite what Max might think, and anyway he didn't leave you because of that, did he? And anyway, so what? This is casual sex. A one-night stand. So it doesn't matter.

There's the sound of the flush, of water booming in the pipes, of the groan and roar as it subsides.

'Any chance of a cup of tea?'

'Only if you put some clothes on.'

He's got his trousers on by the time he comes into my kitchen and sits on one of the high stools at the breakfast bar. All long legs and naked torso, with the kind of grin that's seriously missing a floating cat behind it, sitting with one huge foot hooked over the bottom bar of the stool and half bent over the counter.

I get out two mugs and fill the gleaming retro style kettle. Since Max left, cleaning is pretty much all I've done. I've taken everything that might be considered Max's and folded and boxed and filed it away in the second bedroom, because although he might come back, I don't want to make it easy for him. I've turned out cupboards, I've bought new cushions, I've sat in the kitchen and I've cleaned my kit and my gun, as if it really was an AK-47, stripping it down and disinfecting every part of it. Even though I'm not working and am having a year out because of everything. I even contemplated adding some more work to my left thigh, but decided against—never tattoo yourself, or someone else, in anger. But all of this, even arranging the mugs in the mug cupboard, first in rainbow order, then in shape order, then alphabetically by slogan, made perfect sense. Until now, with this boy sat waiting for his cup of tea like a six-foot eight question mark.

'This yours, then?' he says.

'Yes.'

'I mean, you own it?'

'Yes, I own it.' Because I'm a grown-up, right? The kettle vibrates on its stand, the water rolling to a boil. He needs to leave, he needs to go, so that I can pretend he didn't happen. So I can clean up.

'Nice.' He cranes round again, like he's doing an inventory. 'I mean, you've made it work, you know? How long you lived here?'

'Five years or so.' I put the kettle back on its stand. 'This some kind of credit agreement or what? You want to see utility bills next?'

He grins. 'Two sugars please.'

He really needs to go.

He is cute, though. When he drinks his tea, he watches me over the rim of the mug, as if it's me he's tasting. Which, you know, feels nice, because it feels like it's been such a long time since I've been looked at that way, when someone hasn't been looking at me to gauge when I'm going to bite their head off.

'Look, you've probably got a busy day ahead grinding bones to make your bread or whatever.' I say.

'Nice!' He gets out a cigarette, holds it between his fingers and points at me with it. 'That's a giant reference, right? Not bad, thought I'd heard them all.'

I can't help the smile, can't help feeling pleased he got the joke.

'People usually go with, "You're tall", like I hadn't noticed.' He laughs.

It's like a cross between Sid James and Kenneth Williams, like a music hall clown—waugh, waugh, waugh, waugh. He laughs like a seventies sex comedy, like confessions of a—'You're not a window cleaner, are you?'

'Oh,' he frowns. 'Because I wouldn't need my own ladder? Not so original.'

'What do you expect, it's bloody early?'

We both look at the kitchen clock, we both see that it's not that early. That's right, I was trying to encourage him to go, wasn't I?

'Well, okay, so it's late, so—'

'What do you get, then?'

I pause, lean my back against the edge of the counter. 'What do I get?'

He runs his tongue over his teeth. 'I'm guessing you get ... are they real, did they hurt and ... what about when you're older. In that order.'

My tattoos, of course.

'You don't have any, do you?'

He holds his hands out to his sides, pulls his shoulders back. He's against the light, back to the kitchen window. 'Blank canvas,' he says.

I put my mug down. 'Right,' I say.

So he's one of them. Needle whores, Big Al calls them; told me about them when I first started working for him, when he trained me in the art of skin ink and tea with three sugars. Tattoo groupies hoping for a freebie.

Oh dear, I have been a complete twat, haven't I? There's me thinking this was a guilt-ridden slice of revenge sex, and it's even worse. I've been a big enough idiot to be taken in by a needle whore, some idiot who thinks he's in line for a cut price tribal arm band, or some shit like that, some shit I don't even do. Well thanks a lot, Max, you've successfully kicked me hard enough in the emotional bollocks, for me not to even see this one coming, to not even—

'Don't want one, anyway.' He eases a lighter out of his jeans pocket. 'Not my style, besides, scared of the pain.'

'Great big thing like you?' I say.

'Serious, don't do needles. Like yours though, like books, innit? Give you something to read while you're—' Lighter in one hand, he throws his cigarette into his mouth and mimes taking me from behind, breaking off in mid thrust to read, tracing something with his finger, then considering it in the manner of a sage, finger to chin, nodding.

I laugh, when I realise what he's doing, because it's so childish, and yet endearing, somehow. I'm laughing at myself, because there I was, getting all self-righteous, thinking he was just using me for my needle, when all along he was just using me for sex. Ah, bless, a simple creature after all. I really must learn not to be so suspicious.

'Look, I think you better go, though,' I say. Hurt pride aside he did make me laugh, and that's kind of why he needs to go. I feel worse about the laughing than the sex. Max always used to make me laugh, even during the worst of it, well, not the worst of it maybe, but he always used to make me laugh when I was being a bitch, being up myself, when I was quite determined I wouldn't let him. And laughing like that with this boy, as he says, 'Go on, admit it, made you smile, didn't I? Cheeky fucker, aren't I?' Then lights his cigarette without asking me if it's okay. Fucking him is one thing, one I might be able to forgive myself for, brush under the carpet when—if— Max comes back, but laughing with him? That's bad.

I lean back against the counter again, the mug I've filled and emptied a second time held against my chest for want of a shield.

'It's just I'm really blasted, you know, from last night?'

The boy picks up his lighter from the counter.

'I mean, I've kind of, well.' I exhale, feel my fringe flutter against my forehead. 'I've kind of been dealing with some shit, and, well, I know that's … I mean that's nothing to do with anything, really but…'

He gets up, nodding, looking as if he understands, as if he was just going to say the same thing. He sniffs, wipes his hand under his nose. 'It's late,' he says.

'Yes, and—'

'You've been through some stuff.'

'Yes, and—' He's surprisingly close to me now, in a lean, firm-bodied, dusky-skinned kind of a way.

'So I better go,' he says. Then he takes the mug out of my hand and puts it on the counter.

Oh shit, I really hope he is twenty-eight.

IT'S DARK WHEN he finally leaves. He doesn't ask for my number, I don't offer it or ask for his. I even tell myself that's the way I want it, and I'm quite convincing. It's for the best, of course it is, like I said, the sex is one thing, but the laughing. The lying on the bed afterwards and just enjoying him being there, that's not part of the deal, is it? I walk down the stairs to the street door with him, making sure he's actually gone, I suppose. He looks back at me once, that grin thrown over his shoulder. Christ, I hope no one sees him. This is it, though, no more of this shit. I've done the revenge night out and sex thing now.

The lights from a taxi pulling out of the rank opposite light him up like a director of photography getting one in the bag, and that's when I see her again, for the first time since the night Max left. The rude girl.

A few days before Max decided he needed closure. He'd taken us out to dinner in this place we both like, the one that looks like nothing but is all organic. We were walking back from the tube, Max's arm across my shoulders, the two of us leaning together like we were newly in love and were still behaving properly with each other. She'd come up behind us then cut in front to cross the road, so close to Max that he'd had to pull up to avoid stepping on her.

'Look out, love,' he'd said, or something like that, nothing nasty, nothing angry or rude, laughing as he said it, and let's face it, there's always something endearing about the Birmingham accent, something you can't help but love.

'Fuck you,' she'd spat. Just turned back and snapped it at him, all slicked back hair and gold hoop earrings. 'Fucking weirdos.'

'Alright love, no need for that,' Max said, taken aback by the viciousness of her tone. Because Max is always surprised at just how nasty people can be in London, even now, even after living with me.

'Leave it,' I'd said as she flipped us the finger, turning back half-way across the street to do it, the taxi headlights lighting her up the way they do the boy now.

How old is she, for Christ' sake? She can't be more than fourteen. Skipping across the road outside my flat, hoodie up and arms folded across her chest. Where does she get so many taxis to?

Then all I think about is throwing myself into bed and sleeping for as long as the world will let me, before it starts to ask me what the fuck I think I'm playing at.

CHAPTER FOUR

Only pretty girls
get to be fairies

My BALLET TEACHER told me only pretty girls get to be fairies. I don't remember even wanting to do ballet. Mum wanted me to do ballet, or just assumed I would. I did it because it seemed to be what I was meant to do.

I wasn't a fairy, because I wasn't a pretty girl. They were issued with rolls of brightly coloured tulle and packets of sequins for their mothers to make into fairy costumes. Not mine though. Not because she couldn't, because my mum made pretty much everything we wore, but because I wasn't going to be a fairy. I was going to be a mushroom.

True, I was going to be *the* mushroom, and I do re-member the dance teacher trying to impress upon me how pivotal I was to the dance of the fairies.

'Without you, dear, they'll have nothing to dance around, now will they?' That's what it's like, when you're a mushroom girl. You have to be grateful for the role life has handed you, because it's a pivotal role. You will be the one who organises things, so people don't have to go to the bother of forgetting to invite you to them. You will be the one the pretty girls will use both as a prophylactic against unwanted attention, or to peer from behind and look coquettish. And, if you're lucky as a mushroom girl, when the unwanted suitors have their little hearts broken, and turn away from their pursuit of the fairies, there you'll be, ready to clear up after them, absorb their tears and, who knows, become a consolation prize. That's what mushrooms do after all, they absorb the shit other people leave behind.

So I got sent home with two large squares of red felt and a smaller square of white felt, and the instructions that my mother was to make a mushroom hat. I was also to be bought a white, close fitting polo neck top and a pair of white tights, in which I was to perform my pivotal mushroom role. Stretching up on tip-toes and solemnly turning round three times, before adopting my crouched mushroom stance. See, pivotal.

I didn't want to be a mushroom. I thought I wanted to be a fairy, until the pretty girls caught me in the stone-cold church hall toilets, and poked and jeered at me until they made me cry about being the mushroom. Then, I decided I didn't want to be a fairy either. I wanted to be something else, something better. But I wasn't sure what that was.

When the night of the performance came, and Mum squeezed me into my white tights and polo neck, and pulled the red felt hat onto my head, and had me look at myself in the mirror, saying, 'There, you look lovely, even if I do say so myself, and who wants to be a boring old fairy anyway?' I had to agree. But even through the dull ache caused by the tourniquet grip of the mushroom hat, I knew I wasn't a fungus.

The pretty girls were all in the room behind the stage, which smelt of old shoes and cabbage. They wisped about in lilac and pink and lime, too excited to even notice me. When the moment came for junior dancers to take the stage, I was ready. Just in case the humiliation of the brain cracking mushroom hat wasn't enough, the music we were to dance to opened with a few bars played on the euphonium. It was a community affair with music provided by the Sea Scouts silver band, and as I made my debut under the blue-white spot light, the oom-pa-pah, oom-pa-pah of the euphonium welcomed me. I began my stately twirls, and a ripple of laughter ran through the crowd, and I thought of Mum, Nan and Lauren, five years younger but already the star of twinkle toes starters and hotly tipped to play the sugar plum fairy at Christmas, and wondered if they were laughing too.

My turn complete, I limped to centre stage, and dropped into the curtsey I was meant to hold for the rest of the performance. The euphonium was replaced by a volley of trumpets, heralding the fairies. As their little feet thudded behind me, my curtsey became a crouch and I grew ready. I was no mushroom, and they were about to find that out.

The fairies danced around me in a ring, and then, at the climax of the piece, which was at least mercifully short, the prettiest of the pretty girls was to jump over me, the mushroom, aided by the second and third prettiest girls, lifting her from either side. The moment came, I braced myself. As I was under the expansive mushroom hat, I cannot say if the prettiest girl was smiling as her feet left the ground, but I imagine she was. I know I was as I flinched upwards, in such a way that no one, not even the back row, could have thought it was an accident. The prettiest girl didn't, as I'd hoped, continue her forward momentum off the stage, breaking at least two of her legs and, preferably, her nose into the bargain, but she did collapse sideways with a scream, and both she and the second prettiest girl, smacked into the stage and skidded into the gaggle of minor fairies. Then I used a bad word, one I'd heard the builders doing our front drive use. But everyone was laughing. I'd made them laugh. Me, the mushroom girl.

'I've never been so embarrassed,' Mum said on the way home.

'It was an accident,' I lied.

'Accident, my foot,' Mum said. 'Goodness know what your Dad's going to say—' though that was an empty threat, as Dad would only ever say what she'd said. Before telling me to leave it alone now, give Mum a rest now, get on with something else, why don't you go and do some drawing, eh?

'Oh, come on Gail—' sitting squashed in close to me, Nan gave my knee a squeeze. 'Cheered everyone up at least, gave them a laugh.' I looked at her hand on my knee, at the way the sickly orange streetlight made all her rings look like amber.

'Don't you encourage her,' Mum said. 'And don't think you've got away with anything, madam. I had to apologise to Katie's mum, you know, apologise for your behaviour, and your bloody language.'

'And your bloody language,' I muttered. When I looked up, Mum caught my eye in the rear-view mirror.

'You're so sharp, you'll cut yourself one day.'

I'M THINKING ABOUT this now as I'm just about to have an after party debrief with Cassie, and I suppose I'm kind of doing the same thing, or I was doing the same thing when I was fucking the boy at the weekend. Exacting revenge on Max for consigning me to the rank of mushroom again.

Maybe I really am a mushroom?

He's right.

I'm a piece of shit.

I hate myself.

Must do better, must do better.

BEFORE I RING Cassie, which I time for her coffee break even though she's got her own office and can have a good gossip whenever she feels like it, I count out my vitamins and supplements.

Because I *must* do better.

I line the bottles up on one side of the chopping board, then move them across to the other side after I've taken the required dose from each. I like the omega three oil the best. When I hold it up to the light it glows amber, like Nan's rings did on mushroom night, looks fat and warm and like it's really going to do me some good. Pointless, all of it. Without the magic ingredient that Max will no longer be supplying, these pills can boost my immune system and supply me with micro-nutrients all they want, but nothing's going to happen.

But he hasn't gone forever, not yet.

Have to make amends, have to do better.

I take them, pill pop, pill pop, pill pop, because I've been taking them for almost two years. Like I've been taking my temperature at six forty-five every morning with a digital thermometer that has "*baby mad*" written on the side, in tiny, pink letters. But look, no baby.

I get my phone, and see there's a missed call from

Lauren again, but no voicemail or text—well, sorry, sis, but you're not what I need right now, telling me how I really ought to phone mum back, because didn't I know she's been trying to ring me? Yes, Lauren, I do know, because that's kind of what phones do these days, tell you who's rung and what they wanted. I know she wants to speak to me, I just don't want to speak to her, okay?

When I speak to Cassie, I don't tell her about The Boy. I feel my way through the weekend debrief and give her the bones of the aftermath, while redacting the truth as subtly as a CIA spook on the stand. I'm being over cautious, because Cassie is not one to bother with lines, let alone reading between them. She doesn't know who I left with, hasn't been told, hasn't been given any hint of it. She's worried, mostly, about how I am after letting my hair down so spectacularly, she's worried about post-drug blues kicking me in the ass with their usual forty-eight hour delayed hangover—steak knife Tuesday. I tell her I'm alright, then I find I'm telling her about the girl.

'D'you remember that time I said I was outside my place with Max, and that girl flipped us the finger?'

'No, not really.' Cassie says, then her phone clicks and I hear the sound of her fingers on a keyboard. 'Sort of, maybe, you said she was young?'

'Yeah, I was just…' She doesn't notice the pause as I rearrange my reason for being on the street. 'I went to the shop, to get munchies, about eleven-ish?'

'You were still awake then, after an all-nighter? Blimey, I crashed out about six, and there's me thinking you were out of practice.'

'Like riding a bike, innit? But I saw her again, that's all, when I went to the shop. She was crossing the road to the taxi rank.'

'What happened?'

'Nothing.' Just a girl crossing the road to get into a taxi, and me watching the boy walking away, his grin seeming larger than his face. 'She was just really young to be out so late, getting a taxi.'

Thing was, she looked back at me too, when she crossed the road. I sort of got the feeling that she was going to laugh at me, to point—look, there's a mushroom, a stupid, fucking mushroom, thinking she's a fairy, like she's a pretty girl. But she just looked at me, then looked back again as she was crossing the road. A mushroom herself.

CHAPTER FIVE

Four is the Chinese word for death

IT STARTS AROUND seven in the evening—the edge of steak knife Tuesday sawing at my mind. There's no way, not really, but look—what if I'm pregnant? I mean, I'm not, there's no way, right, but Max and I did have sex the night before he left. And then there was the weekend, and all of that. What if it's happened? Don't be stupid, I tell myself, because you know you're not pregnant, you know you're not.

But look, what if it has happened, and I've just hit the poor little bundle of cells with a ton of MDMA? And alcohol, and not sleeping and not eating—what if that's what I've just done? Killed it already, snuffed out the spark of it in the black hole of my womb.

This is stupid, there's nothing to indicate that there's the slightest chance, but now I've thought it and the horrible, itching, nasty of it is creeping through me. You filthy bitch—three years of being good and healthy and doing it all right, and this will be the time it happens, and this is the time it will work, but your baby will be damaged and hurt and it will be all your fault, you nasty, nasty girl. My mind now takes the opportunity to sneak in and remind me of a few of my other greatest moments, just to underline how nasty I really am. Hell, it even goes over my infamous entrance to the world story, the one about how mum nearly died giving birth to me, and I nearly died being born. So Dad was going to kill himself. Yes, that one—hurrah!

I'm on the sofa by nine o'clock, curled up on my side in the dark, a pillow clutched against my belly. It's going to happen again. I'm pregnant and I'm going to lose it again, just like before, and this time it really will be my fault; blood on my hands. There's no one I can talk to now either, because I can't tell Cassie and I can't tell Max. It's all going to happen again, just like it did before. So then I replay that too, just because I can.

The fourth time was the kindest. The fourth time was the worst. I didn't go to A&E, I didn't go to the doctors. I didn't do anything. I was at work. Part way through an arm piece of a retro style, 1940's mermaid with a knowing wink, resting on a backdrop of waves, on the arm of a 1940's-style-girl. I turned to say something to Big Al and when I turned back, there was a kind of clicking sensation from inside me, a crack. Not even a pain as such, but something like the snapping of a twig. I knew straight away what it was.

I made myself finish the hour on the girl's arm, because despite everything, I didn't want her to walk out with a half-finished job that looked terrible. Was it the worst time for being the third second chance? The time we'd both told ourselves really would be the last, because we didn't think we could go through it again, only of course when I said that, I had been saying what Max wanted to hear. It was the worst, and it wasn't, because as soon as it happened, as soon as it snapped inside me, and I felt the pain begin to build, I knew I could go through it all again.

I drove home and went into the bathroom to check that I was bleeding, even though I knew I was. Then I went and sat on the sofa. It was only eight weeks; it had hardly even started this time. Didn't need hospital, didn't need a doctor. I knew my body better than they did, I knew what to do. I was just going to sit there and I was going to relax and when it was gone, when it had all bled away into nothing, I'd pick myself up and we would try again, alright? Because I could take it, because I am stronger than it, and I can put myself through anything, if I have to. Because really, I am not strong, I don't think, not strong enough to ever give up trying.

When I told Max he said: 'I can't do it. I can't watch you go through this again. You said it too, you said, if it happens again, then that's got to be it.'

'Yeah? Well, I lied.'

THE ONLY LIGHT in the flat now comes from passing car headlights on the wall, and the soft, sodium orange glow of London. When I open my eyes, this is still bright enough to hurt. Not enough though, not as much as I deserve.

That's why it's never worked, I don't deserve it.

I get out my phone and look at the app where you record your temperature every morning, along with all the other signs and hints and wonders of the female cycle. It's ever so helpful, it colours in the days you're not fertile in white, and the days you might be fertile in spring green, and the days when you're probably going to ovulate in deep green. It even puts flashing hearts on the days when you should fuck, the days where you have the best chance of conception, and then it colours the rest of the month in blue, calming blue, contemplative blue—blue for the days you sit and wonder if maybe, just maybe, this time it will work.

Yesterday was the last of the flashing heart days, which means that The Boy, him with all that lovely young, healthy, fresh from the box, best before date sperm, and I were together right in the middle of the do-it-now, zone, the at-it-like-rabbits zone, the don't-matter-if-you-orgasm-just-fuck-you-idiot zone.

CHAPTER SIX

One foot on the floor

BUT WE USED condoms. So I'm probably, definitely not pregnant, and I did not poison my unborn child with my drugs and drink binge. I have to put it all behind me, go to bed, fresh start tomorrow, new day. I will start again, I will be good, I will make amends for being the nasty girl I truly I am. I will start pretending that I am a good person. I will do it all and maybe Max will believe me, and maybe this time it will work. Something in my life will work.

I WAKE LATE. In the kitchen I make myself a coffee and troll through Facebook on my laptop, unable to face eating. There are a couple of messages, three in fact, and none of them to Asylum Tattoo's page, which means they really are for me, and not from clients asking when I'll be coming back. Even though I'm on my self-imposed exile, I told Big Al that I'll still handle the social media crap, as he calls it, because Big Al is very much a man of his generation, and social media crap will forever fall below his radar. He's remarkably forward thinking in many ways, he gave me my first job after all, at a time when a lot of male tattooists wouldn't have, but he still likes to feel that what he considers secretarial work is my domain, even if he denies it utterly to my face. Likes to think of himself as liberal, does Big Al.

The Facebook messages are from men I've known for a number of years, none of whom I consider friends. No messages from Max. Which is fine, obviously, as it's him giving me space. Besides, he wouldn't Facebook me, he'd ring, or text. So, yes—the three men; they're also about my age, within five years either way, and from what their Facebook statuses obligingly reveal, in different degrees of singleness and complication. Of course they are.

Fragments of the weekend have been surfacing. Not The Boy, he's been running in my subconscious like my own personal porn film, to the point of becoming a brain worm—note to self, stop it, stop it now, for God's sake—but moments of conversation, of people asking how I was doing, with varying degrees of sincerity. These three men had all popped up during the evening, one baldy, one chunky with a ponytail, and one with sandy hair and eyebrows. They'd each bought me drinks, shouted into my ear about how they were doing at work, while neglecting to ask me the same in return, and given me the cigarettes I really shouldn't have been smoking. All three of them have now sent me *good to see you over the weekend'* messages, ending with *'be great to do it again sometime'*, wrapped around some pointless padding *'saw that guy with the cage on his head again later....saw that article about your shop in the metro...'* all very transparent.

Perhaps not. Perhaps I'm fooling myself, a jumped-up mushroom girl only popular now all the fairies are either married, or twenty years younger than they are. Funny how a couple of months back, at the last thing Max and I went to together, pretty much the same crowd was there and I might have talked even longer and more coherently to all of this trio, and yet that didn't prompt them into messages of concern and gratitude. What are they after this time, now everyone knows, or thinks they know, that Max has (not) dumped (but is just taking some time out from) me? Bit of casual forty-something sex, with someone on the alternative scene still interesting enough to hang with, but old enough not to make demands on them long term? Bit of ink work thrown in perhaps?

More than that even, each getting round to realising that their twenties are a dim and distant memory, their thirties are about to go the same way. They're single, and suddenly not quite as attractive as they once were, not now they've a divorce and debts to service. Hell, not all men actually find twenty-year old girls that attractive after the initial fuck-fest has faded. It's a sobering thought indeed that your girlfriend dresses like you because she thinks it's retro.

Oh, but what the hell do they see in me? They can't know, can they? Not the whole truth of it, my disastrous three years. Scare the hell out of them if they did, or worse, give them the idea that their majestic sperm will succeed, where poor old Max's didn't. Short men, all of them, shorter than me anyway, and well, that's a red rag to a bull. Planting the flag, climbing the peak. Is that what they imagine, being the one to tame the dragon no other man has, and get her successfully knocked up?

I doubt it. Quick charity shag is nearer the mark. Just like the idea of doing it with someone they've heard is a bit dirty and will say yes to a bit of bondage or whatever, without the bother of having to talk them into it with months of gentle emotional black mail. That's romance for you.

'Just blackmail with chocolates,' I say to Nan's picture, because that's what she used to call it, Valentines' Day, all of that. What she said when I didn't get a card, which I never did. I like this picture of her, one she let me take even though she was all *"What do you want a picture of my ugly old mug for?"* about it. She's against a blue sky at her seaside house, you can just see the edge of the garden wall behind her head.

'I just want a memento of you, all right? Come on, you're practically famous now, aren't you, front page of the paper and all. Look, just smile, for fuck's-sake!'

'Why?' she asked a second after the camera clicked.

'Am I going somewhere?'

Seeing as I'm on Facebook I do a bit of stalking. While refusing to admit that what I remember most about The Boy is his smile and the jokes, I discover that he is not the part-time shag, of the part-time lesbian flatmate of Mary-Mary. I track down who I thought he was through a series of eliminations, and am quite pleased to see it's not him, this one having long, dark hair and less than perfect skin, even after the judicious application of Photoshop. Then I feel deflated at not finding him, which I shouldn't do if The Boy is nothing more than a forgettable one-night stand.

Must do better.

I've let Max down, I've let me down, I've let everyone down.

Everything I'm feeling is peeled back for the world to see. I got so far out of my skull for the first time in years, it's hurting as I try and crawl back in. Stands to reason that I'm going to fixate on someone who's been a bit nice to me, even if my definition of nice could stand some reconsidering. The best thing I can do is acknowledge this, and administer a suitable punishment for my bad behaviour. Which comes down to a choice between returning my mum's call and going for a jog.

I go jogging.

The taxi drivers have a good look as I set out, but they're more used to me now so I'm less of a novelty.

They ran out of blue hair jokes once they'd exhausted smurf references; and seeing as I do occasionally put work their way, they're reduced to staring. On the corner, a group of Neds falls back on a kind of 'oi-oi' to rhyme with saveloy chant, that filters in through the gap between songs, but then an especially nasty track from an anonymous hard house compilation kicks in, and I'm deaf to the lot of them.

In my bubble of noise, I dodge across the street and weave through the pedestrians, until I can cut across the market square to the park. When I first moved here, the market was a real proper London market, mobile phone accessories next to fruit and veg stalls. Some of that's left, but there's an awful lot of artisan bread, vegan falafel and craft made cheeses sneaking in round the edges. Don't get me wrong, I'm as much of a foodie as the next middle-class indie freak, but there's a big part of me that's nostalgic for the days when markets were more goblin than gourmet.

As I hit the park, memories of The Boy slide under my conscious mind, until his image has distracted me enough to shut my inner voice up, and I allow myself to indulge.

It was the evening. He had his jeans on, though he'd unbuttoned them, and was sat on the edge of my bed. He'd got out a tobacco pouch from his pocket and was skinning up, laying out papers, licking them, sticking them together in the time-honoured way. I watched his tongue on his fingers, the way his hands moved, their dexterity as he crumbled skunk into the papers and plucked out tobacco.

'Like your jacket, the one on the stand. Is it Westwood?' he said.

'Yes.' How'd he know just by looking? 'Got it on eBay.'

'I love clothes. It's what I do, fashion.'

'You're in fashion?' I couldn't keep the surprise from my voice, the slight incredulity. He stopped what he was doing to look at me, not hurt, amused, the whites of his eyes very white, his irises very blue despite his pupils being saucer wide.

'What, you think you got to be gay to be a man in fashion?'

'Oh, I wasn't worried about that, as it goes.' I smirked.

'Never understood that, why clothes are for birds,' he said, looking at me to see my reaction, to see that I know he's being ironic. He should be called something like Alfie, or Freddie, this should be 1960, and he should be a photographer.

'Photographer?' I asked.

'Fuck that,' he said. 'Designer pattern cutter. I make frocks, innit.'

'You make frocks?'

He got his phone and tapped in the code.

'Four fours? Your code is four fours? Seriously?'

He grinned, shrugged. 'I can't remember shit like that.' He shows me a few pictures, fabric pinned on a tailor's dummy, an unsmiling girl in a blue jacket.

'All my own work,' he said, then tossed the phone and carried on rolling his spliff. 'Good with my hands. Me dad has a stall, always had one, fabric and stuff. Was working on it for years, 'til I sorted my head out enough for college.'

He lit the spliff, the flame painting in the side of his face for me. With the end glowing as he inhaled, he chucked the lighter on the floor and moved so that he was sitting astride me, balancing his weight on his heels so that he held himself above me, rather than on me.

I've nearly done my circuit when I get to remembering this part, have cut back through the market again. Is this why I'm being all nostalgia stupid about the good old market days, because I think his dear old Dad is here somewhere, and therefore, so is he?

I'm like a beaten dog, craving any hint of affection. Why am I doing this to myself, giving him this power over me?

He sat astride me and held the smoke. I could almost see him counting, eyes closed, the hand holding the spliff resting against his forehead, the other hand gripping his thigh. He was so obvious, leaning back a little so that his stomach was pulled taught, skin caramel cream over muscle. Not gym muscles, scant ones made firm by the effort of just keeping all those bones in order, all those ribs running up his flank. He looked good, though. Lickably good, like all the boys your mother warned you about, the ones your best friend warned you about, the ones you hate yourself for thinking about. I hate myself for thinking about him.

And he exhaled, the smoke billowing round his face as that grin pulled his cheeks into apples, his body shook with a giggle that rippled up from his naval.

'Here,' he said, and held it out to me, and I, the non-smoker, the three years without drink and drugs, took it. I put it to my lips, and as I did, he reached into his pants and lifted out his cock, hard and getting harder, inside its rubber second skin, moving so that he was poised to slide into me.

'Go on,' he said. 'Breathe.' And I did, and through the haze of smoke his eyes were very white and very blue against his sandy skin. My lungs burned, my lungs filled to bursting, and as I breathed out, as the rush hit me, he was inside me, moving slowly, deeply, supporting himself on his elbows as he fucked me, rolling his hips and—

'Hey—'

The Boy, his voice in the pause between track seven Stone Temple Pilots and track eight, System of a Down, sitting on the three steps that lead up to my street door, great long arms, great long legs, folded up in front of him, pulling the strings of his head phones from his ears, as he grins up at me. 'Good run?'

CHAPTER SEVEN

Self-harm

MY HEART RACES, I mean, actually races; the blood pounds in my cheeks. This is because I was running though, not because he is here. Honest. Right?

'What the fuck are you here for?' I say. I'm nice like that.

He pulls an amused face. 'For the sparkling conversation,' he says. 'And the tea.'

'So what, you just turn up? You don't call first?'

He shrugs. 'You didn't give me your number.'

'You didn't ask for my number.'

He puts his hand up to his ear, like he's making a call. 'You in later? Thought I'd pop round for tea.'

'It's not such a good time,' I say, fighting the urge to smile.

'No tea?' He puts his hand on his chest. 'I'm beginning to wonder if you're just using me for sex, seeing as you haven't called an' all.'

'I don't have your number,' I say. Right on cue, my

phone rings. It's on silent, but it vibrates in my pocket. I take it out.

'Answer it,' The Boy says. He stands up, and because he's so tall and because he's standing on the second step up, he towers over me. I look at the phone then shove it back into my tracksuit pocket.

'It's nothing,' I say, even though it was Max.

Of course it was Max, timing being everything.

'Seriously though,' The Boy says, coming down the steps, hands in his pockets. 'I can fuck off if you want.' He shrugs, pulling on his pockets. 'I was just passing, saw your road, the taxis, you know?' He nods over the road.

I find I need to look, as if the rank and its neon lit office are something new he's showing me. Two of the drivers are loitering by their cars watching us. One of them does that sort of head bob thing, saying to the other one, *'Look, it's that crazy tattooed lady'*, which is how I hope they talk about me, because *'Old blue-haired woman'* would suck.

So I do something stupid. My default setting these days.

'Two sugars, isn't it?'

THREE YEARS AGO, when I got pregnant the first time, I did the right thing. I told Max he didn't have to stay if he didn't want to, that I had plenty of money put away, I had the house by the sea, all of that. I told him he could be as involved as he wanted to be, but I'd understand if he didn't want me in with the deal—three months we'd been together, I mean, that's hardly a relationship, is it? Nobody would blame him, least of all me, because hell I wasn't easy to live with, everyone knew that, right? I offered him the door, I offered him the role of part-time dad. He listened to me, then he got up and kissed me.

'What makes you think I'm going anywhere?' he said. 'Have you told your mum yet?'

'Oh,' Mum said when I told her. 'That's a surprise…' which was her reaction to everything, to my going to art college, to my quitting art college, to my becoming a tattooist.

'You are sure?' she said after that. 'I mean, look, you've only been with…Mark—'

'Max, Mum, and yes, I am sure—aren't you pleased?'

'Of course, of course I am,' and she'd given me one of her ironing board hugs, her eyes all wet, and said she hadn't meant it like that. 'I'm over the moon, and your Dad will be too, it's just that, you know, it's…it's really hard when you have a baby, even with having your father there and everything, not that men did much then anyway, but just having him around, because you were such a—I mean, lovely but, such a—'

'Max is on board with this,' I said, tap-tapping my fingers on the kitchen counter, counting myself calm again. 'And yes, before you ask, it was an accident, but it's what I want, it's what we both want.'

Mum put her hand to her face, touched her mouth and smiled, a tear breaking over her cheek.

'Oh, bless you, well, don't tell the baby that, will you?'

'No Mum.' Was all I could say, because hearing her say it like that made it really real, like it was a thing that really could happen this time, not something I could fuck up. After that, I did all the right things. I ate well, I stopped drinking, I exercised in a sensible, life affirming way. I was even nice to my sister. I stopped being me, and in the end, none of it helped, none of it made a difference. No baby, no Max. So I figure I deserve some being bad, that I'm owed a bit of no strings sex. That's the crap my subconscious is coming up with anyway as we climb the stairs to my flat, him ducking his head as he follows me inside.

'I should shower,' I say.

'Should you?' he says. Why does that make me smile, make the soles of my feet tingle?

I go to the kitchen, as if I really am going to make him a cup of tea, and he comes with me, as if that's what he's really here for. I want to ask him where he works, if he's skipped out early because it's not quite four yet, or does he work his own hours, or do they only get busy in the season, because they have that, don't they, fashion people? They have seasons, like the way other creatures migrate, so maybe this is off season, and that's why he's at a loose end.

'So, do you, like—'

He puts his hand over mine on the kettle switch. 'Okay,' he says. 'I'm not really here for the tea.'

So, we fuck again. In the kitchen, in the sitting room, on the sofa, on the armchair, over the table, in the bed, out of the bed, on the floor, in the shower, against the wall. Like we're working through a list, like it's a great big game of top trumps. Fuck trumps. And yes, I think about Max, and how much this would hurt him, and how I'm doing a bad, bad thing, and I let the Boy, do everything he wants to do, everything I want him to do, because I am doing a bad thing. I'm really quite impressed with myself, in a kind of detached, well look at you girl, kind of a way.

And as I fuck him, part of me tumbles away back in time, all the way back twenty years, as if I'm unwinding to a younger me, a simpler me.

Then we're lying on the sitting room floor on the fake tiger skin rug Cassie got me for Christmas a few years back, the flat screen on one side of us, the long, low black glass side table on the other.

'Fuck,' he says. He leans his head back, hand over his eyes. The day's still bright outside, the rectangle of the window blue above the grey blocks of houses. I don't want it to be bright and sunny, I want it to be night and dark, as if that will make it all better, as if that will make this last longer, make him forget he's got somewhere else to be later, which I'm sure he has. So I get up and pull down the blind—metallic silver in contrast to the battle ship grey wall—and switch on the standard lamp by the arm chair. It casts a yellow light that's kind and soft, that mellows the room into shadow. I think about putting some clothes on, but don't and lie back down next to him. He moves both hands to the back of his head, and it's then that I see them.

The light from the lamp is catching him at an angle, and where it laps the skin under his arms, it reveals the marks. I hadn't noticed them before, or just seen one or two and not thought much of it, but now, at this angle, lying so close to him, I see them properly. Cut marks, thin, neatly done. In the body-mod scene, scarification was big a few years back, but it's never made the mainstream quite the way other things have. This is not scarification, not done by a professional, though they're really quite well done seeing as they're self-inflicted and all. Lots of them though, some older, some newer. How could I not have seen them before? Because I wasn't looking.

'Fancy a bump?' he asks, dragging his fingers through his locks. Has he seen me looking? Does he even care? He's hardly hidden them from me. Badge of honour aren't they, these days? What all the cool kids are doing. And what, when it comes down to it, is that different from the artwork I've scrolled on myself over the years, filling in my own blanks?

The Boy pulls on his trousers and fetches his jacket. I get shorts and a washed-out Asylum tattoo t-shirt, well, it's my house and all, my shop too, near enough, and come back to sit on the floor. Today, his trousers are pin stripe, with a high waist and silver buttons. They've got braces, and he pulls these up over his shoulders before he sits on the sofa. He sprinkles crystalline powder from a small grip-seal bag onto the coffee table. I don't ask what it is. It's Wednesday. There's no way I'm going to take class A drugs on a Wednesday.

'Who's the bloke then?' he asks. He's taken a credit card from a wallet he folds back into his trouser pocket, and is using it to crush the granules, rolling it about. He hasn't looked up, but I know he's talking about the picture of Max and me on the mantlepiece.

'That's Max,' I say. Perhaps by naming him, it will remind both the Boy and I that we really should make this the last hurrah.

'At work, is he?' The boy asks, not breaking his stride. He begins to cut whatever it is he's cutting, working it back and forth over the glass, breaking it into two lines, three, then reforming them into one pile.

'I wouldn't know. We split up.'

'He's a cock, then,' the boy says. He looks at me, his long, hollow face failing to suppress how pleased he is with himself, how cheeky he thinks he's being.

'Perhaps I threw him out?' I say.

'Did you?'

I could say anything, I could say that I was simply bored of Max, that he couldn't get it up, that we had an open relationship, so open it allowed for him to travel to India to teach blind children to roller skate, or save donkeys in Peru—I could say anything, but what I do say is, 'No, he fucked off, as it happens. Said it wasn't me, it was him.'

'He seriously used that line? That's lame.'

And he doesn't ask any more. He pinches his nose, sniffs, then bends his face to the table and snorts a line of whatever it is through a rolled up five-pound note. Then he holds it out to me. It's Wednesday and I'm too old and too fucked still from the weekend. But I take it anyway.

'Did you make your trousers,' I say, when we've tangled ourselves on the sofa, his pinstriped grasshopper's legs trailing over the arm.

'I did, yeah, can you tell? Have to. You try buying off the peg when you're six seven.'

'I'm the same though, nothing I buy fits me. Too short in the arm, too short in the leg. Where did you study?' It's getting too comfortable, his being here, lying with his head in my lap, one arm kind of up and round my waist, my legs around his torso. I'm making conversation as if we're getting to know each other. He's scrolling through my iTunes.

'You got a lot of Lady Gaga.'

'So what? I know everyone hates her, because she's…oh, but so what? I like a bit of camp sugar pop every now and again.'

'I like her too.'

'Fuck off, straight men don't like Gaga.'

But he knows the words, and he sings along and dances, camp, laughing, pulling me up and making me take a pose. And I do, I dance like the drunk Aunty at a wedding, and he knots my washed out t-shirt tight round my midriff, pulls one shoulder down, and stands back to admire me, tweaking at my hair as if he's dressing me for the catwalk, his grin like it's graffitied on his face in magic marker pen. Then we do Beyonce *Single Ladies* then Sound Garden, to kind of clear the air, to make amends to the rock gods I say, which makes him laugh. Then he sticks Goldfrapp on shuffle repeat all, and we end up, after another line of what he tells me is the last of the weekend's MDMA, folded around each other as the light behind the blind softens and fades, and the place becomes night, lit only in yellow.

Lying there, so warm, so relaxed with him, I imagine keeping this going for weeks, months even. How easy it would be. He'd just send me a text, because he's taken my card this time, or just turn up, nothing regular, now and again, midweek on the low season, weekends for our own after party, casual, like. He'd have all his best lines ready, all the jokes, little bit of banter, and then we'd shag and take drugs and he'd be off again. I'd be his mistress, I suppose, in the way gifted young men had them in the eighteen hundreds, or forever, I imagine. Older women still well turned out, experienced, cultured, with plenty to teach them. Grateful for the attentions of a younger man, but wise enough to know that there isn't any future in it. I mean, in those stakes, I'm pretty good. I'm not famous, not in real terms, but people know me. They know my work, they've seen it in magazines, they might even have seen me at conventions, when I did that sort of thing. No, I'm not famous, but I'm known, like the way I know the people who run BitchSmack, enough for them to say hi, to shove the occasional guest list at me. So I'm quite a catch, for a young man who's up for a bit of no strings fun, I'm quite the connected, richer, cougar aren't I? Easy, then, to keep it going for weeks, as long as I need him. Treat it like therapy, treat it like a new hairdresser, be casual about it, because I'm the one in charge, I'm the older woman.

But that isn't what will happen, is it?

'So, tattooing, yeah?' he says. 'How did you, I mean, where do you, like, start with that?'

I want to hurt myself. I want something else to hurt me, other than my own body, and he's just, well, goddam perfect for that, isn't he? Lying on my sofa in the tangle of him, with the warmth and the smell and the thought of him, like something dangerously expensive I've just slipped into, like a silk chemise.

'Oh, well, you know—it was just something I got into, really. I'm just an Art school dropout, that's all.'

'What d'you mean?'

'Nothing, just...went to a big, posh old Art school and they were all...you're brilliant, you're gifted, at the start, but when it came to it what they wanted, wasn't what I did. Drawing wasn't in anymore, it was all...painting yourself blue and crying an' shit like that, piles of newspaper and stupid puns, so fuck that shit, right? Nobody wants someone who's shit at drawing doing a tattoo, do they? So, whatever, it worked out for the best, in the end.'

'But you're really good, though.'

'Yeah, but not good enough.'

Never good enough, not me.

It's because of Max. I'm going to blame him for it. Not because of what he's done, but because of what he'd said. It's not you, it's me. That's so fucking wrong. That's just shorthand for: No, I can't face it anymore, what you've put me through. I don't think you're stronger than me, I think you're madder than me. I think you're letting this thing destroy you and if I stay around, it will destroy me as well. Never mind that you can't escape it, that it's part of the very cells of your body, the marrow of your bones, it's in your blood, because I'm getting out while the going's good, while there's a break in hostilities, and I'm leaving you to face it alone. Because it *is* you.

'You just got into it? Bullshit—you've got a whole business, you've got awards and stuff.'

'Been looking me up, have you?' Oh shit, has he? I narrow my eyes at him and see at once that I'm right— he's not that good at lying. He tries to cover it up, does a little shrug, but he has, of course he has. That wakes me up.

I get up, slip out of his arms and collect our glasses from the table, take them to the kitchen. He swings his legs round, feet back on the floor, watching me while I do it.

'Look, it's what I do, okay? It wasn't part of a grand plan or anything, I just found I could do it, and I worked my ass off to be as good as I am, okay?' I look back at him. 'Right place, right time, I guess. Know what I mean?'

Backing off because this feels as good as the beginning with Max. And that's a lie. It has to be.

CHAPTER EIGHT
My hero

FEW YEARS BACK, I bumped into Big Al, him walking one way, me walking the other.

'Bugger me, it's my little apprentice, how you doing, Harpy gel?'

We went for a drink and he was all the big-I-am until the truth serum of three pints got it out of him. He'd lost wife number two and the shop after getting a Lithuanian girl half his age and weight, pregnant and giving her all his money before she vanished with the kid.

'Don't know what I'm gonna do, Chicky,' he said.

But I did. Right time, right place.

First time I met him when I was twenty-three and crashing out of my life that was right time, right place too. He'd done my first tattoo, the wings on my back, from my own design, looked through the rest of my sketchbook and he liked my style. So when I unceremoniously crashed of the legitimate art world and needed a plan, Big Al was the first thing that popped into my mind.

'Oh, it's you, chicky,' he said when I'd burst into his shop. 'Harpy gel. Thought I'd see you again, what is it this time? Wings on your heels?'

'I want a job,' I said. 'I want to be a tattooist.'

'Oh, does she, now?' he said. 'Thinks it's as easy as that, does she?'

'No,' I said, 'I don't think it's easy, I think it's bloody hard work, but that's okay, that's what I want.'

'I see, and what do you think I want, hmm?' He shrugged the meaty expanse of his shoulders, pulled his hawk-eye expression. 'You think I'm short of artists, do you? Think I don't got them knocking on me door every other day, asking me to given 'em a shot?' He waved his hand about, encompassing his world. 'Opened this place before you was born, chicky, what makes you think I need an apprentice?'

'You don't,' I said, folding my arms. 'But you need someone to make the tea. How many of those artists is willing to do that, and sweep the floor, and do the washing up? I'll do all of that, and clean your windows, for six months, and you won't have to pay me. If you're happy with me after six months, then you can train me.'

'And how you gonna eat, for them six months while you're making the tea?' he said, but I knew I'd interested him. Later he'd say this was the reason he gave me a go, because I was the first person in years who'd come to him and not expected to be doing a full back piece the next week, who'd understood that before you were let near skin, there was months and months of learning the basics of health and safety, hygiene, and drawing and drawing and drawing, and that this was a good thing, this was how it should be. I was the only person in years, he said, who respected the craft over the art.

'Well then,' he'd said and held out his mug. 'Two sugars, let the bag sit for at least five minutes, don't play with it, don't squash it with a spoon, and don't you go near it with the milk until them five minutes are done. You understand, chicky?'

I understood. And got a bar job over the road.

When I bumped into him that day, when we went for drinks and he told me the truth about what was happening. I'd been working in two studios, one in Kingston and one in Earl's Court, renting a bench in each and doing pretty well but I didn't have quite enough money to open my own studio. The small share of cash Big Al could muster was nothing compared to the value of his thirty-year rep and all the contacts he had which, added to mine, were worth three times anything a bank might lend us. Less than a year after those pints on a grey and raining Thursday afternoon, we were opening The Asylum on Holloway Road. The Lithuanian wife had resumed contact with Big Al so he could see his baby boy, and I was my own boss at last.

So yes, that's part of how I did it, my glittering career. It's how I met Max, too, as it happens.

Back stage, on the opening night, Big Al and me sharing a beer.

'Officially, this is a good thing,' he said. 'My slinging my lot in with you. Sounds better than the truth, don't it?'

'Don't be so melancholy,' I told him. 'Come on, Al, shit happens. New start, and all that.'

'You,' he pointed a thick, blue scribbled finger. 'You're my apprentice, gel.'

'I was your apprentice. Now, I'm your partner.'

He smiled, his big, broad forehead folding into creases. 'Don't mind me, Chicky. Old dog, new tricks, that's all.' He looked around the place, picking at his gold teeth with his fingernail. 'Nothing like my old shop, this is, right smart. Mine was over a hardware shop once.' He looked back at me. 'Gave you your start, didn't I? When no one else would 'ave?'

'Do you want me to play the violins yet?' I struck a pose, bow poised over invisible fiddle.

'Shut me up, give me a drink. Listen to me, going on, you're right, fuck the bitch, fuck the world.' He picked his beer up from the desk and clinked it against mine. 'Here's to you, me old darling.'

It was a good night. Enough of the relatively famous-in-their-own-lunchtime people I invited came, and all of the glorious collection of freaks I called friends, and the faces who knew Big Al. An interesting crowd. Interesting enough for bloggers and journalists and magazine people to turn up and take pictures too. There was something of a buzz. We even needed the security Big Al provided, which was nice. Dad came for half hour, stood at the edge of things like a genial bouncer, letting Cassie look after him. 'Just to show my face,' he said as part of his goodbye. 'Mum's orders, show my face, job done. Would have loved to come, but she had one of her heads, you know love? But she's really proud of you, really she is. We both are. Well done, Lydia-O, swanky do!'

The highlight of the night was one of Cassie's more intellectual friends deep in conversation with one of Big Al's, about the nature of morality, which Big Al's mate, Gripper, probably knew inside out. They're still together, as it happens; a lovely couple.

Anyway, through the crush and canapés and spon-sored beer of it all, Cassie brought me Max. He wasn't her date, she was already with her lovely man by then, but someone she'd met in the café by her work where she has lunch.

I remember looking up and seeing this big ox of a man, like Big Al almost, only all muscle and much better looking. I remember his hands, and how soon as I saw one stretched out to take mine, I thought how good it would feel to have them running over my skin, how they'd make me feel smooth and lithe under their touch. As the party burned out and the appointment book filled, we got talking, until even Cassie and Big Al had gone, and it was just us and the caterers.

'You free for dinner next Friday?'

'Yes,' I said. And then, 'No. It's my sister's wedding. I'm a bridesmaid'

'Just have to take your number then,' Max said.

IT WAS MUM who asked me about being a bridesmaid; not asking me officially, but just sounding me out before Lauren did, because if I didn't want to, then I could just say no to her and she'd pass the message on. This of course meant I had no choice but to say yes, because, well, reverse psychology is a bitch, so I said I would.

'Well, you will promise me that you'll, you know, behave?' Mum said.

I had agreed to do that as well. Luckily, Asylum Tattoo's opening night was the same weekend as the hen night, so I was spared pink cowboy hats and sashes, if that's what Lauren was into.

'No there was not,' Mum snapped when I asked if there had been a stripper. 'We went to one of those pot painting places, and then did a boat trip.'

'Wild,' I observed. 'Let's hope the hangover's better by next weekend. Touch and go I imagine.'

THE BIG DAY was bloody freezing for May, and I was the tallest, oldest, thinnest and ugliest bridesmaid, buttoned up to the neck and paired up with someone's twelve-year-old son, as all the others were married to Lauren's team of ushers.

'What's your name, kid?' I asked as we shivered outside the church.

'Mark,' he said to his shoes.

'Mark? What you into, then, Mark?'

He shrugged. 'Nothing.'

'How many swears do you know?' That at least got him to look at me.

'Three?' he offered.

'Well, we'll soon fix that,' I promised.

'You two making friends?' Mum said, cutting in with her breeziest of smiles.

After the bad hymns a small, crepe-skinned pastor got up from her seat and gave a long, rambling address, which threatened to reach a point but never quite did. Michael stared at Lauren, really stared at her which was a bit weird, and cried, which was even more weird. He cried when they exchanged their vows, when he held her hands and when he kissed her, just as if he really meant it. I was glad that he meant it, don't get me wrong, but you know, chill out dude.

I sat on the end of the top table, sweating now we were inside, the underarms of my lilac dress going dark.

Mum had chosen the dress. Picked, I imagine, because of the long sleeves and high neck. Doing her best to cover me up.

There was crap food, crap speeches, thinly veiled jokes about how all the bridesmaids looked pretty, even Lauren's sister, and then it was the first dance. I realised with horror that each usher was heading over to the top table to collect his respective bridesmaid, and among them, was the diminutive Mark. I looked at him, he looked at me, and thank God he sloped off in the direction of the toilets, his face crimson. I'd had enough.

'Excuse me,' I said to no one in particular, pushed my chair back and strode out of the room.

There was a bar not far from the banqueting suite, so I went there and ordered a double vodka and lime. The bar man eyed my lilac dress. When he brought me my drink, I went to get out my wallet, then realised that of course it was in my room and I couldn't remember my room number.

Then a voice said, 'Don't worry, it's on me.'

Max. Standing next to me as if it was the most natural thing in the world, as if he'd every right to be in this godforsaken hotel in the wilds of Hertfordshire, in a grey suit with a red tie, looking like a young Elvis.

'What the fuck?' I said, when I'd finished staring.

'Cassie gave me her invitation,' he said. 'Hope you don't mind or nothing.'

CHAPTER NINE

Insomnia

I DON'T REALISE I've fallen asleep until I wake up. Cotton mouthed, I snort and put my hand to my face. Have I been drooling? I'm alone with the light from the standard lamp, no sign of The Boy. My first instinct is to look and see that the scatter of Apple products is still where I'd left them, which is a shitty thing to do, but then hell, you hear about that sort of thing all the time, right? Whatever, they're all still there, so my bad, but hey, look—the table has a smudge of white, like a powdered sugar fingerprint.

I pick up my phone. Eleven forty-six, and a text from an unrecognized number. I know it's him before I read it.

'Bye bye, sleeping beauty.'

I need a drink. Juice. I go to the fridge. Right, so I guess he must have sneaked about picking up his things and leering down at me, letting the old sleeping dog lie. Couldn't even wake me up to say it properly, what the hell? Scared I might demand something of him, a kiss, a phone number, or that he take the bins out? But then, why send the text, why give me his number if he was just going to sneak out? Maybe he was just being nice letting me sleep. People do that. Be nice.

I stand at the window drinking my juice, watching the yellow light flash at the taxi rank. It flickers across me as it strobes round and round. I watch it a lot, when I can't sleep, which is most nights. I should be grateful to the Boy, that's got to be the first time in months I've fallen asleep without noticing. There's that word again, gratitude.

The girl appears, walking down from the main road on the same side as the taxi rank. Despite the dark, I recognise her. It's that ponytail, Croydon face lift they call it, pulled back so tight it must feel as if someone is constantly yanking her back. She's in a hoodie, of course, and a mini skirt. Her skinny legs look like they don't belong to the hump of her upper body. It's warm but she looks cold.

Head down, she walks up to the front of the taxi office, where they're sitting behind a scratched Perspex screen. She's talking to someone inside, her face touched by the yellow light.

How old is she? It's only because I've seen her close up that I even ask myself this. From up here, she's just a woman, small, sure, but the way she's standing, leaning against the window like that, well, you wouldn't know just by looking. I still have the feeling that she shouldn't be out this late.

A man comes out of the office to talk to her. One of the younger ones. Perhaps she's his fare for the night. Maybe she works at the supermarket and her mum, or her boyfriend, gives her the money for a cab home when she works late. Can't have much change from that sort of hourly pay, so that's what I'd do, if she were mine, pay for her cab. I mean, if I were her mum, or something. Because that's what mums do, don't they? I mean, say what you like about mine, as much as she annoys the hell out of me, she would always do that; if I said I was going out it would be all, 'And how are you getting home?' and I would roll my eyes, and Dad would say I only had to ring, that he'd get up, then Mum would say that no, he wouldn't, because some of us had to work in the morning and would give me money for a taxi, which I had to promise not to spend. So that's what I would do too, I would always give my daughter money for a taxi. I'd go hungry or without wine or anything, to make sure she got home safe.

I'd be a good mum, really I would.

The girl hasn't got into a cab though. She's walking back the way she came with one of the drivers, him having to bend to the side to listen as she talks at him. She looks excited, the way a puppy might if it were going for a walk with its new owner. I move closer to the window so I can see where they go. When they reach the main road, they wait for a car to pass, and then as they cross, he puts his arm about her shoulders. Someone to see her safely home after all, then. Older brother, let's say that, right? Or Mum's boyfriend, or her Dad, why not that, her Dad—her Dad who works there, right?

Why am I even thinking about her like this? I'm just tired, I guess. I fixate on shit when I'm tired.

I haven't slept well for months, not in the way I once could, not in the way I did when I first met Max. That's almost the thing I miss most about him most, the way we could be unconscious together, like it was something we built into our week. We both of us worked most weekends, it goes with the territory, the weekend being when most people want to get inked or to pretend like they're going to buy custom built motorbikes. So Monday was, if not our weekend, our day to sleep. Monday mornings melting into Monday afternoons, breathing in concert. There'd be that sleepy, only half aware moment when we'd roll together, and Max's big, strong hands explored me, making me part of the dream we shared. Sleep so heavy it was hard to shake off. That was the knitter up of all our troubles, when we didn't have troubles to knit, only hope.

Now I go to bed at one, maybe two, and my skin itches with ant crawls, until I have to get up and shower, or sit in the dark to try breathing exercises. I count through the alphabet, naming bands for each letter—

Adam and the Ants, Bauhaus, Cure (The), Damned (The), mining my adolescent record collection. When I get to Xymox, Clan Of, only purists of exactly my age and experience are still with me. Second time round, it's X-ray Specks, which even I only know from compilation albums released after the fact; third time the letter 'X' sticks in my brain and becomes a fly buzzing against glass, a rattle that finally, almost reluctantly, sends me into a fitful, dream-light sleep.

My phone buzzes with a text before I get to the last X.

'You awake?' the Boy asks.

'Go away,' I reply.

'Love you too,' he replies.

At three am, it's too hot for London, it feels more like Vegas or Ibiza. The sky's lurid orange under the black-grey of what passes for night, I swear I can see a hint of brightness over towards the city already. If the Boy was to come round now, I'd fuck him, just because it might help me get some sleep, just because it might stop the thoughts from scratching about behind my eyes. I even get out my phone to text him again, like poking at missing tooth wanting the pain.

'You awake—,' no, delete, 'hey, what you dreamin—,' no, delete, 'Guess what I'm dre—' no, delete, 'I'm dreaming of your great bi—' oh for fuck's sake!

Disgusted, I throw the phone on to the counter, take a great handful of my hair and pull it tight against my scalp. You're meant to be cooling it off with him, you're meant to be gently manoeuvring away, because you can't face the straight-out telling him thing, and you're hoping he just loses interest and drifts away, like some tectonic plate. This is not that, this is not what you said you'd do, sexting him at three in the morning is not that.

I leave my phone on the counter and go pull on some jeans and a vest top. I force my feet into a pair of trainers, so busted up and worn down I don't need to undo the laces, and take my leather flying jacket from the hall cupboard. It's too hot for leather, and it makes me sweat, but I can't go out at night in a t-shirt with no bra, I just can't. Even with my A-cups, it's just one of those things no one does, like sitting upstairs alone on a night bus, or taking a short cut through a park in the dark, or getting into a mini-cab you haven't called.

Outside the street smells of burnt out summer and asphalt. There's no cold in the air, not even a hint of it, just a kind of less heat. I should sell up and go and live in my place by the sea that Nan left me. Still not really my place though. It still feels like Nan's, which is why I don't go there, I guess. No, it's because she's not there anymore to tell me to come and stay for a bit, to tell me I need a breath of sea air to sort my head out. That's the real reason.

'I expect you'll sell it,' Mum said after all the paper-work was done. 'I still can't imagine what she thought she was doing, leaving it to you at your age, I can't imagine what she was doing leaving it to you at all.' As if Nan had planned to die when she did solely to be awkward. Maybe that was why I didn't sell it, because Mum thought I should.

The taxi rank light flicks my shadow on and off, until the mild white light of the twenty-four-hour shop paints it softly on the pavement behind me. The trays of vegetables are all inside now, as if the place is a snail that's drawn in its horns. Christ knows how it keeps going now that the supermarket has opened up in the space behind it, but it does. Oh come on, I know how. It keeps going by breaking the licensing laws, as if it was an act of post-colonial rebellion. Under the counter vodka is how it keeps going.

They know me in there enough to do the eyebrow raise hello to me. As the man behind the counter is counting out my change, there's a scuffle at the door. He looks up and his immobile face bursts into life.

'Hey,' he demands over my head. 'You, get out, get out of my shop!'

I turn. It's the girl. She's standing under the strip light over the door, rabbit-eyed and sneering, a scowl twisting her lips but her eyes confused, as if she's not sure he means her or me.

'Hey, I told you before, you're banned! You don't come in here, okay?'

'I only want—' she begins, but he cuts her off.

'I told you before, get out.'

There's something desperate in the way she'd started to speak, something pleading. For a moment I think she's going to cry, or that she's trying to work out what to say to argue her case.

'Fuck you, you Paki bastard,' she spits instead, a beetle-browed expression darkening her face. 'Fuck you, you fucking Paki cunt!'

'Get out of my shop!' the man demands again, furious, slamming my handful of change on the stack of papers, slamming the till shut, slamming his hand on its closed drawer.

I want to say something, tell her she can't use words like that, ask him what the matter is. I feel my mother's voice rising up inside me. *Now, now, no matter who did what, I'm sure we can sort it out, if only we all just calm down and—*

The girl darts forward and snatches at the display shelves directly opposite the door. She grabs a packet of biscuits and sends a whole stack flying to the floor.

'Thief!' The shop man yells, and I jump forward as if to catch them.

'Fuck you,' the girl screams. Then to me, 'And you, bitch!'

A little unnecessary, seeing as I'm the one juggling with the mess she's made. Then she's gone, running out into the night, up towards the main road, from what I can see.

'Oh, my God,' the man says, hands up, shaking his head. He comes round the counter and over to where I'm bending down to pick up the biscuits. 'No, no, it's okay, you leave it, please,' he says. More slide off the shelves, a small earthquake of brightly coloured biscuit packets, a veritable confectionary landslide.

'You see this?' he says to me, hand out as if addressing a larger audience. 'Every night, most night they do this. Her and the others, come and steal from my shop. Every fucking night. I call the police, I tell the police, what do they do, huh?' He looks as if he's expecting me to answer, as if this is a quiz.

'Nothing?' I venture.

'Nothing,' he echoes, nodding as if I'm so right he can't imagine why I've not been made mayor of this whole goddam city. 'Nothing, see, you understand.' He holds out his hands for the biscuits I've rescued. 'I blame them, you know, where are they?' Before I can ask, he explains. 'Where is her father, hmm? All the same, you know, blacks like her, running wild.'

'Is she black?' I say, which is not what I meant to say really, but because I hadn't given it much thought until he said it like that.

'Course,' he says, and stoops to pick up more biscuits. 'Half black, mix-up mongrel, innit, no father, mother some crack whore.'

81

I assume he's not really talking to me anymore, or hope he isn't. From deep in the recesses of the shop, someone calls out to him and he stops his muttering rant and stands up to bark commands. A younger man hurries up to see what the problem is, and I can work out what they're saying without losing anything in translation.

'Okay, well, I'm gonna go now,' I say, and the shop man breaks off from demanding why it is he's expected to deal with shit like this, to say, 'Yes, yes, you go, and if the police ask, you say, yes? You say what she did, if they ask you?'

'Sure,' I say, and he holds out his hand to me. I look at it for a moment, the broad, pink brown palm, fleshy fingers, then we shake hands.

'You tell them, what she say? I don't have to put up with that racist shit. I'm running a shop, that is all,' he says, and he nods. 'Thank you.'

I go then, and I wonder if he's asking me to back him up, because even now, a white woman's word will hold just that little more weight with the police, than his? White privilege in action.

When I get back into the flat, tiredness finally eating hard enough at the back of my eyes, that I think I might even sleep, I leave the peach juice unopened in the fridge and pick up my phone. There's a text message.

'Hey, can't sleep, thinking of you.'

It's from Max.

I'm disappointed.

CHAPTER TEN

A.A.

THERE WERE OTHERS before Max, of course there were, but most of all, there was Cassie.

I met her on a night bus when I was twenty-one. I'd been on a date with some bloke, friend of a friend scenario, who I initially thought was a lot more interesting than he turned out to be. So I said I had somewhere else to be, said I wasn't looking for anything right now, and when that didn't work, that really, he'd be better off without me.

That left me in Euston too late for a tube and with no cash, just before everyone started having mobile phones. The cash point at the station was broken and I'd had a few too many Newcastle Brown Ales, so I got on a night bus to throw myself on the mercy of the driver.

No night bus driver in London has any sympathy left for the stories they're told, and who can blame them. But just when his expression had hardened beyond the point of no return, someone came up behind me and offered to pay, and that was Cassie.

She was in full on Goth mode then, all in black apart from her hair, and unlike everyone else I was friends with then, wasn't at college.

'What would I go to college for?' she said. 'How can you tell what you need to know, until you've found out what you don't already?' Or something like that, which sounded incredibly clever and deep at the time.

We swapped numbers, old school, pen and paper, and she rang me and we just started hanging out. She came to college parties, she slept with a boy on my course, she helped me with my infamous graduation exhibition, where we papered the whole thing with photocopies of our arses, confirming to all and sundry why I only deserved a third, and then we moved in together, in a shitty flat in a shitty part of Turnpike Lane. I worked with Big Al, and she started on another one of the endless jobs she did before she found one which recognised her many talents and paid her accordingly. We went to gigs, we got stoned, we hung out in Camden Town and had our hair put into dreadlocks, we wore shoes with enormous soles, we got bits of us pierced and, when I was good enough, I tattooed her back with an octopus, which is far more beautiful than it sounds.

'I want to be a Bond villain,' she said. She got her hair cut in a severe, blonde bob, and wore ultra-violet lipstick and silver clothes. Because back then people chose a colour and stuck to it for accessories, furnishings, shoes, kind of like a tag. She glittered, Cassie. A human disco ball.

Just before I turned thirty, I got bored working on the clients Big Al had in his Crouch End shop, even with the odd interesting one he threw my way. So, when the shop was quiet, I worked on my own stuff. I collected images of war time pin-ups, and fine art, and folk art, and I tried to work them together. I looked at black work embroidery, white work embroidery, Scandi prints and textiles and fashion design. I read so much—Angela Carter, Sylvia Plath, Neil Gaiman—anything which made good pictures in my head, anything that pushed my hand faster across the paper, made my fingers inky.

'I never see you these days,' Cassie said. 'You're always head down, working.'

I stuck huge pieces of paper on my bedroom walls and drew on them, stories and characters and cameos; my own style with smoky edges cut through with sharpness. I spidered my thighs with damask print and venetian masks, bird skulls and fairy tales. Then Frances Del-Gatto came into the shop.

He was American, and being American, and having tumbling playing cards tattooed down his arm, and being handsome, in a kind of blonde thatch of hair and dark glasses way, I read him completely wrong.

And yes, I was restless at Al's. My own work was really

starting to interest me, like I was falling in love with my skills after college had beaten that out of me, and yes, I was single. But I had Cassie, and we had fun. And I was happy, I wasn't needy, I wasn't down, I wasn't looking for anyone beyond myself.

Frances spent a long time looking through the designs in the shop, then he looked through some of the ones I had up in my corner and asked for an arm piece, said he wanted something unique.

I ventured into my dark portfolio, the weird, dream-like work which had been pouring out of me, but which felt too fragile to be exposed to the sunlight yet. He came back to see it, said he loved it but it wasn't quite right, that he wanted me to "push it", go deeper—which meant he'd seen something in it, surely? I went home terrified, but I worked harder, worked longer into the night, because working for someone else seemed a thousand times more important than working for myself. With the second one, which I presented like an eager pupil, he was not exactly unimpressed, but it still wasn't right. I'd done a good job, but he wanted something which hurt for me to give to him, something which was more mine than his. I thought he was good for me, that he was getting the best from me—that he validated me.

The third design was perfect—because he said it was perfect. He pinned it to the wall, made me stand back and look at it, clapped his hands to his thighs. Strode up and down in the empty shop because he liked to meet there after hours so we wouldn't be disturbed, telling me I'd done it, given him what he wanted.

'I have to be in the States next month, so book me in after that, I don't want to travel with it healing, don't want to rush the process. So, not sure what your plans are, but might I buy you a soda? There's something I'd like to run past you.'

'Make it a beer and you're on,' I said, already thinking how I'd describe him to Cassie, how I'd mimic his voice as he said, 'Whatever you want, darlin'.'

He said he'd come to Big Al's under false pretences, because much as he wanted some of my work on his body, he really wanted to put a business proposition my way. He'd seen me in a magazine article about Big Al's, in which I got to show off a little. He wanted to open a tattoo parlour over in Kingston, was looking for artists with a difference, artists who were hungry and wanted something new, and I listened and heard everything I had ever dreamed about hearing. Then he left, said he had another appointment, but that he'd be back in touch real soon.

I told Big Al, because we'd always been straight with each other, and as much as he can be an awkward, stick in the mud old fucker, he's honest.

'You go and spread your wings, chicky,' he said. 'Get yourself round them conventions, get known, that sort of bollocks. You're bigger than Big Al.' He slapped me on the shoulder with the flat of his hand.

Cassie said, 'Fuck him, and go on working with Al,' but she'd just been dumped and wasn't feeling very positive about men.

FRANCES WANTED TO see my portfolio so we arranged to meet up. He called when he was a half hour late and arrived full of apologies, with a story of how he'd been held up at a meeting with some guys who were looking to invest. He asked if we could talk at my place, because he couldn't concentrate with all the background noise if we met in a pub. We spent hours with my drawings spread out around us, drinking and talking about them, him telling me, 'What we're gonna need, is a whole heap of your designs down on paper, your best work ever.' He touched my cheek and said, 'You're gonna blow their tiny little minds, darlin'.' Then his phone rang, and he had to go, and I'd promised him a portfolio in a week, thinking I could have produced one in a day, I was so excited to finally have someone believe in me, in my work. Just like the nice man at art college had.

The next morning, he rang and said he had a meeting arranged with the investors in three days' time. It was near Gatwick, because they were flying in for it and were on a tight schedule. He'd booked us into a hotel by the airport but didn't say if that meant two rooms or one.

I was tired, I'd spent hours working on the portfolio, buying beautiful paper and tearing it into pieces that made me think of skinned animals, and working them over and over with my designs. New pens, new paints, all of it, working and working because Frances Del-Gatto believed in me, more than anyone ever had, more than I ever had. It was in the car, on the back seat when I picked him up at the train station.

'Hey, you even put the seatbelt round it,' he said.

I laughed and said that was because it was my baby.

My first baby.

He told me to wait in the lounge while he checked us in. When he came back, we went to the bar and he talked a lot about who these guys were and why they were interested in me. Then he got a phone call. He went to the far side of the bar to take it, and when he came back said they weren't coming after all. He was really sorry, angry, on my behalf.

'Made me drag you all the way out here to this god-forsaken shit-hole of a place.'

'Really, it's okay, we can just meet them another time, and—'

'No, it's not okay. Nobody dicks me around like that, nobody. You wanna drink?'

So we had one, and he stared at his hands. Then he said we'd better get our bags from the room, seeing as we were wasting our time.

He said he'd fetch my bag, then, as we were crossing the dreary reception area, he got a call. He was walking a few steps behind me, so I didn't hear it ring. He became involved in the conversation, nodding, animated as if he were waiting to jump in on an argument. Then he came to a stop and got out a room key, and mouthed, 'Get the bags, would you, darlin'?'

'Sure,' I said, and went to go, but he held out his hand again. When I didn't get what he wanted, he cupped his hand over the receiver and said, 'You wanna leave that here, darlin'? Save carrying it up all them stairs?'

So I did, I gave him my portfolio, to save carrying it up all those stairs.

I gave it to him.

Stupid thing was, it was worth nothing to anybody but me; they were mine, then they were gone. The woman behind the desk seemed genuinely surprised when I asked where exactly room thirty-seven was. She looked at me through her large, pink framed glasses, and said there wasn't a room thirty-seven, and besides, that wasn't a key from their motel.

When I asked her where Frances had gone with my portfolio, she said he just walked out with it.

I DROVE HOME having rung his number and screamed at his answer machine, as if I expected him to ring back and say, 'Oh shit, darlin', I don't know what got into me.

Sure, I got your drawings, they're all safe with me.'

When I got in, Cassie was in her dressing gown, her face avocado green with a face-pack and eating ice cream. I fell through the door, hardly able to get a word out for the tears, and her crying just for the shock of seeing me like that, and saying, 'What's happened? What's happened? Did he hurt you, are you hurt? What did he do?' Me trying desperately to tell her that it wasn't that, it really wasn't, not what she and everyone else might think, what with me going to a motel alone with an arsehole I hardly knew.

It took me so long to tell her that the muck on her face cracked off, and her ice cream turned into a brown puddle of mush.

'He did all of this, all the…the lies and the calls and making me do all that work, and talking about it with me, because, because of what? To steal what?' The humiliation of it rose up again in me and had me gasping for air.

Cassie snatched up a towel to rub her face clean.' He's a fucking fantasist,' she said. 'A psycho. You need to call the police.'

'And tell them what?' I said. 'He set me up to steal some tattoo designs, a portfolio that's worth jack-shit?' Just like me, stupid, idiot me thinking him or anyone could see any good in me.

'It's your work, for fuck's sake,' she said, jabbing her finger at someone who wasn't there. 'It doesn't matter what anyone else thinks, it's your work.'

All I could see was me and him, my drawings spread out on the floor, and him talking and talking about them, as if he understood, as if he got me.

'Maybe he was going to do worse,' Cassie said. 'Shit, I don't want to say this, but—'

'Yeah, I know, I got off lightly, he could have arse-fucked me in a broom closet or some shit like that.'

'Well, he could of,' she snapped. 'That's the point. What if next time he does do it?'

'I need more evidence first.' Because I thought, some-how, that would make them take notice of me, prove to them there was something more going on than just my hurt pride.

I rang everyone I could think of who might have known him, from the places he said he'd hung out, people he'd mentioned that he knew that I sort of knew too. There were notes all over the sitting room floor.

Cassie came home to find me unwashed and just getting off the phone to yet another person who ran a shop in the market, who was sure he'd come in with another girl about two weeks back, remembered because he'd bought her some of their top of the range boots.

'She said it was weird because he had this black credit card, a type she'd never seen before, and everything went through fine at the time, but a week later…'

'Babe,' Cassie came and got hold of me and made me

look at her. 'It's doing your head in. I spoke to the police, right, and they said that—'

'You did what, why?'

'Because this is their job, not yours.'

'But why did you, when I asked you not to?' Then I cried, because I didn't want to speak to the police, because speaking to them would be like admitting what an idiot I'd been. And why was I getting so upset anyway, what was the big deal? It wasn't proper art, was it? Just a load of my drawings out of my head, and anyway there was nothing original in me, nothing a photocopier couldn't do just as well. That was what they said at university, right? That silver-haired tutor, the one who'd encouraged me to apply for fine art, smiling and telling me I had a nice little talent. I mean, who cares about a nice little talent?

'I'm just looking out for you, yeah?' Cassie said.

'I don't think his name's even Frances,' I said.

'Probably not.'

She made me go and report it. I went because I want-ed to find out who he was, call him out, stand with my finger pointed at him and scream in his face what he'd done. The police recorded it as a crime, they took a statement and listened patiently as I talked through my crazy research. They asked if I might be able to draw him, this Frances Del-Gatto, seeing as I was so good at drawing, but I couldn't do it. Under my pen his face extended into a cartoonish mask of horror as my hand juddered over the paper, my fingers stiff and unwieldly. They never got back to me and, let's face it, the weird little fucker could have simply got on a plane with the drawings and gone back to the States, so what did I expect them to do? Cassie suggested I tell Big Al I'd had second thoughts. Big Al nodded and said, 'Good thing too, chicky, I'd have missed you brightening up the place,'

'There,' Cassie said. 'You've done it. Look, let's go out and get pissed shall we? Make you feel better?'

'Yeah,' I said, 'if you like.'

Only I didn't feel better. I started having this night terror thing, waking up with this sensation like a cat was sitting across my neck, so real I swore I could feel its fur, even its claws prickling the skin of my neck, and its purr, vibrating into my breastbone. Cassie would hear me screaming and come into my room, and I'd be thrashing about in the bed, until I'd sit up in the orange dark of a London night and cling onto her.

'You have to let this go,' Cassie said. 'Come on, no one died, right? You're just letting him win, this isn't like you, yeah?'

I got Big Al to tattoo my neck, so that the pain of the thing choking me in my sleep felt like mine, like I was doing it to myself. Then I pulled myself together.

I redrew my portfolio. The lines I used were evil, sharp, and the images I pulled together were vengeful and bitter, cruel and beautiful. I don't know if they were better, but they were harder and cleaner and angrier. I took them to a place in Kensington that was run by a dickhead with money, who was British and so unable to beguile me with Louisiana vowels. He offered me a chair at an extortionate rent so I doubled my hourly rate. I started doing the whole social media thing, which everyone was suddenly all very excited about it, and a friend of Cassie's helped me design a website full of the dark excesses of my new style. I had a My Space page, when that was what everyone had, then Facebook, then a Twitter account and tweeted pictures of my work as it gnawed its way across other people's skin.

But it still wasn't okay, somehow.

Then everyone was getting inked, which is a phrase I love as much as I love the drooling, celeb-wannabes that use it, but hell, who's counting? I got to hurt them and they paid me a lot of money for it. Then your actual minor celebrities started coming. Footballers and their WAGs, TV people and media people, and musicians I'd heard of, bands I'd downloaded. I got invited to their parties, in shitty-glittery night-clubs in the West End, that were all cocaine and spray tans, and Cassie was always my date, every time, no matter who else was around.

'You know why we never pull at these things?' she said. 'Because we always get pissed and end up snogging each other.'

'You're crazy,' I said. 'That's why we *always* pull at these things.' Which was pretty much true. We even had a threesome in some hotel with a kid's TV presenter, seriously, no shit. In his day job, he leapt about being a tree or some shit like that, but at night, he liked women and coke, and was one hell of a laugh. He got caught by some paparazzi with a couple of call-girls the week after, which was a shame, because that kind of put pay to his career. He'd been going to get an arm piece from me, once he'd come back from filming elephants somewhere, with a puppet.

'He must have thought we were a right cheap night out!' Cassie said, and we'd laughed about it, lying side-by-side on the floor of our flat, stoned out of our minds.

'It's good to have you back,' Cassie said. 'I've missed you.'

I saw him, Frances Del-Gatto, just once more. I was in Camden Market—afternoon off, browsing, taking myself out to lunch. Turned the corner and there he was. Sheltering from the rain under an awning. It was so crowded he didn't see me. I went to run, but people were pressing all round, so all I could do was turn my back on him as heat rushed through my cheeks, my heart hammering. Then I made myself look again, to make sure.

His hair was dark this time, but I could see the edge of the playing card tattoo on his neck. He was with a dark haired, pretty woman, about my age, wearing a large, black hat. He was talking to her, looking at her the way he'd looked at me, as if he was seeing something more in her than everyone else did. Maybe not, maybe that was just me making shit up, because he couldn't just be ordinary, could he?

I remember my pulse beating high and hard in my chest—this was it, I could do it, call him out. I went towards him, threading through the crowd. I was going to go up to him jab my finger into his shoulder and yell, 'Hey, you fucking arsehole, where's my drawings, huh?' And watch the look of comprehension break on his stupid, smug face, and hear him stammer out some excuse, or pretend he didn't know who I was. Do what the police hadn't done and catch up to him. Prove my work was worth it. Prove I was worth it.

I heard him say something, caught the end of a sentence '…weather in this country, wouldn't think it was nearly summer.' And he was speaking in a British accent, straight up London, like he was local or something.

I couldn't say anything. I watched them for a moment longer, then turned and pushed away through the maze of stalls, with the splash of rain underfoot and the smell of cooking, and sweat, and cigarette smoke, and the sense that there was something sitting on my throat, stopping me from breathing.

'I'm thinking of getting my own place,' I said to Cassie.

'Was it something I said?' she asked, and then we both pretended she was joking.

I needed space to find myself, find my work again, to see what I could do without someone like Frances, or even Cassie, telling me I was good enough. The more they said it, somehow the less I believed it.

So I got my own place. Then I moved Max in and I kind of forgot all about that, and the space I'd made became full of everything else again, a tide filling up the beach of my life.

When was the last time I sat down and drew something new, something for me?

CHAPTER ELEVEN
Not everyone talks like that

THE DAY SEEMS wilfully hot when I wake up, not enough hours after I fell asleep for it to really count. I make real coffee with cream in it and drink it leaning against the counter, wishing the clock on the wall didn't say eight-fifteen. When I pull up the kitchen blind, leopard print with a grinning skull knob on the cord, the world outside is cracking with heat, the span of the buildings opposite sun-baked all the way to the supermarket and beyond. I should seriously think about moving to Nan's cottage, but right now the thought of that and the conversations I'd once had with Max about how we might do it when the baby came, are like something written in dust on a windowpane, just as fragile, just as real.

The taxi drivers are milling about outside their rank, three of them, out early. They're all wearing jackets despite the heat, as if this English idea of summer is nothing to them, hardly breaking their stride. A police car pulls up outside it and that's when I notice the twenty-four-hour shop is closed. The shutter's down and has a vast splat of white paint across it. Was that there last night? I'm pretty sure it wasn't, and neither was the word, "Paki" scrawled alongside it.

I finish my coffee and go for a shower. I'm meeting Cassie for lunch. The only thing that annoys me about her is that her indefatigable sense of fair play will mean that she will have spoken to Max. She met him a little before I did, so she counts him as her friend too, I mean, as well as friend because he's my boyfriend. Was my boyfriend. This means that she believes it's unfair to take sides, even if she's acutely disappointed at what he's done. This also means that it's probably not a good idea to tell her about The Boy, even though I've broken it off with him. Which is what I'll say if I accidentally let slip about it, and which I haven't actually done.

My phone beeps. The Boy.

'Hey, woke up with a big fucking—'

I turn it face down, as if even reading it while I'm getting ready to see Cassie, might mean she'd know about it.

I'm standing by the wardrobe having chosen a pair of high waist shorts and a sports bra, when the door buzzer sounds. Yes, there's a moment when my heart does that stupid hard hammering jump, and I think it might be The Boy. But I know it isn't, because I've made him swear he'll text first before he comes round, and besides, I get the feeling he's not a morning person.

It's a policeman.

He looks both younger than me and older, a child soldier given an android's bulk by his stab vest and squawk box. And yes, like everyone, even though I've done nothing, I feel both guilty and alarmed by him filling up the doorway with his shoulders.

'Sorry to bother you, Miss,' he says, which at least isn't madame. 'I'm P.C Barnes.' He shoulders his ID towards me, as if the uniform wasn't enough of a clue. 'I've been called out over an incident of racial abuse, and the gentleman says you were a witness?' He glances back over at the twenty-four-hour shop. 'The owner says you were there when it happened?'

It's about the biscuits. I hadn't really considered the possibility that the shop guy would actually call the police, but then I remember the white spray paint on the shutter.

'Would it be okay to ask you a few questions about the incident?' he asks.

I imagine him writing me up in his note book, if they still do that, recording an interview with a female witness to the event, who lives in a flat opposite the location, and was apparently in the shop at the time, though goodness knows what she was doing there, bit 'suss' if you ask me, m'lud.

'Okay, sure,' I say. I can see the taxi drivers and a

couple of guys from the shop are on the street watching us, though they're not standing together. They're in two quite distinct groups, drivers, shop men, both are staring at me. I feel the need to conduct this interview, however brief, upstairs.

'Why don't you come up?' I say.

'DID SHE MAKE any verbal threats at all?' PC Barnes asks. He's actually writing everything down that I say, or an approximation of it I suppose, like they do on TV and everything.

'I'm not sure what other kind of threat she could have made. There's not much of her.'

'But did she … did she make any further threat, after her use of the racially abusive term?'

I wonder how he might refer to the shopkeeper with his mates? Not in his report of course, but in the infamous locker room you hear about, the culture of which was meant to be so hostile to non-white, non-male officers? Interviewed this right one about that Paki shop thing today? Tattoos bloody everywhere, she had.

'No, she didn't,' I say. No, I can't see him doing that, not this nice PC Barnes. He's a new generation, all that shameful stuff drummed out of him, and a good thing too. He's probably got black and Asian friends in the force, and is mates with a female officer, and a gay one. A proper community liaison police officer. I imagine kissing him, imagine what it would be like to be pressed up against that stab vest, all those buckles and zips. Quite kinky, really, PC Barnes. Then I think about the girl, and how she should have been in bed.

'She's not very old,' I say. 'I was surprised to see her there, that time of night.'

'Why were you there, if you don't mind my asking?' He shrugs. 'I mean, I just wondered?'

'Insomnia,' I say, because there's nothing like a vaguely medical term to close down a line of questioning. 'Thought I'd get some juice, that's all. Dehydrated.'

'Right,' he says.

'Do you know who she is?' I venture. He doesn't look up from his notes. 'I mean, I've seen her about a few times recently.'

'Have you?' he asks. 'Where?'

'Just hanging about, you know, locally?' I'm not sure why I don't tell him about the time I'd seen her walking up the road with the taxi driver. Maybe it's because it's her business who she's with. Like when my sister, who was only nine, saw me in the record shop near home and told Mum about it. I wasn't doing anything, just leaning against a rack of twelve inches and talking with the man who worked there. True, I was fourteen and he was twenty one or so, but at the time I was just furious with her, because he was just a guy in a shop and even though I really wanted him to ask me out, he never did, so it was fine, right? God, he's in his late forties now, and so far more suitable as an alternative to Max than The Boy, only then of course the six or so years between us was quite a different thing. When Lauren told them, Mum and Dad sat me down and gave me the talk, you know the one, and all the time I felt humiliated and horrible and angry, because nothing had happened between us, and nothing was ever going to, and he was nice. So maybe I didn't say about the girl and the taxi driver, because of that, because it felt like I was snitching on her.

'I've an idea who she is,' PC Barnes says, because of course he isn't about to give me her name. 'There's a few of them you get every year, kids like that. The girls can be the worst. We've had a spate of it. Trying to be as tough as the boys, out to impress some spotty Herbert no doubt.' He smiles, clearly scrabbling through, "The big book of phrases only your Dad would use" for something to say as he can't really tell me anything. 'There's not a lot a I can do, other than have a word, but we'll see.'

'Isn't it on the CCTV?' I ask as he gets up to leave. 'I mean, in the shop, isn't it recorded, her coming in and that?'

'No, which is a shame, their system's down or something. No idea who did the outside of the shop either, not for sure, but...'

WHEN I TELL Cassie about it over lunch, I tell her that it

was like having a character from a PlayStation game come to life in my flat.

'I dunno,' I say, twirling green spaghetti round my fork, 'there was something a bit unreal about him, like close up he was going to be all pixels.'

Cassie, who always eats as if someone might take her food away from her if she were to give them an inch, has already folded her knife and fork together on her plate, and is crunching one of her ice cubes. We're in a bright, busy place over the road from where she works, which is a cross between a cafe and a bistro, with an outside seating area crammed with suits. They all stare at me when I come in, and I stare back at them, enjoying it. They're city types, though not the worst city types, and it's too early for them to be drunk and coked up enough to get abusive at the mere sight of my illustrated thighs. I wonder how many of them, especially the women in their crisp blouses and glossy, business-ready hairstyles, hide secret ink beneath it all. Chances are a fair few of them have half sleeves and back pieces to boot. Hell, I'm practically mainstream these days.

I tell her about what happened by way of telling her what I told the policeman and make my first error in letting slip that I was in the shop at three in the morning.

'What the hell were you doing up at three in the morning?' she asks, frowning.

The spaghetti I've been eating, slimed with a home-made pesto, is starting to be just too much of everything, too oily, too herby, too cheesy, so I push my plate aside before trying to be casual about it.

'Oh, you know, just one of those nights when you get woken up and can't get back to sleep. I had some weird craving for peach juice, so I thought fuck it, I'll go and get some, you know? I can do shit like that, what with me being young, free and single, don't you know?'

But Cassie isn't put off the scent that easily. 'Is this every night, or just a one off? You not sleeping again?'

'It's probably just the after-effects of the weekend. Really, that's not the point. The point is that the girl was there, the one I told you about.'

'Which girl? Oh, this kid you said about, the rude one.'

'Right, and what was she doing there at three in the morning? Fuck, she can only be, what, fourteen, tops?'

'Kids look older these days, but even so, I suppose. What did she do?'

'Not much, really, but I got the impression that they've had a run in before, the shop man and her. He told her to get out soon as she appeared, and she told him to fuck off.' I can't use the word Paki, even in a direct quote, not in public among all these suits and slimy spaghetti. 'He got angry, then she sort of snatched at a shelf, tumbled the biscuits down and ran off.'

'So he didn't know for sure it was her, then?' Cassie

says.

'Nah, just fishing, see if I saw something during one of my night rambles.'

Cassie has a portable phone charger and we've both plugged our phones into it. I glance at mine, and Cassie sees me looking.

'Have you heard from Max,' she says, in a tone that suggests she's been waiting to say this since I arrived and wants to be kind about it.

I smirk, pull my mouth to one side, don't look at her when I say, 'The other day, we spoke on the phone. He's gone back to Birmingham, staying with one of his sisters, can't remember which one, the middle one I think.' I look at her. 'It's okay, we're okay.' All of which is a lie, a huge one, because Max hasn't really called, just like he said he wouldn't.

'Are you okay, though?' Can she tell, Cassie? Can she see the lie, and the shame of it, burning in my cheeks? Because really, shouldn't Max have called me by now?

'Of course I'm not, but what you gonna do? Going to the loo.'

After I use the bathroom, I stare into the washroom mirror. I should probably try and eat a bit more of my lunch before Cassie starts to worry about me not eating. I keep coming back to the girl though, her face when she first came into the shop, the way she looked as if she really wanted to come in, as if she really hoped it would be okay, and before her face had gone all angry and hard, there was a moment when she looked so small, as if she might be going to cry.

As I thread my way back through the tables, letting the gaze of the suits slide over me unheeded, I see Cassie at our table, watching me come toward her. She smiles as I sit down, takes a sip of water, then says, 'Tell me to mind my own if you want, but who's the Cockney Fuck Buddy?'

It's not that I'm shit at lying, I'm quite good at lying when I need to be, *Sure, that's a great idea for a tattoo, I'd love to work on that for my hundred and fifty pound an hour fee*, but I'm shit at lying to Cassie. Besides which, she's caught me totally off guard, because for a stupid moment I can't think how the fuck she's come up with that name, the stupid one I use for The Boy on my phone, because I haven't told her about him. Then I remember the key word in all this, my phone. I look, and it's still sitting innocently next to hers. When I touch it, running my tongue over my teeth as if I might find the right words to say to her there, its treacherous little screen lights up with, Cockney Fuck Buddy: 'So, I'm texting first this time, you in for a fuck?'

'You really don't have to tell me,' Cassie says, in the voice that means I really do have to tell her, and that she's a teeny-weeny bit hurt that I haven't told her already.

'It's nothing, really,' I begin. I unplug the phone and

stick it back into the pocket of my shorts. 'Shit,' I say, and flop back against my chair.

'Look,' Cassie hold up her hands, 'Max did a shitty thing, you know I think that, and so, sure, you're going to feel—'

'It's just sex, alright?'

Cassie's eyes widen, now she's more than a teeny-weeny bit hurt.

'Shit, I'm sorry.' I slump my head onto my hands, elbows on the table. 'I really didn't want you to find out because it really doesn't mean anything. Because it's over, because it was nothing, you know?' I peer at Cassie through my fingers.

She blows out a huff of air, the loose strands of her blonde hair rising and falling. Everyone must be looking at the two of us and thinking, how the hell are these two friends?

'It's okay, you don't have to explain.'

'But I do, yes I do.' I put my hands down and she takes one of mine and squeezes it, and I see that she's blinking away a tear. 'Cassie?'

'It's just that you've been through so much,' she says, and lets go of my hand to pick up the napkin and dab at her face. 'So I do understand, I really do.'

We have this exchange then, with neither of us really saying anything at all.

'It's just—'

'You don't have to—'

'It's not about—'

'I know, I know—'

Then we're both doing that girl crying thing and saying we love each other, and we get up and hug, and someone, some delightful soul at the back of the café, does a low whistle, and Cassie pulls away from me and barks, 'Hey, arsehole, back off!' As we sit back down. Because she's a lot better at doing that kind of thing, than I am.

'Who is he? What's his name?'

'Well, not that, anyway.'

She's waiting for me to tell her, and when I don't, this annoys her.

'He's just someone I met, and now it's over.'

'It doesn't sound that over,' she says, and clicks open her bag to fish out her mirror.

'Well, of course I'm going to tell him it's over now, that he can't come round.'

'He knows where you live?' she says, and this time I get an eyebrow raise. Cassie could never play poker, her eyebrows seem to conduct a facial semaphore of their own to anyone who knows her.

'No,' I say, making the quick calculation that the message didn't actually mention a venue.

'And, he was at the after party?'

That I can't get away from, and I'm hoping to God

that she doesn't remember him, that I was standing with him leaning on the balcony smoking. Something Cassie has never done and does not approve of, and thought I'd given up years ago.

Then she says, 'Was he that tall kid?'

'Which tall kid?' I manage, because I'm in my stride now, she no longer has the advantage of surprise. I'm even better than I thought, or she's deciding to go along with it for now, because she seems to discount that and then says, 'Wait, not Alan, Alan A?'

He's one of the ones who messaged me in the aftermath. It's not him, of course, but if it was him, that would make more sense to Cassie than some random tall kid, who isn't connected to anyone, as far as I can tell.

'It's not Alan A,' I say, 'really it isn't, though funnily enough he messaged me afterwards.' Because a little bit of truth, and all, wrapping up your lie.

'Did he?' she says, her interest momentarily deflected. 'I always thought he had a thing for you.' Then she narrows her eyes again, 'Look, alright, whoever he is, and you really don't have to say, and, leaving aside the whole Max thing, I just don't think you're, well…are you sure you're strong enough to, well, not get involved with him?'

I love Cassie but the one thing I fucking hate about my best friend of all time, is that she always knows exactly the truth of me. She knows that I've been awake at three am for the last three months on and off, and that I'm not eating, and that I'm cleaning and running as if both were a punishment from a drill sergeant, and all of that really fucks me off at times. And she knows me so well, that even though I'm angry at her for saying this, for knowing that this is the absolute truth of the thing, I'm even more angry at her for not knowing me well enough by now, that by her saying I'm too vulnerable to shag The Boy, she's pretty much made certain that I'm going to do exactly the opposite. Hopefully twice.

'Don't be stupid,' I say, hating the way I shrug back from her, the way I push my half-finished plate of food away. 'Look, I know I'm messed up right now, but I needed to blow off some steam, you know? I just wanted to feel attractive again.' I can't quite bring myself to use the word wanted.

She's nodding, she's understanding, I'm using the words she might use about me, if she was talking about all this to her Lovely Man.

'I mean, however hard this is for you, and Christ it has been, maybe this was just what you had to do, the way Max had to have some time out, some space to recover too. Look, I know this is hard for you to hear, but he's hurting too, and he probably just doesn't know what to do for the best.' The traffic in the street behind is moving at speed, the flick-flick of cars passing, the sunlight flashing off their windscreens. I find that I'm watching them, letting my eyes flick-flick too, leaning back in my chair and only half listening to her, hearing the clatter and chatter of the cafe behind, feeling the sun on my face. I'm waiting, much as a cat waits by a mousehole, waiting for something. And, there it is.

'He probably needs to get a sense of perspective, of closure, before he feels able to move on with you, and...'

Perspective. Closure. Those are Cassie's words, and the last time I heard them, Max was saying them.

The world sways away from me; my vision goes hot and a rush of anger lights me up. It was her. It was Cassie. Understanding and reasonable, Cassie, being her usual fair and balanced self. It was Cassie, sorting things out how she thinks they should be. Just like she's always done even when I never asked her too.

I get up.

'It was you, wasn't it? You told Max to take a break from me, didn't you?'

Cassie's too stunned to say anything at first.

'Fuck. You told him to leave me?'

'It's not like that,' she begins, her face going a weird combination of white and blotchy pink. 'I just—'

'Made it easier for him?' I say. 'Gave him the right words to use, the right oh so very-fucking-much not like Max phrases to make me understand.'

'I know what it looks like, but I'm talking to you both, I'm just keeping you both—'

'Please tell me you didn't tell him to say it's not you,

it's me? Because I'm gonna forgive you everything else, eventually, but I sure as hell ain't gonna forgive you for that shit, not ever.'

CHAPTER TWELVE
A whistling sound

TO RUN IS a cowardly thing to do, because I know Cassie can't follow me. She's an honest, upright person, so the last thing she will do is run out after me without paying. I've also inadvertently made her pay for the lunch I haven't really eaten too, and the wine I've drunk, the wine that is fuelling the hurt and anger which is propelling me at speed past Southwark tube onto Blackfriars Bridge. Then I break into a run, cutting round shoals of tourists looking for the South Bank.

Surely Cassie never approached Max, it must have been the other way round. Poor, confused, hurt, scared Max went to Cassie for help, because who else knew me better? He couldn't talk to me, because I wasn't exactly talk-able too, was I? Crouched like a spider on the couch, barking out instructions like, 'We'll try again, we've done it before, we'll do it again.' Looking at him with flinty eyes. And he knew there was no talking me out of it, must have, not when I arranged with Big Al to take a year out, one last chance, and went overdrive on the supplements, Chinese herbs and yoga—fucking yoga, me! Screaming, 'We've got to relax, we've got to be calm, otherwise we won't conceive again.'

So what else could he do, except look after himself? Except talk to Cassie, because he couldn't talk to me, because I couldn't even hear him, not anymore.

Well, he should have tried to talk to me. And what about Cassie? What the fuck was she doing agreeing with him that he needed some space? The two of them could have come together and talked it over with you, if she was so keen to get involved. She'd have loved that. The two of them talking you down, being reasonable, being concerned, helping you to see sense, to take a step back from it all. Perspective, right, get some perspective, they could have said that together.

And Cassie too, so happy with her lovely man, her lovely, rich man, Sebastian, bloody Sebastian, after all the shit bags and arseholes she'd been through in her twenties, and thirties, the two of us mostly on our own, mostly single. Then I meet Max and she meets him, and so what? The idea of my having a baby freaks her out? Cassie, who has always said she never wanted one, didn't think she was the right sort of person, and she's so glad that Sebastien doesn't want them either, despite all his money and the stately pile because yes, he does have one, he's actually that rich. This is the most implausible thing I have ever thought, and possibly the nastiest, and even as I think it, I know how terrible I am being, but I think it anyway. Did she talk Max into leaving in the hope that he'd eventually convince me to give up on the whole baby thing, so there I'd be, still available for nights out, and dinner, and holidays?

And then, right then, when I'm almost laughing with the joy of it, with the power of feeling so fucking hard done by and so right, and so wrong, my phone rings.

Max.

Has Cassie rung him?

I won't answer it. Fuck the both of them. Now is not a good time to speak. I answer anyway.

'Y'all right, babe?'

'You fucking cunt,' I say. So loudly, that the people I am standing next to, nice, middle class people with their children, clutching guidebooks and cans of drink and bags-for-life, turn and look at me. If I were not so furious with Max, I might have glared at them, or kicked myself for conforming to their vision of what I must now look like, some foul-mouthed tattooed bitch on the phone, junkie, whore, delete as appropriate, but I'm actually too busy being furious to give a fuck.

'Babe?' he says. Then there's a pause and I can see his expression as his mind scrolls desperately through the last few weeks, wondering what the hell he's done.

'Did you really think I wouldn't find out?' I demand.

'Babe, oh, shit, now, just take a moment, calm down—'

'Calm down? Seriously? You're telling me to calm down?'

'Babe, I don't know what you think's been going on, but—'

'Did you really think you could hide something like that from me? When was it, Max, when did it start all these,' I wave my hand, 'what shall we say, Max, conversations? Little chats?'

'Babe, what are you—?'

I slither to a halt, my sweat soaked feet sliding against the soles of my gladiator sandals, the leather straps biting my ankles. I'm next to an Italian suit shop that has had a sale on for the last five years. I can see myself in the window, laid over the red 'Closing Down' banners and I feel as if I am, as if everything in me is shutting up shop.

'I lived with her, longer than I lived with you, you sorry shack of shit!' And I do say shack, not sack, and when I say it, I think how much more appropriate that is. 'I know how she talks, and I know how you talk, so I know you went to her and—'

'Oh no, don't you have a go at her, she was only looking out for you, and if you would let yourself see that for once, for one actual moment, instead of jumping in—'

Somewhere, far above me, from a sky that is high and blue and bright as glass, clawed through with vapour trails, a penny begins to drop. It falls hard and fast. I can feel it accelerating as it plummets towards me, even hear the high-pitched whistle of it coming closer.

'She was bloody brilliant, as it goes, came round when you were at the studio that time, and she really helped, actually, she—'

There is a long silence as I stand there, the sound of the penny dropping to earth rebounding through me.

'She told you to leave me,' I say.

Max is silent too, far too silent for far too long for him to be able to come back from that, for him to even attempt a lie. I am cold, inside the city-tacky slick of my skin, too bitterly cold for tears.

'Babe, please—'

'She came to you, and she gave you the words to use when you fucked off and left me, didn't she?'

If I just stride off now maybe I could leave all this behind. I could get onto a bus or turn down an alleyway and become someone else, be somewhere else, leaving only the ink on my skin as an afterthought in the air behind me, as if it's a skin I need to shed to become someone else.

'I spoke to Cassie, yes, I did, I'm sorry. I just didn't know any more what was going on in my head, babe, I didn't—'

'Well, I hope you two had fun, had a good laugh behind my back.'

'It wasn't—'

I hang up.

CHAPTER THIRTEEN

Dog saloon

I GET ON a bus, and I text the Cockney Fuck Buddy—the Boy—him—Martin. His name is Martin, and I text him. The motion of the bus combined with the penny drop shockwaves make me feel sick when I look down, but I do it anyway. I don't even justify it to myself, I don't even question if I should, or remember deciding what to write, I'm just texting, 'Hey, Dog Saloon?' and hitting send as if it were a reflex reaction.

Because neither Cassie nor Max would think this is a good idea, right?

I pull my shades down from my hair and hide behind them. Glare out of the window. I'm not going to cry. I'm quite good at not crying, so good that you'd hardly know I was not crying really hard behind my shades. If he doesn't text back, doesn't come, that's okay too, because the Dog Saloon is on the same long stretch of Holloway road as the shop. My shop, of which I own seventy percent, with its cubby hole of a back office smelling of disinfectant and newspaper, and its worn leather swivel chair, into which I will climb and sit and take off my glasses and cry properly. I will say hello to Big Al, who will say something like 'Stone the Crows, it's me boss, look lively troops!' And wink and give me a hug. I won't let him, of course, because I never do, and because if he were to do it, I would cry in front of him and I will not let myself do that either. I will say I need to make a call, that my phone has died, that it is a long call and that I am not to be disturbed, and then I will lock the door of the office and cry. It's my office, it's seventy percent mine, and as I've not been in there for some time, it owes me.

What if he doesn't text back, the boy?

Of course, Big Al will guess there's something up, he may be a bull-headed old git, but he's not stupid. But he also knows me well enough not to ask. Or maybe he will ask, because I clearly don't know people as well as I thought I did, but even if he does, it will be alright because he's Big Al, and what he wants me to say when he says, 'You alright, chicky?' is something like, 'Oh, it's nothing, just the usual shit mate, you know?'

And then he'll nod, pulling his mouth into an upside-down smile for understanding, jut out his bottom lip and say, 'Yep, I know, chicky, I know. Chin up gel, if it hurts, it works,' or something else that makes no sense and yet does.

And if the....if Martin does text I'll have time to pop

in the shop to wash my face and sit for a while with two iced coke cans from the machine on my eyes to take the swelling down, and put some make-up on, fix my hair, wash my arm pits, all that sort of stuff. Whether he comes or not, I will go to the Saloon and I will buy myself something to drink. It's the sort of place where I may well bump into people I know well enough to have a drink with. People who will notice when the Boy turns up, if he does, and we drink and flirt and play pool together, and perhaps even mention something to Max, maybe? Maybe not. Maybe they'll be far too busy with their own lives to care, to remember who I was with, because why should they?

The bus is moving in bursts of speed between long stretches of idling, its engine chugging and rattling. I lean my face against the window and somehow the hard, flatness of it helps.

What if he doesn't text?

I will go to the bar, I will get drunk, and maybe that might make all of this hurt less.

Cassie told Max to leave me. She went round when she knew I would be out, and told him to leave me. Or at the very, very, very least of it, she went along with him and told him how to phrase it, how to put it, and that of course, yes, he should do just that. No. She *told* him to leave me, because she thought that was being a friend.

My phone vibrates. It's him, the Martin boy. He's got

something to finish then he'll head over. I text a smiley face then drop my phone into my pocket.

A woman gets on, her face set in a down turned mask as if she's never smiled in her life, then a man who can only be her son, then three Asian women in jellybean colours all trimmed with gold.

Or maybe I won't do that, the whole getting fucked thing. Maybe I'll just go home and turn off my phone and lie on my bed until I fall asleep, and perhaps I will fall asleep now, because at last I'm tired enough?

No, I don't think that's going to happen. I don't know if I even have the capacity to think any more about any of it. But then the memory comes back to me, sneaking in under the white noise in my head as if it thinks I won't notice.

It's the third time. I pissed on a stick, in a café toilet. We didn't have any tests left in the flat, because by then I couldn't bear to wait for my period to find out if I was or wasn't pregnant, and so would use them up days before they could really tell me anything, over and over in case they were giving a false negative. Someone said once they never give false positives, but they can give false negatives, so that would make me try almost every morning, because, you know, it might just be lying to me, right?

So we'd gone to the high street pharmacy. We'd talked about everything but what we were there for, of course. Because it couldn't be, not at last, not after all this, could it? Me and Max, looking in the crazy-ass windows of the sell-everything-and-nothing for a pound shops, seeing stuff we really wanted and saying we'd get cash out and come back for it, knowing that either way, yes or no, we wouldn't.

We'd gone to the café because I couldn't wait to find out; not in an excited, stomach fizzing way, but just because it was a thing to be got over. It would be another negative, I just needed to get it done, go back to what passed for normal. And Max didn't even ask if I wanted to do that, go to the café, but just walked a little ahead of me, to a place four doors down from the pharmacy, and went in and sat us down and said, 'What do you want, then, babe?' Knowing that he was ordering for me while I was in the toilet, doing what I had to do.

I turned my back on the stick while I waited, leaving it perched on the closed toilet lid, as if I looked down and saw it before it was ready, the result would somehow be wrong, or rub itself out, or change its mind. I stared at the toilet paper roll on the wall, and where someone had scratched a phone number, no message, just a number, the figures squared off rather than rounded. I even thought about ringing it just to see what would happen, just to stop that sinking, dead stomached feeling of dread.

What if I'm not?

What if I'm not?

What if I—?

Then I looked, and I saw the cross that meant I was pregnant again, and the horrible, hollow rush of grief and happiness hit me, and the hope, the bloody, bastard hope that this time, this time, it would really, really happen.

What if it works, this time?

What if it works?

What if—?

I couldn't get the lock on the door open; my hands seemed to have turned to boxing gloves and wouldn't work. When I finally got out, bringing the stick with me as if I needed to prove it to Max, as if I'd ever have lied about a thing like that, only then making myself drop it in the waste paper basket because, well, I had just pissed on it. I remember thinking I should leave a note for the person who was going to empty the bin and might see the stick, explaining that it was a happy thing and hadn't been left by some desperate teenager thinking her life was over, then almost laughed at the ridiculousness of that. And, when I sat down and cried, Max came and put his arms around me and knew that it was positive, and why I was crying, all without me having to tell him.

'It's gonna be alright, babe,' he'd said, looking up when the waiter came over with our breakfasts and having a wordless conversation with him in answer to his un-voiced query. Then he turned back to me, 'It's gonna be alright, this time, I promise, babe. This time it's gonna work, right?'

And I looked at him and didn't believe him, but really, really wanted to.

THE BUS IS picking up speed, the air a fraction cooler now. When it next stops, a woman gets on with a buggy. I say woman, but she's hardly that, one of those hard-bodied girls with arms like knotted twigs, her skin slick with sweat, making her look almost sculpted. Her tight, black leggings moulded to her perfect, petite legs. Her hair scraped back into a long plait, as if it had done something wrong and she wanted to hurt it. And the baby in her buggy is crying.

The bawling cuts through the noise of the bus, a wail of panic, of fear, of anger. It cuts at me, a cheese grater of noise. I shift in my seat, I'm alone now, people have come to sit next to me, people have gone. Right now, I'm alone. I turn even further round to the window but the baby keeps on crying.

I look up, straining to see where we are, and make out the beginnings of Holloway Road, the college or whatever it is now, all artfully tumbled architectural boxes frozen in their fall toward the pavement. The woman with the buggy is still coming towards me, taking a moment, a long moment to stand by the stairwell to the upper deck, one hand up to her ear and her head cocked as if she's listening to something, waiting.

I'm close to the gap for wheelchairs and buggies. Hers

is laden with bags that catch and snag on the seats as she passes. I glance up and her face is impassive, jaw set and eyes front as if she's on parade, as if the baby is nothing to do with her. Then I see she has headphones in, and then she says something to whoever she's talking to through the headset.

How long have I been on this bus? How long does it fucking well take to get there?

The sun is boiling through the glass, but I'm covered in a cold, itching sweat, as if ants are crawling under my skin. I clutch my hands together between my knees, shift my legs. The baby's crying goes on and on. It tightens my throat, vibrates between my ribs.

I dart a look behind at the mother, but I can't see her face anymore. She's just a shadow against the light blazing through the windows, a thousand miles away from me on her phone, while her baby screams and twists against the straps of its buggy, its fists flailing weakly, face screwed in a tight, pink knot.

It's not mine. For fuck sake it's not yours. It never was going to be yours, never could have been, even if you were sitting here with all four of them, alright? The crying is like a saw working between my shoulder blades, nagging on and on. Pick it up, I want to scream at her, pick it up and hold it, why can't you? The heat is building inside me, and I'm gasping. Trying to breathe. Just a moment ago I could. I could feel the air coming in and out but now, now my chest is jumping, jerking, like there's something trapped inside me. I'm going to be sick, or scream. I'm gripping the rail around the luggage rack in front of me, its diamond pitted surface imprinting on my hands as I hold it, crush it, in my grip.

I'll get out and walk. It's not far now, it can't be. But I can't leave the baby. Other people are looking now, a fat, black woman behind the mother is pursing her lips, her face folding into disapproval. Everyone else must see it, they must.

Take it.

I don't know where the voice comes from, but as I stand up, shaking and sweating and fighting for breath, it comes to me, cold and hard and in control.

Take it. She doesn't want it, and you do. You want it, you take it. It needs you, it needs your help. You know what happens when people don't help, when they walk away. What sort of mother would let a child cry like that, a baby, a little baby?

I'm holding onto the pole by my seat, swaying with the motion of the bus. I'll have to walk past them to reach the door. She's not even looking at the baby, she's staring out of the window as if she can't hear it. It's got a hat on, a pink one that's slipped over its face. It's crying and crying and twisting against it, trying to get it off only it can't.

The bus is slowing down. Someone, not me, has

pressed the bell and the orange sign has lit up.

Take it.

I'm standing right by her now, the baby wriggling and fretting, the buggy shaking with the effort. The mother's not looking at me, she's not looking at the baby. She's not even holding the buggy, she's turned away in her seat, her arms folded.

Take it.

My hands shake. My heart is beating high and hard in my throat. Tears roll down my cheeks, collecting along the inside edge of my sunglasses, a sticky, salty goo of tears, pooling before they break and run and I can taste them. The bus is pulling over to the stop, the one right by the tube station with its maroon tiled front and arched windows. When the door sucks open, the draught of air sticks the fabric of my t-shirt to the sweat coursing over my skin. I reach down to the baby in the buggy.

I stretch out my hand and lift the baby's hat from her face, and as I do, the mother's head snaps round and she glares at me, as if she'd like to hiss at me, all angry cat and spiteful. Her hand snatches the handle of the buggy and she jerks the thing toward her, and the fat black woman behind her looks at me too. I try and smile, but they can see it in me, I'm sure, and it makes the mother lean into her baby, at last, and unclip her restraints and pick her up—because she can see the want in me. Feel it burning off me like a flame.

I step back from them as the baby's leg snags in the strap and the buggy rocks on its wheels and the mother scowls at me.

'I was just—' I want to say about the hat, the crying. About why the fuck she hadn't picked the baby up before, and what the hell did she think she was doing, on the phone like that when her baby was crying? But the words come out in a horrible, weird, twisted sob that makes it worse, that makes me sound like a crazy woman, a crazy, rubber-faced-kangaroo-freak. A baby snatcher.

I run. I fling myself from the bus, my rings clanging on the pole by the door as I let go, scrabbling for a foot hold. The steps are oily, slippery under foot, the door already hissing shut as I tumble through. Wrenching sobs break from deep within. When my foot hits the pavement, the jolt crunches through my knee and my leg jars with pain. I turn, push blindly through the crowd of people milling round, one of whom calls out my name, one of whom catches hold of me—

'What's going on, you alright?' he says, and in that moment, I think only that him seeing me like this is as bad as admitting that I really, really do need him.

Martin.

CHAPTER FOURTEEN
Sleeping together is wrong

I PUSH HIM away, groping in my pockets for a tissue. I don't have one so scrub at my face with my hands. He takes hold of my shoulders and bends to look in my face, takes off my sunglasses, as if he needs any further fucking proof of the mess I'm in, and wipes his hand over my cheeks.

With him so bloody tall and bending down to me, I feel ridiculous. 'Get off, you're not my fucking dad.'

Which makes him laugh. Then he takes control.

He puts his arm round my shoulders and walks me under the railway bridge, a train clamouring and roaring overhead. He talks, even though I can't hear him. Talks so there's a screen of words that allows me to suck back in the tears and wipe the snot discretely on my shorts.

He says he was only in Commercial Road.

'Just walked down to Aldgate tube and changed at Kings Cross, thought I'd be early as it happens.'

'What's in Commercial Road?' I ask.

'My sewing machine,' he says.

WHEN WE SIT down in a coffee place my legs stick to the vinyl seats despite the air conditioning doing its best around us.

'You don't have to say,' he says. He's bought us frappuccinos.

'It's nothing, panic attack.'

As far as he knows, I send him a text summoning him to what he no doubt hoped would be a long summer evening of drink, drugs and casual but athletic sex, only to be confronted by a wailing cougar banshee, which is very much not what he signed up for. This really isn't what I wanted either, but it's not as if I can tell him the revelation that it was my best friend who persuaded my boyfriend to leave me, because that somehow doesn't feel real yet.

'Look, it's a long story, and I'm sure you didn't expect all this, so, thanks for the coffee thing and all, but I'm fine now, so if you want to go and—'

'No,' he says. He doesn't sound angry or pitying. He shrugs, bends to slurp his drink through his straw then says, 'S'alright. Not much going on, got nowhere else to be.' Which is great, until he adds, 'Take your time.' And reaches across the table for my hand, because that means he still wants an answer.

'Really, it was just a panic attack, I get them sometimes, just the heat I suppose.' I shrug. 'It was nothing. I'm okay now.'

He nods, running his tongue over his teeth as if he's chewing over what I've said. 'Yeah, right, if you're okay, then I'm fucking Larry the Leprechaun.'

'Are you? Because, does Mrs The Leprechaun know you're fucking her husband? I mean, it doesn't bother me, I'm open minded about that sort of thing.'

He doesn't laugh, which is a shame because I think it's quite a good come back.

Instead he says, 'Why do you always do that?'

'Do what?'

'Every time I think you're going to say something real, you tell a joke.'

He can see that already? Am I really that easy to read? Well I am not going there, with him. Today. I let go of his hand and pull my fingers through my hair. My sunglasses are on the table and I'd like to put them on, because him staring at me is getting uncomfortable.

'Look,' I hold up my hand. 'Something just got me on the bus, something someone said, and boom, up I go. I'm just on a short fuse these days, and it was a stupid idea to drag you into all this, so—'

'Why?' he says, as if he really doesn't see why it's a stupid idea.

'Because I hardly know you. Because you're, well, you're...' A kid, I want to say, a kid who's very tall and very grown up and all, but you're not even thirty yet, and you just haven't been through enough to understand. 'You're…'

'I'm the person you rang,' he says. Then he picks up his milkshake and tips it down his throat, head back, gulping it all the way down inside him. He's wearing a short sleeved black t-shirt, and with his arm up holding the coffee, I can see the marks again, the little cat-scratch rows of them.

When he puts the drink down, I say, 'I lost a baby.' I put my hand out to touch my sunglasses, and find that my fingers are trembling, my blue painted nails somehow making it more obvious.

'Oh, shit,' he says, and puts his hand on mine again.

'Don't.' I can't bear it. Because this is me ending it, this is it over between us because this is me saying *hey, I'm a desperate, baby-mad old cow, who's clearly going to steal your precious young seed and try and trap you with an unwanted pregnancy, who's on the brink of losing everything and dangerous enough to take everything from you—run, run while you can, you idiot.*

'That's just so fucking terrible.'

Then I'm only bloody saying, 'Four, I lost four of them, alright, and the last one was in February and—' Then I'm not saying anything, not even looking at him because you don't say that, do you? Because people don't want to hear that shit, do they? Which is why you've stopped saying anything that matters to anyone, even yourself. Why it's become the silent, cold thing between you and everyone else.

'My fucking Christ,' he says, and the woman on the table next to us glances up at that particular piece of profanity. 'This was with that dude in the picture?'

I nod, and the woman gets back to her latte and her phone conversation.

'You don't have to stay, please, I'd better go and—'

'Why today?' he asks. 'What happened now?' He reaches forward and touches my cheek with his hand, tilts my face just a little so that I'm looking at him. I wish he wouldn't, because I'm crying again but hell, at least this time they're those kind of elegant, attractive tears; when big ones collect in the corners of your eyes and run down your cheeks like in cartoons.

I move back from his touch and tell him about the baby, and the sun hat, and I say things like, 'And all the time, this bitch was like just on her phone, and she wasn't even listening, I mean, like, the whole bus was looking at her and this baby was crying and crying, I mean, what sort of? I mean just what the fuck?' Then I slump my head into my hands. 'What do I know though, right? What do I know about what shit she's going through?' Because I don't, do I? Maybe the kid had been crying for hours, because I believe they do that, don't they? Maybe the poor cow has been up for hours and was barely able to think and was just trying to shut out that noise, to stop herself from flinging the pushchair across the road.

'I dunno. But she's not with me, you are.' He gets up, lifts his bag off the back of his chair. 'Finsbury Park?' he says.

'What?'

'That's the quickest route, right? Finsbury Park and then about five stops, yeah?' And when I'm still not getting it, he says, 'To your place from here, you daft cow!'

WE TAKE THE tube neither of us saying much, and walk through the dusty, tarmac sticky, heavy dregs of a summer Friday. When we turn down the side street which leads to my flat, there's a group of men outside the taxi rank and the twenty-four-hour shop. When we get closer, I see that it's the head taxi guy and the shop guy having an argument. Martin looks and smirks at them. The lesser shop guys, the cousins or brothers or sons I guess, are lurking in the shadow of the fruit and veg, arms folded but watchful, as if they might be called into action and don't want to be. The other taxi men are leaning against their cars in much the same pose, though they look more up for trouble.

They see us, me in particular, and I seem to break their concentration. The shop guy flaps his hand and taxi guy looks over at me with a head raise, almost as if he's half expecting me to chip in.

'All right, Boss?' Martin says, half laughing the words, and both groups turn away, as if they're suddenly very interested in their respective businesses.

My flat smells hot and empty, even though I've only been away for a few hours, like when you come back from holiday and your own scent seems to have faded from the place.

'Wanna get drunk?' Martin asks. He drops his bag on the floor, making himself at home.

'You think that's a good idea?' I go into the kitchen, run the tap and pour myself a glass of water in a blue, pitted highball glass and drink. I drink as if it were air, the cold of it gloriously painful. When I put the glass back down and look up, he's there, leaning against the kitchen door.

'You said something about getting drunk and fucking?' he says.

'You really want to, still? Me breaking down and all that shit, that does it for you?'

'Nope,' he says, and comes over and takes my hand.

'So what then, your listening fee?'

He grins. 'Not that either, that's free, it's just that I do it better when I'm drunk and in bed. But hey,' he touches my cheek. 'Whatever you want, okay?'

Without my making any commitment one way or another, we end up in the bedroom. The curtains are still drawn so it's cooler in here. He strips off his shirt, and still in his cotton pants, he climbs onto my bed and makes a joint, the way he did the first time. I think the hair pin he used before might even still be waiting for him on the bedside table.

'People don't know what to say to you, do they?' he says. I'm leaning against the headboard, padded red velvet to match the curtains and the carpet, the rest of the room as black as I can get it, and I'm holding the drinks we've made, the second ones, vodka with whatever juice was still in the fridge.

'About?'

'About you losing the pregnancies,' he says, which strikes me as an odd, because it's how you say it if you know about it first-hand. 'So they say nothing, as if that's better. I mean, they say sorry and shit, but then they kind of stop saying anything, don't they?'

'How do you know?' I ask.

He looks at me, pursing his lips, the soft light filtering through the curtains giving me only an abstract of his face.

Then I say, 'Your arms?' He breaks my gaze and I think he's almost shaking his head, not much, just once or twice. 'I saw them, you can't be surprised that I notice skin. It's kind of my thing.'

'Your thing, innit, skin,' he says, as if he likes the poetry of it. He lights the spliff and settles himself next to me, talking without looking at me, saying it to the space in front of us that trails with the smoke of his words.

'What do you remember?' he asks, 'Like, the earliest thing? Tell me.'

'Play group,' I say, because I've been asked this question enough times before that I have an answer down pat. I no longer know if it's true though, or if it's just what I remember saying when asked. 'My cousin holding a jack-in-the-box and turning the handle, and me knowing that the jack's gonna pop any moment, and he's got his fingers over the hinges where he's holding it, so I'm really worried, because I know when it opens, it's gonna pinch his skin, maybe it happened to me before so I knew it would hurt, but he's laughing and doing it anyway to wind me up.'

'How old were you?'

I shrug. 'Younger than three, because I remember where it was, and when I asked my mum, she said I was only there when I was about two or something.' He's going to tell me his now, of course he is, that's why he's asked. As he tells me, I wonder where I was when he was making his early memory. Secondary school perhaps?

'I got this one from primary school. There was this girl with all this hair, loads of curls like spirals. Like pasta twists,' and he smiles, and I can tell he's seeing her again. 'An' all these freckles, an' a red t-shirt, one of them sports ones, Arsenal of course. And I was just watchin' her shirt because it was red with this white stripe on it. She come over and kind of held her arm out to me, like she knew I wanted to touch her shirt, and she was saying it was okay, y'know?' He's looking at me as if I should say something, as if the significance of this should be as obvious to me as it is to him. 'First day at a new school, and they were all told to be nice to me, the other kids. Of course, that's like putting a big sign on your head, innit, hey, the new kid's a freak, right? So soon as they didn't have to, none of them went near me for ages, until she did.' He's rolling his thumb and forefinger together, like you might if you were feeling one of those sports shirts that look like satin, the slip and slide of it between your fingers.

He breathes out a long curl of white smoke. 'Stupid thing is, this shit I'm gonna tell you, is the first thing I usually tell girls. That's how fucked up this is,' and he laughs, not his big, Sid James laugh, a sad, small, dry one. 'It feels wrong, or it feels like more, sayin' it this way round, I—' He shakes his head, risks a glance at me. 'That sounds stupid, though.'

'No, it doesn't.'

He holds his arm up, elbow bent so I can see where the underside is striped with cuts. He puts his index finger on it, the smouldering joint resting between the fingers of the same hand. 'Know what this is? It's how I pull, mostly.'

'Really?'

'That's just a side effect though. It's not why I do it,' he says.

Do, not did.

He drops his arm and offers me the joint. 'Looked after kid, wasn't I?' he says.

He was one of five, he says, the youngest. Five seems excessive. Five, really? That's just plain greedy. He says how he thinks he always knew, that he wasn't just the youngest, that there was something different about him.

'My dad, my…first dad, he had bright red hair. And my mum, she was blonde.'

He doesn't say first mum, or real mum; there's just something in the way he says her name that shows that's what she must have been.

'And my sisters and brothers, they were blonde too, right?' He touches his hair, his dark brown, short scruffy dreadlocks. 'My mum died when I was about five. Cancer of course, isn't it always?' His voice becomes cold, matter of fact. 'We went to the funeral, all of us, in black, fucking penguin suits. He must have hired them, my dad, none of them fit and they all smelled damp an' old. There was all these people clucking about. Loads of sausage rolls, all piled up on a big plate, and I really wanted one, because I love sausage rolls, right,' he glances at me, smiles. 'An' this woman with a big hat, dunno who she was, she came and gave me loads of them on a plate, and she's all cryin' and I think it's because of Mum being dead, you know? But while I was eatin' these sausage rolls they was all looking at me, like funny, you know? There was me, wiv my dark hair all curly, and there was me brothers an' my sister, an' they was all blonde and—'

'Shit,' I say, because I realise I know what he's going to say.

'S'right,' he says. He leans back, lies almost flat and pinches the bridge of his nose between his thumb and forefinger, closes his eyes. The spliffs gone out and we don't relight it. The drinks are gone, but we don't move to get more. A slight breeze stirs the curtain.

'Next day, Dad says we're going for a drive. Where to, Dad? Going to see someone, that's all. He took a bag.'

I press my fingers against my lips to stop myself swearing. How could he?

'Pulled up outside this house miles away. Couldn't look at me, said to wait in the car. I watched him go down the path up to this door, and he rang the bell or whatever, and I felt so scared. I think, I—'

'Fuck,' I really want to hold him, but I don't let myself. I can't do this.

'Man come to the door, they talked for a while then Dad, the man I thought was my dad, come back and got me out of the car. I didn't say a word, an' me Dad just walked me up to this bloke by this house and he said something like, "This is yours," an' he left me.'

He tells me he didn't try and go after him, the man

who wasn't his dad, says that he kind of knew that was the end of it. Says he didn't stay with this man for very long either. But he saw him again a few times, his biological father, when he'd grown up and found out that he'd worked with his mum, they'd had a fling.

'Says he never knew about me, said Mum left, an' he never even knew she'd died.'

'I don't know what to say.'

He shrugs. 'S'way it goes. Don't get all sympathetic on me.'

'You didn't stay with your real dad, then?'

'Nah, like I said, looked after kid, innit? My Mum an' Dad, like the ones I think of as me Mum and Dad really, took me a bit later on. Bit of a time in a care home, not too long and nothing too Saville,' and he winks at me with an appalling leer. 'Nothing like that, an' Mum and Dad took me in then, and they're lovely.'

'Fuck,' I say, 'that's—'

'I had a sister too,' he says, and though he's smiling, he rolls a little away from me. 'We grew up together, but we weren't, you know, related.' Then he looks back at me. He holds his arm up again. 'Things got a bit shit when I was older, right?' He taps the side of his head, 'Like crazy shit. Went though some stuff an' used to cut myself, don't do it so much anymore. But now it gets me laid. I tell them my story, then I say as I how I don't do relationships. Say I won't call, I won't text, I don't want their number, because I'm not,' and he does speech marks in the air, 'in a good place right now. Works like a fucking charm. On a certain type of girl, anyway.'

'And old bats like me?' I mean it as a joke, but he turns to me, his face sharp.

'Don't put yourself down like that.'

'Okay, what do you want me to say? You still fucking all these girls too?'

He sits up, 'No, I'm fucking not, I'm trying to tell you, alright?'

'It's okay if you are, it's not like we're—'

'I'm not, alright? I used to, I used to tell them all about me, an' they'd go all gooey eyed and, oh no, poor you.'

'You went for the sympathy fuck?' I say, incredulous because I couldn't imagine him needing to.

'Yeah,' he says, 'the sympathy fuck. Because I'm a cunt.'

'We all need an angle,' I say. 'Me? I'm something to read in bed.'

He smiles, but he doesn't laugh. It was his joke anyway. I'm losing my edge.

'I hate it, though, what I do. Make them feel sorry for me. I hate myself, when I do it.'

'So why are you telling me this, I mean this way round?'

He sits up and he moves our empty glasses to the

floor, and the dish I've let him use as an ashtray with what's left of the spliff in it, then he sits up next to me and kisses me. He does it with one hand on the side of my face, kissing me as if he really means it.

'Don't,' I say when he stops kissing me.

'I just like you more,' he says.

'Don't, please, this isn't right, we're not—'

'What? We're not what?'

'We're not,' I say. Because we aren't, and he needs to understand that. Because he's given me his story and it's too much, this is too much. 'I'm too tired, please, I need to…I don't want to.'

'S'okay,' he says.

He lies next to me and holds me, and I feel the warmth of him and the space between our skins softens and dissolves, and he doesn't try and change my mind. I think how it's wrong, what he does, but how I also understand it, which probably shows just how wrong it is.

Then we sleep.

CHAPTER FIFTEEN
Well, that was alright, then

AFTER THE THIRD time, I made them refer me to a clinic. I found out about it from a woman I met online, one of those support groups you get, who told me to make a fuss. So I did, and Max and I got an appointment.

I was driving, because I didn't want to arrive with helmet hair. We'd got out of the habit of the bike a bit, because when I was pregnant, neither of us wanted me to ride pillion on Max's Honda, and then when I wasn't, I didn't quite go back to it either.

'Maybe we might move out here,' I said, as Max had been quiet for a while. 'I mean, you know, if it all works this time.'

'It's gonna work,' he said, more forcefully than I was expecting him to. 'Naw, babe, it's gonna work, I know it.'

'I've got to get pregnant again yet,' I said.

'We will. They're gonna find out if there's anything wrong, and they're gonna make it all right, aren't they?'

'There still might not be anything wrong, you know, I

mean, that they can find,' I said.

'But there's got to be something, right? I mean, it just can't keep on going wrong like that, without there being something up with your...' he waved his hand about,'...you know, your womb and that shit.'

My womb and that shit.

'They're gonna find out what's wrong, and they're gonna fix it,' Max said, not looking at me. That's how I was to him, to all of them, I realised. A wheezing mass of pipes and tubes that needed fixing. A faulty bit of machinery that they couldn't get at. He'd like it if they could open me up, like one of his bikes, and find the sprocket or the valve or whatever it was, the baby hatch or the egg delivery tube or the feed line, whatever broken part of me it was that kept on doing this. He'd like that to be the truth of it, Max, because then he'd feel that he was doing something, could do something. I looked at his great big hands, like spades, fingers strong enough to tighten nuts and bolts, but I'd defeated them.

'I don't think it's anything,' I said. 'I think they'll just say they don't know, it's just one of those things. Like they did the last three times.' I kind of wanted that to be true, because then there wouldn't be anything anyone needed to do. Then I could still fix it myself.

IT WAS A big, expensive looking building that looked more like a hotel complex, from the outside anyway.

Inside it was just the same as any hospital, three clicks above school, five clicks above prison. We sat in a waiting room shared with a podiatry clinic, old people inching painfully back and forth on a variety of walking frames. A little Filipino nurse came out to find us, the two of us towering over her when we stood up.

'You pregnant?' she hissed, and I smiled and said no.

Then we had to wait in another room, an inner sanctum.

'How long they gonna be?' Max asked after five minutes. 'They said three thirty, right?' He looked at the clock, then got his phone out to double check.

'There's always a wait.' I was glad. Calm, composed and waiting to find out my fate. The longer we sat there, well, then I didn't have to know. The nurse called my name.

In the doctor's room orange curtains framed a hedge that was shifting in the wind. It made it look as if we were at sea in a ship, floating on green water.

The doctor didn't look at us. He watched the hedge sea, the light from the window illuminating his aquiline black face, catching on the thin wire frame of his glasses. He didn't ask us to sit down. We sat anyway, and Max coughed into his fist. The Doctor looked round and flipped open the file on his desk, glanced at it then looked at Max. He made a small blowing out sound, pursing his lips and then letting them pop closed again. Just when

Max was about to speak, he said.

'The blood tests from three week ago. We tested for a number of things, all the usual things.' He picked a pen up from his desk and looked down at my notes, then used the pen to tap them.

'What did they—' I began, before Max did, but the Doctor got there first.

'It shows that the wife has antiphospholipid syndrome.'

What was that? I felt it slide cold and strange into my mind, felt it beat under my skin. I reached for Max's hand, and he took hold of mine. 'It's what they call Hughes Syndrome, the sticky blood.'

He explained how this meant that my blood made micro clots, blood clots that didn't affect me, wouldn't cause me a thrombosis or anything fun like that, but meant that they would block the tiny vessels of the placenta. Sometimes it would be okay, enough of them would remain clog free for the baby to grow, but then, thwump, one would block something vital and that would be it, the baby would slowly die inside me.

He explained all this to Max.

He didn't look at me, not once, not really, his eyes only occasionally flicking my way. How dare he? It was my body, my babies. But I sat and listened to this expert tell Max what was wrong with me, that it was my fault, that it was my body, my nasty, underhand, devious body, my dirty blood, killing our babies. The anger beat inside me like a drum. I wanted to vomit and had to swallow it, along with the terrible, desperate urge to cry. Because it was me, after all, not Max, it was me.

'How does it happen?' I said, all of sudden, cutting across him, the only time I did, the only time I stood up for myself.

His gaze slid over me, expression unchanged. He looked a little bored.

'How do you get this, sticky blood thing?'

He exhaled gently, a controlled calming breath. 'It hereditary,' he said, as if I should have known that, as if everyone knew that apart from me. He glanced at my neck tattoo. 'It nothing you catch,' he said. 'Not like the Aids.' Then he looked out of the window again. 'If the wife get pregnant, if it happen at her age, then we inject.'

That was low, that was enough to make tears itch at the back of my eyes and tighten my throat. My age.

'I write you a script for the drug. She inject every day into the belly.'

'Does she do that now, like?' Max said.

The Doctor was writing the script using a maroon pen with a gold clip, a nice, fat expensive looking pen. He had nice, fat, expensive looking handwriting, lots of loops and curls. He pushed the script towards me.

'If she become pregnant, the moment she get positive test, start to inject. Get the prescription now, so it all ready.' Then he leaned back in his chair and turned to the window, raised both arms above his head, then lowered his hands to hold the back of his neck, elbows up in the air. He remained staring out of the window, watching the green sea of the hedge.

'Thank you very much, then,' Max said.

I got up before he did, was at the door before him, striding away down the corridor, dodging my way round shambling old people, and fat people, and pregnant people who, when the little nurses hissed 'are you pregnant,' at, could fucking-well hiss right back that yes, they were. The soles of my boots squealed against the floor as I broke into a run. I heard Max call after me and come after me, light on his feet for a big man.

'WELL, THAT WAS alright, really,' he said.

I looked at his hands on the steering wheel, holding it more correctly than he would usually, ten and two. 'Alright?'

'Well, you know, they know what it is, now. You got the prescription, you can get the injections, so it will be alright now, won't it? Now they know, like, what it is and that.' He nodded, face serious but positive, determined and optimistic. 'We'll be alright now, you'll see,' he said.

When you're under the care of the frequent miscarriage clinic you get to have early scans. I'd read on the internet that there's a link between early scans and miscarriage prevention. It's not that they do anything to you, but it's to do with the physiological sense of security, and that someone's taking an interest in you, which is what they think makes the difference. You relax more, so you're less stressed, so your baby has a better chance. Get stressed, and your body might just think, 'Hey, things aren't looking good out there, this mother needs all her energy to survive, better ditch the freeloader downstairs then.' Or so the story goes.

'You're not gonna be stressed, are you?' Not now they're looking after you.' Max said.

Soon as I got the positive test in the cafe, I went back to the flat and ripped open the sealed packets of hypodermic needles they'd given me, pre-filled with the anti-coagulant.

We went back to the clinic two days later and I got to have my moment when the tiny nurse leant into me and hissed, 'Are you pregnant?' And I got to hiss back, 'Yes.'

We saw a Dutch doctor this time, who did look at me as he said, 'I'm really sorry, but there's no slot for you to have a scan, today.'

'I thought I was supposed to have one?' I said.

'Sure, sure, you should have one, but today one of the scanners is down, so we don't have enough slots.'

'But—' I said, and it was already happening, tears were itching along my eye lids, my throat going tight, 'I was meant to have a f—'

'It's a long way for us to come,' Max said, forestalling my fuck.

The doctor was sorry, and I was annoyed at Max, at not getting an early scan.

'Don't suppose they would have seen much, anyway,' Max said as we drove home.

'You can see the heartbeat,' I said.

'Well, they said next time. Just try not to get stressed about it.'

The next time I had to go alone, because Max had a work thing. I waited my turn, then I was shown in to see another consultant.

'I'm really sorry,' she began, 'I can see from your notes that the previous consultant you saw, stated that you were to have a scan as a matter of urgency.'

Urgency—the word flared in me.

'But one hasn't been booked in for you, must have been some—'

'You're fucking kidding me?' I said.

'I'm really sorry—'

'No,' I said, 'I'm really sorry, and I'm fucking furious, do you know what it's like waiting for—' Shit, crying again, unable to speak because of it, and all the anger inside me twisting into panic, which for once made me polite.

'I'm really sorry, the best I can do is to try and schedule one at your local maternity unit as soon as possible, if you can tell me where that is then—'

'I don't know, I've never got far enough along to find out.'

She made two phone calls in quick succession, and I was booked in at Barnet Hospital for the next day. They said I must have as full a bladder as I could manage, so by the time Max and I had driven to the unfamiliar hospital, paid for parking, got lost three times and were finally on the seventh floor, I was in agony.

'I need a piss so bad,' I said, 'It's starting to hurt.'

'I'll ask how long they're gonna be,' Max said.

'She's next,' the woman said.

'I really can't wait,' I stood up, the pressure in my bladder making me sweat.

'You can let a little bit out,' the receptionist said, 'but not too much, yeah?'

I did a penguin walk to the ladies. The relief was amazing, so good it was bordering on the orgasmic, until I remembered myself and stopped midstream. Still uncomfortable, I hobbled out, to find them all waiting for me, Max, the receptionist and the scanning woman.

Inside, her room was dark, blue lights, green lights, a large flat screen TV, a computer monitor.

'I'm just going to pop some jelly on your tummy,' she said once I'd laid back on the padded bench and revealed my purple blotched skin to her.

The pressure of her machine skating on the thin ice of my belly made me want to go again, but I didn't care. Max and I held hands and stared at the flat screen TV. Grey, cavernous hollows of my body rolled and slicked about, silver and black. A ship on a night ocean, and we're the light house, looking for it in the dark.

'No,' the woman said, 'no, I can't see anything yet … I'm going to have to use the internal.'

She got out a shiny white dildo, onto which she placed a condom.

'Bit late for contraception,' Max said.

She didn't reply.

'Can you slip your bottoms off, dear? Don't worry, it doesn't have to go in that far, just the tip.'

'That's what she said,' Max said.

The medical dildo slipped an inch inside me, under the cover of the green paper tent she'd spread over me. I tried to keep calm but the muscles in my neck were rigid. Surrounded by machines and cameras lying on the black leather bed, it all started to feel like I was part of some terrible medical fantasy porn film. I tried to make myself think about that, because it was better than thinking about the screen. The silver swirl, the looming, ghostly shapes of my crapped out reproductive organs, blinking in the light like deep sea fish exposed to a diver's spotlight.

'There,' the woman said, and I saw it and Max saw it too, because he gripped my hand more tightly, and we both flinched toward the screen. I saw a pearl, a pearl in all that blackness, a bubble of white.

'There it is,' Max said. 'I can see it, look!'

But the woman, her dildo still pressed against my bladder, said 'How many weeks do you think you are?'

'Eight, nearly eight.' Though it was probably seven, seven and a half, but eight sounded further along. Safer.

'Is there any chance you've got your dates wrong?'

'No. No, I'm not wrong.'

'It's too small,' she said. Her dildo sucked back out of me, leaving the flaccid condom and a slick of warmed up KY jelly, both of which she wiped away with the paper towel, leaving my shaved and tattooed bikini line exposed. 'You can get dressed, dear.'

'You mean, I'm earlier on than that?' I slipped down from the bench.

'No, it's just too small. It's probably not viable, that's all, not growing. You'll have to come back in a week, see what's happened, then if there's no change, you'll have to have a D & C.'

'What's that?' Max asked, 'Is that gonna help, is that gonna—'

'I know what it is,' I said.

CHAPTER SIXTEEN
Bad shit

I WAKE FIRST. It can only be a few hours later, but the room has cooled and the edge of light around the curtains has faded. I leave him sleeping and go to the kitchen, look at my phone, rubbing my eyes to make them focus. I don't turn on any lights but stand in the shadow of the half pulled blind, letting sleeping dogs lie.

There is a string of messages from both Cassie and Max, missed calls, texts, an email even, among all the spam and the special offers. Cassie is sorry, Max is sorry, they are worried, they are still sorry, they never meant to hurt me. Then Cassie is a little angry with me, why am I being like this, can't I see that maybe we do both need some time out to sort things out? Then Max is sorry, again, and really wishes I'd stop ignoring him, and then Cassie is sorry for what she said before, and hopes she didn't come across as to judgmental, and now they're both going to give me some time and space to get back to them when I'm ready. Which is nice of them. I wonder if they've rung each other yet, and just which one said sorry the most? Oh and actually, maybe they should both just shut up and leave me the fuck alone, because I have given them the very clear message that I don't want to speak to either of them. That's what I'd really like right now—someone to actually listen to what I say to them instead of telling me what they think I should do. Banging on at me all the time like demented crows, crashing against the window, going 'caw-caw, caw-caw'.

I sling the phone on the counter where it skids toward the kettle and flashes up at me resentfully.

I've got to end things with Martin now, of course. I drink tap water staring out of the window. I should have ended it after the first time, the second time, I should never have let him come back with me now, but most of all, I should never have listened to his story, because now, now he's definitely not the Cockney Fuck Buddy anymore, is he? I pick up my phone, go to my address book and delete the words 'Cockney Fuck Buddy' and type in his real name.

Martin. The only little dark-skinned kid at a funeral, the odd one out, the one his dad allowed to eat sausage rolls before getting rid of him. The kid who tells his story to make girls feel sorry enough to sleep with him, because inside he's so little and scared he doesn't think they might just want to do it anyway. That's why I have to break up with him, because what have I just done? I didn't tell him

I was all broken up because Cassie was the one who gave Max the words he needed to make his escape, because that wasn't a big enough thing, was it? No, I've done just what he hates himself for doing. I've taken the biggest and worst thing in my life and I've given it to him like a big gift wrapped present. Look how tragic I am, how devastatingly broken, this is serious shit, this is the big one, you can't leave me now, can you? But maybe, just maybe, *you* might be the one to fix me?

I press my face against the window. I like the way its flat, and hard, and solid, and yet not there at all, like an invisible force keeping you safe. And now, of course, I'm going to tell him it's over, that I won't call or text, and just like it works on all those little girls he does it to, it's going to work on him too. And part of me wants it to, but part of me wants him to come back again and again, and I know how desperate and sad that is. Oh shit, you know what I need to say to him? That it really isn't him, it really is me.

Ha, ha fucking ha.

It's dark enough now for the lights to be on at the taxi rank. The yellow light strobes the ground. The pale glow from behind the controller's plastic window with the holes drilled in it, like he was a hamster needing air.

Then the girl appears, and this time she's with another girl. This one is fairer perhaps, though it's hard to tell, and has a mop of curly hair scraped back in a pony. They look as if they're having a laugh, they've got their arms around each other and they're singing or shouting something.

Just like Cassie and me would have been, once.

Now they're laughing and drinking, passing a bottle of coke back and forth, though maybe not just coke. We used to do that too, pour half away, top it back up with vodka, thought we were smart, because that way we could sneak it into clubs.

One of the drivers comes over to them. Don't have a go, I think, because although they're so much younger than Cassie and I were when we first met, even, I mean, five years younger at least I'm guessing, I can see an echo of us in them. I bet they're gonna cause some trouble and do some stuff. You go girls. Don't let the bastards grind you down, you do whatever the fuck you want.

The driver holds out cigarettes to them. That's not on, surely? Come on, mate, they're just kids and yes, I'm queen of the class A's, B's and C's this week, but they're just kids. They take them of course, and let him light them for them, and hold them as if they're not sure how, but are terribly pleased to be doing it. Like it's such a big thing, holding a cigarette.

And now they're getting into his cab. The girl is, anyway, stepping forwards as he holds open the door, but the friend isn't so sure. She's saying no, the one that would be Cassie, hanging back. One of the other drivers comes up and puts his arm on her shoulder, talks to her. The girl reappears for a moment, her dark head bobbing up above the car's roof when she steps back onto the pavement, saying something to the friend. While she's speaking, a third man gets into the driver's seat and turns the engine on. The car's rear lights come on, and the girl reaches for the friend as if they have to hurry now the car has started, and the friend gives in to her. In seconds they're both inside, and the first man gets in the back with them, and the other man gets into the front passenger seat, and the car pulls away.

I watch as the car heaves round the corner onto the main street. My heart's beating fast, dry and hard at the back of my throat. They're too young, too young to be smoking and getting into taxi cabs like that, and it's not right, three men in the car with them.

I fish out some tracksuit bottoms and a sweatshirt, darting into the bedroom as quickly as I can so as not to wake Martin.

I'm not going to have a word with the drivers. I don't look at them, in case they know I was watching and are keeping an eye on me. I glance up at my kitchen window, but it's nothing but a grey square of glass, just like all the blinded eyes in London, not seeing, not being seen.

I go into the shop, go to the sweets section and pick up a bar of Fruit and Nut. Shop guy's positively animated when he registers that it's me. I get a nod and something close to a smile.

I need him to talk to me, so I try, 'Had a word with that policeman this morning.'

He doesn't say anything, just nods again.

'Said he knew who she was. Did you see her earlier? I mean, just now, when I was coming out, I thought I saw her?' But that's already wrong, I can tell.

'Where you seen her?' he says, but he's thinking about biscuits and spray paint, looking outside to see if she's lurking there, can in hand. 'I tell him, they're all the same, all of them.'

'Do you see her a lot?' I try, but he's holding his hand out for my money.

'If she come back, I ring him again,' he says as he slams his till.

'But did you see her just now? Getting into a cab, did you see her?'

At the mention of the word cab, he stops squinting outside and narrows his eyes at me. It's like the shutter over his alcohol section has come down. Whatever community spirit he'd grudgingly felt towards me after I'd spoken to PC Barnes, has gone.

'I not see,' he says. He puts my change on the stack of newspapers on the counter and seems to shrink back into the shadows with a shake of his head.

'Okay, I just wondered, that's all.' I pick up the chocolate. 'Bye, then.'

When I get indoors, Martin is in the kitchen. It strikes me how odd that now sounds, his name, how much more of a stranger he is now he's got a name. He's drinking water, using the same glass I'd left there. I put the chocolate on the counter with my phone and keys, on the end of it that's furthest away from him.

'Sweet, love a bit of Fruit and Nut, me.'

'Hey,' I say, 'We kind of need to talk.'

CHAPTER SEVENTEEN

It's me

'LOOK,' I SAY.

I put my index finger on the edge of the counter, and because that seems too much like pointing at him, I walk the next one along with it, two steps, then I stop, because I've no idea what I'm doing. 'I...I'm kind of in, well, I'm...you saw what a mess I was earlier, yeah, not good, right? Well, erm, I kind of...it's just I think I should probably, kind of be on...'

I could really use Cassie right now, or Cassie half an hour ago to talk all this through with.

'I think we should probably kind of ease off a bit for now, you know?'

He's put his t-shirt on again, and his shoes. This is a good thing, because it's going to be easier to say this when I'm not distracted by quite how much there is of him when he's not wearing clothes.

'Early night?' he says. 'I should probably head anyways.'

Part of me wants to take the easy out he's just thrown me, only it would be like picking up the ball a puppy dropped at your feet only to throw it over the hedge.

'No, I mean, yes, you should probably head. I've had a fucked-up day, and, you know, you were great, really, but, this…' I shrug, hoping to God that the word "this" will somehow convey to him everything I can't bring myself to say. 'I don't think *this* is a good idea right now.'

He puts his hands into his trouser pockets and leans against the fridge.

'Why?'

What do I say now? Go for the big guns, or state the obvious? 'Look, I'm forty-one, Martin.' This doesn't get any obvious reaction. I realise I'm a little disappointed that it doesn't, and that I was kind of hoping it would be a big reveal, and that he'd spring back in amazement.

'So? You still looked hot when I first saw you.'

'You were high when your first saw me.'

'So were you.'

I put my hand to my forehead, then drag my fingers through my hair. 'I'm still forty-one, and you're…you're not even thirty yet, are you?'

'So what?'

'So how old are you?'

'Twenty-seven.'

He says it too quickly and too pleased with himself for it to be real, like he knew this was coming, and he'd got an answer all ready, worked out twenty-seven is nearer to thirty than he is, and yet not so close he thinks I'll spot the deception. 'Anyway,' he says, 'I'm tall for my age.'

'Oh, Martin, please, you can't, you can't want—'

'You getting back with that Max bloke?' he says.

'What? No.' But saying it like that sends a stab of something through me, because if I say goodbye to Max, then what else am I saying goodbye to? He's looking at my phone now where I'd put it with the chocolate. He moves to pick it up just as the fucking thing cheerfully flashes up Max's name.

'Give me that.' I go to grab it but he jerks it out of my reach, just for a second, then gives it back to me.

'You think you've got the right to…to take my stuff like that?'

'I was after the chocolate.' He's grinning at me, all Cheshire cat again. 'Think he wants you back, though,' he says. 'Seems real sorry 'bout something, really—'

'Shut up, what do you know? It's not up to him or you or anyone what I do, and you don't just switch off your feelings for someone, not all of them, not just like that—'

'No,' he says. He's smirking at me, enjoying my rage as I buzz about at his feet, wasp in a jar, then goes quite still. 'You don't, do ya?'

There's something uncanny in his stare, as if a part of him has slipped away and revealed something I should have seen earlier. Still in his calm, *I'm being controlled so you know I'm being serious*, kind of a voice, he says, 'I know what this is.'

'What is it?' My throat is tight and my heart's going crazy hard in my chest.

'It's what I said, you think you can't trust me now. S'all right, I understand that.'

Something in him relaxes, the darkness melting as his lips twitch with a smile again. It was nothing. He's just a hurt kid who doesn't want to get dumped. I'm just jumpy and paranoid.

'It's not that, I don't care about that—'

'Yeah you do.'

Oh God, whatever this is, I just need him to go now, I really do. I keep thinking about the girl and the taxi drivers, and her friend not wanting to get into the car. I keep thinking that I do need him to go, because I want to think what to do, see if I can contact PC Barnes or something, because right now that seems much more important than all of this.

'It's all right, you got every right. I just need to prove it to you, that's all.'

'Prove what to me?'

'That you're different.'

'I'm not different, I'm just the same, I'm just another fuck and hey, it was great.' I hold my hands out, feel myself become animated, all teeth and eyes and exaggeration, comic defence shield at maximum. 'But I'm a serious, grade A, fucked in the head nightmare, and I can't deal with your shit as well as mine, okay?'

'So…?' he says.

'Martin.' Christ, I'm blowing steam now, which is good. I'm going to say some horrible shit to him now, I'm going to really hurt him and then he'll get angry and go. I mean, not too angry, not smashing things angry, please, and not hitting me in the face kind of angry, but hurt male pride and all that, enough to get out of this for his own good.

'Space, final frontier an' all that. I get it,' he says. He strides into the sitting room, picks up his bag and slings it back onto his shoulder. 'Sweet,' he says. 'Look, you're fucked up, I'm fucked up, it's cool.'

'What does that even mean?' I say.

He bends to kiss me, a peck on the cheek that's too fast to return and too fast to avoid.

'It means it's cool,' he says, and goes to the door.

'Martin—'

'It's cool,' he says. 'I understand. So this is me, giving you space.'

And he's gone, with a wink and a grin, and there's me, trying to pretend like I'm not disappointed.

CHAPTER EIGHTEEN

Tele-phoney

I'M STILL THINKING about the girl and her friend when I get up in the morning. I've gone all the way from, 'I need to dial nine-nine-nine,' through 'There must be a way of finding a number for that nice PC Barnes,' to 'Look, you don't know what was really going on, do you?'

Underneath all this, I can't get away from two basic facts. One, I am going to have to call Cassie and speak to her, because she's way more sensible about this stuff than I am; and would probably be able to deal with it better than me anyway. Two, I am actually missing Martin. No, that's not quite true, I'm missing when he was the Boy, because he was less real then, and I thought I had a handle on him. He was basically doing what I wanted, which is always endearing. I am both annoyed that he didn't put up more of a fight for me, and heartily relieved. Although his leaving shot of saying that he understood my need for space, was definitely a cover for the humiliation of being dumped by someone he no doubt assumed would be grateful as hell for his attentions, and also because he'd played the whole story exchange thing wrong. It's had the opposite effect, because it had made me realise that he's a real person and not a sex toy. The intimacy of it is way too much for me. Martin has gone from the easy to handle Cockney Fuck Buddy to a scared, lost little boy, dumped out with the rubbish in a way that made me feel sick to my stomach. Sick and angry enough to want to find his so-called father and demand what the fuck he'd thought he was doing? There's no way I can get freaky with him now, no matter how awfully big he's grown since then.

I call a national charity help line for when you're worried about a child in danger. My heart actually pounds when the nice woman answers my call. As I stumble through my concerns, bless her, she does her absolute best to encourage me, making little, "mmm" and, "oh, dear" and, "uh-huh" noises in the background.

'I mean, it's just…they don't look very old, that's all. Not when the one, the main one was in the shop, close up, you know, she didn't look…. I mean, I know it's very hard to tell these days—oh f…flip, that makes me sound so bloody old, but—'

'But you think she is a young teenager?'

'Do they count as children, still?'

'Yes, I know it can be hard because they do look so adult, and often strive to do so, but yes. We're concerned with young people up to the age of sixteen; or people who might have suffered abuse at that age and are only reporting it now.'

She makes me feel good, using words such as "concerning" and "understandable", and tutting, and saying that I've done absolutely the right thing, which feels bloody good, actually. It feels as if I haven't done the right thing for some time now, so it's a nice change.

Then she says, 'Now, do you have a name for this girl by any chance?'

Which of course I don't. 'There was that policeman, though, he said he knew her.'

'Yes…I don't suppose he mentioned a name to you? No, he wouldn't have, of course. Safeguarding,' she says, answering her own question. 'Okay,' and her voice gets brighter and efficient sounding again. 'I'm going to log all the details of this in a report, and it will then get passed to your local social services.'

'And the police?'

There's a click on the line. 'Well, if they feel that a crime has definitely occurred, then—'

'I mean, they can ask PC Barnes about her?'

'I'm sure they will. But you might like to contact them directly yourself.'

'The police?'

'Your local social services. Of course, they'll get this report, but they might respond quicker to it, or you might find they're already aware of the situation, if you speak to them directly.'

So now I'm on the council website, looking for a number. There's a link to "*I am worried about my own or someone else's safety,*" which leads to a little white box on a grey screen, mostly talking about adults at risk and domestic violence, but not children.

I look back down the menu on the left, and find Children, Young People and Families, which leads to more green text in white boxes, divided into twelve sections, one of which is "*Safeguarding children*".

It's amazing just how much stuff there seems to be out there for families, stuff I'd never even thought about. That could have been me looking for a child minder or toddler groups, all of that mundane, puke and buggy pushing kind of stuff that comes with the whole baby thing. I distract myself from that by noticing that under the heading, in small print it reads, "*Popular in this section: child sexual exploitation*". Which seems a highly inappropriate way of phrasing it.

Top of this list is child protection, and that has "*Report it*" in large letters at the top, and suggests I dial 999 if I'm really worried. I was there in phase one, but as it's something I saw last night and am not currently witnessing, I decide against this. Below that are numbers for the Referral and Advice team.

It's answered on the fourteenth ring, and I go through

it all again with the woman who answers. While I'm talking to her, my phone buzzes with a message, but I ignore it and answer questions about the date, the time, the location.

'And, do you have a name for this girl?'

'No, but there's this policeman, PC Barnes, the one who came round to talk to me about the incident in the shop?'

'Yes, there should be a record of that, then. And with luck, we can trace her through that. If it's the same girl, of course.'

'I'm sure it's her,' I say, eager, pressing my case. 'I've seen her about a lot—'

'I mean, if this girl is the one *he* thinks he knows,' the social worker says. 'There's always a chance he's thinking about someone else.'

'Sure, but—'

'So, would you say she was being forced into the car by these men? Did you think about calling the police?'

'No, well—'

'I mean, that might have been the better option, if you thought that a crime was being committed.'

I feel a guilty prickle itch over my scalp. 'Well, she wasn't being forced, I don't think, I mean, not pushed or anything?'

'What about verbally? Was there shouting?'

'No,' I say, seeing them laughing, arms about each

other, sharing the coke, being offered cigarettes. 'There wasn't any shouting, from what I could see.'

'So, they got into the car of their own free will. This is a taxi rank, right?'

'Look, they're young, and it was late.' I get up as I say this and go to the window and look out at the taxi rank, innocent in the sunshine that's breaking through cloudy sky.

'It was around nine o'clock, you said?'

'Yes, but—'

'On a Friday night?'

I go to the kitchen and start putting things back into the cupboards. 'Last night yes, but look, the other time I saw her, it was in the middle of the fucking night, and there's no way a child of that—' Now I'm wiping the already clean counter.

'Could you modify your language please?'

'Sorry.'

'We have a job to do, and we have the right to do that job without suffering abuse or—'

'Okay, I wasn't swearing at you, I just meant the middle of the night, I was just—'

'Would you mind modulating your tone of voice please?'

'Look, I...' I force myself to breath out slowly, and she waits for me to do it. 'I am sorry,' I say, with all the sincerity I can muster, and begin lining up the cups so their handles are all the right way round. 'I did not mean to raise my voice, I am just very concerned about this…this thing I saw, and I would like to know what you can do about it, please.'

The woman clears her throat. 'Do you have a name for this girl?'

'No, like I said, I—'

'A nickname perhaps? Or her friend? Or any of the men, you referred to, these drivers, do you have any of their names?'

I look at the taxi rank, at the large yellow and black sign, which reads, AAA Number One Taxi, and which I've already given her.

'I don't have their names, no, but I imagine that if you look them up on some council register, at least the owner would be logged there?' There's a beep from my phone, I have another call waiting.

'Yes, he will. I'll put together a report based on what you've told me, which will go to the child protection team next week, who will also contact the police.' My phone beeps again.

'And they'll investigate?' I ask.

Beep. I quickly look to see who it is. Cassie.

'The first stage will be to try and trace this young person, establish if they are a child or not—'

'They can come round my flat,' I say, and close the cupboard door. I close it firmly, hard, three clicks down from a slam. 'They can come round my flat and watch out of the window any time, it's fine, I won't mind.'

'That…really wouldn't be something we could consider right now, but thank you for—'

'If you had a name, would you do something?'

'We are going to do something, madam. We're going to alert the safeguarding team, and they will consider what the—'

'But if you had her name, that would help?'

'Yes, Madame, that would help, but—'

In trying to juggle the phone so that I can pick up the kitchen spray, I press the wrong button with my cheek and suddenly Cassie's saying, 'Hello?'

'Shit,' I say, and give up on the spray. 'Hello?' I've cut the social services woman off, and I've used abusive language with her, and raised the tone of my voice, all of which makes me look like a bitch, and more than that, an unreliable witness. And now I'm on the phone to Cassie.

'So, you're going to talk to me then?' she says, which makes it impossible for me to say I hadn't meant to answer the phone to her.

'Seems so,' I say. Now I think about it, she doesn't seem as apologetic as I was expecting. 'Have you spoken to Max?'

'No. He did ring, but I didn't pick up.'

What's this, a little bit of honesty in the way of an olive branch, a pledge of loyalty? Or trying to make Max look like the real bad guy? Wow, I really am annoyed with her. I pick up the kitchen spray and aim it at the cooker hob, which is mirror bright and spotless. I close one eye, aiming my sight.

'Well that's all right, then,' I mutter, which she chooses to ignore.

'I don't think,' she begins, her voice much harder and sharper than it really should be. 'I don't think you realise how hard this has been for Max.' She sounds quite self-righteous about it.

'Wow, hard for Max?' I'm striding now, gesturing at the fridge as if it were Cassie. 'Jesus, my heart bleeds for him. Wait a minute, it wasn't my heart, it was—'

'Max is my friend too—'

'I've been your friend for twenty years,' I say, knowing that I sound as if we're in the playground. 'So why are you talking to him?'

'Because I can't talk to you,' and then she's yelling, so suddenly that I jerk the phone away. 'Because you've shut me out for so long, I've been wondering what the hell it is I've done to you, to make you like this!'

I'm reeling, my mouth hanging open as if I can't get enough air in otherwise, 'What the fuck? Cassie—'

'You need to hear this,' she yells. 'You need to hear this, for your own good, you're own—'

'Cassie!' I sob. I feel as if she's just punched me in the throat.

'I've been trying to tell you, to get through to you. I know you've been through the worst shit ever, the really worst, I do know that—'

'That's big of you—'

'But it's taken over your life, it's taken over Max's life, you've closed yourself off to everything else and—'

'How fucking dare—' But my legs have gone all weak, and I have to sit on the floor, I have to suck air in so hard I can't speak.

'I know you hate me right now,' her voice chokes through her tears. 'But you're letting this ruin your life. You don't talk to me, you don't talk to Max, and when I do see you, you're only half there. Fuck, you're so skinny now, I know you're not eating, and you're not sleeping, I know you're not.'

I should be so angry, I am so angry, but all the strength has gone out of me. She's wrong, of course she's wrong. I sleep, I sleep, I want to yell. Okay, I've been a bit up and down, and I eat, I fucking well eat, I…'We had lunch,' I say, through a whole lot of gasping for air.

'That was the first time in weeks, months, even.' She's quieter now, trying to be reasonable.

'It wasn't—' When was the last time we had lunch? And the night's out, and the…that hasn't changed, that hasn't. Has it?

'That's why Max was talking to me, because you've stopped talking to him, and I've been talking to him because you've stopped talking to me, because—'

'Well excuse me for my miscarriages ruining your fucking social life!'

'That's not what—'

But I don't care what it's not. I hang up.

CHAPTER NINETEEN

Park life

BALLED UP ON the kitchen floor against the fridge, I stuff my hands in my mouth and then scream through them, because if I let the sound out, I'll shatter myself into a thousand pieces. Am I being unreasonable? Did she really say that? Yes, yes she fucking did—I'm not the person she once knew? Oh no, well, I'm so sorry and all that, but the person she once knew has turned into a fucking abattoir on legs. So sorry, my bad.

Calm down, calm down—you are not to blame for what's happened, you are not to blame for the miscarriages, and you are not to blame for what she said.

Whose voice is that in my head now, being so reasonable, so supportive? Oh right, yes, Cassie.

I lie flat on the kitchen floor, make myself blow out a huge, deep breath, then another, then another, eyes closed, hands over them for good measure. This too will pass. This too will pass.

When I get a bit of control over my racing brain, I

begin to flick through the last twenty years with Cassie like it's so many old photographs. Her and me when we first met, arranging to go for a drink like it was a first date. It was a first date, the two of us tentatively making what we both hopped would be a connection—saying how neither of us had friends at school, like best friends, like real friends.

'What about college?' she'd asked and me doing a kind of shrug, a sniff, like it didn't matter.

'Don't say that, your course is important to you, it must be.'

And of course it was, but it was only her who'd seen it, who'd said so, who'd let me say so.

'Art college?' Mum said when I'd told her about the silver fox guy at the interview, who'd been so…who'd begun by being so nice about me, about my work. He was all, *"Your work shows great maturity for someone who's only finished their foundation year. Are you sure about applying for illustration, because there's so much in your work, so much depth, so much intelligence, have you thought about fine art?"*

'Well,' Mum said, as if making her mind up for herself. 'University is university, isn't it?'

'She could always be an art teacher,' Dad said, coming to put his arm around Mum's shoulders. 'Couldn't she, love?'

Then he looked at me, with that look. The one that

meant, all right, Lydia, let's just say that, shall we? Don't bother her any more with it, let's give her a break, eh, Lydia? Just like always.

'An Art teacher,' Mum said. 'That makes sense, I suppose.' Which was all she ever said about it, until Cassie came round and told them all the things I could be, the very first time she met them. Cassie sitting in the room as if she'd known them for years and telling them I could go on to do advertising, posters, records sleeves, even web-design, which was only really just taking off so she had to explain to them. When she said it to them, they listened to her.

'Such a lovely girl, really, and so bright, why isn't she at college? You're at college, I'm sure she could be too,' Mum said.

'You're fucking great with them,' I told her.

'What, they're cute?' she said, her face all wicked. 'It's always easier to talk to other people's parents.'

Which is true, I guess. I've only met hers a few times, as they live in Spain somewhere with all the other Brits out there, pretending like it's Southend.

'They listen to you,' I said.

'Because I believe in you,' she said. 'Your work's amazing, anyone can see that.' Only of course they hadn't, despite what she said.

On art degrees, you work nine till six, later if they'll let you, and along with all the physical stuff, the plain energy expended in moving brush over canvas, there's the weeks of sketching and thought and research before you even start that bit. I liked working, though. I liked the self-sacrificing, arm-aching slog of it. I liked the craft of it; of making paintings bigger than me, filled with a creeping ant's tread of line and shadow and shade and colour, of building form from illusion. I liked anything you had to hit with a hammer to inch into shape, I like fire, and steel, and work. I liked work so much I didn't bother to look around me, because I was so busy doing my art. The rest of my course were doing different things, but sure, if one of them wanted to paint themselves blue and stand on a box, that was cool, that was their "thing".

'That's bollocks,' Cassie said.

If they wanted to write the name of every guy they'd fucked on their skin in sharpie pen, and have someone photograph them with a pig—that's cool, right?

'Oh please,' Cassie said.

When it came to the final exhibition, we were all given a piece of the main hall to call our own, subdivided with nice, white pin-up boards, then called in one by one to have a chat with the tutors so that they could give us some pointers.

'Thing is,' the silver fox from my interview three years previous said, stretching his arm up above his head, 'I mean, no one can deny your facility with...with form, line, and the quality of that line is superb, but...'

'You've never taken direction well, have you?' the woman said.

'Disappointing,' the third one said. 'Really. Potential, sure, but there's no development. Of course, you can capture an image but—'

'But so can a photocopier,' the woman said, narrowing her eyes.

'Really, you've never challenged yourself, have you? Been all too busy...being busy. Perhaps illustration would have been more your thing?' Silver Fox said.

We had one day left to set up before the examiner came and we were locked out. I spent most of it on the floor of Cassie's bedroom crying and saying I wasn't going to bother. I'd worked, I'd been good, hadn't I? Wasn't that what you were supposed to do, be good and get your reward?

'They're arseholes,' she raged. 'Fucking idiots, your work's amazing!'

'I've wasted my time,' I told her. 'I'm useless.'

'Don't you fucking dare,' she said, and pulled me up and shook me, actually shook me. 'Are you really gonna lie there and take this shit? Really?'

So at five o'clock, when everyone else was finishing up or had left already, Cassie and I hid ourselves in the Ladies by the main exhibition hall. We'd even made sandwiches, and I had my photocopier card.

Most of the machines were tucked up for the night in

the library, but there was one solitary behemoth of a copier in the anteroom outside.

'Sorry about this,' I told it as I unbuckled my belt. 'But this is gonna hurt me just as much as it's gonna hurt you.'

'How many copies are on this card?' Cassie asked as I climbed aboard, knickers round my ankles.

'Three hundred; wanna spilt it fifty-fifty?'

'Fuck yeah!' she grinned at me.

When we'd papered every corner of my exhibition space with hundreds of photocopies of our arses, floor as well, we stood back to admire our handy work.

'You know it's funny,' Cassie said, stepping right, then left, 'how they kind of ... follow you round the room?'

'What do you think the title should be?' I asked her.

'Bunch of cunts,' we said as one, and I wrote it across them all in purple spray paint.

She was pleased, Cassie, I think. When everything crashed down, when I fell out of art college and into Big Al's.

'You don't need them, anyway,' she said. 'We've got each other. For always.'

For always.

Cassie.

I'VE NO ONE to get drunk with, nowhere to go and get

drunk, and there's no way I'm going to stay at home drinking on my own. I slam my shades on in case I start crying again, or in case I turn someone to stone with my gaze. You know, either way better be prepared.

The world outside is stifling and smells of fried chicken. I cross the street, running through a list in my head of people I might ring to get drunk with, discounting each of them before realising I've left my phone in the kitchen, so it's not as if I can ring any of them and have them turn me down anyway. Fuck them all. I can't be bothered to hook up with people I have to pretend with.

I'll buy cigarettes, because there's nothing like doing the one thing Cassie hates me doing the most, to make me feel even shittier, getting back at her in the most pathetic way possible. I look at myself in the window of the place on the corner, the afro hairdressers, because it has big, plate glass tinted windows that act as mirrors. I can't see what Cassie's talking about, I'm not that thin. And if I am, it's all the jogging I'm doing and the gym stuff, and that's to keep fit, not to lose weight or anything. I've always been thin and I've never slept well, so what's new?

I don't buy cigarettes. When I go into the newsagents a few streets away towards the market square and tube station, it all looks too shiny and clean for me to admit to wanting to smoke. And actually, I don't want to smoke, because I have only done it in the last few weeks when high, as I gave up years ago. Plus I could never smoke in the daylight. So I buy a can of coke and keep on walking, figuring I'll work out where I'm walking to, as I go.

The bigger and cleaner the shops get, the more advertisements about the Olympics there are. For a moment I can't remember if it's happened already or not. It's like the rest of the city is planning a party I've been invited to, but it was only a casual invitation, and no one will really mind if I don't turn up. I won't have to watch any of it. Go me, young free and able to watch exactly what I want on the television. Not that I can remember when I last turned it on.

I go through the older part of the market that sells new things, then the newer part of the market that sells old things, then the plaza with the shit art and cushion stalls. Then it's the park, and on this lovely sunny day the park is full, the swings and slides and water feature all full of laughing children and happy couples and dog walkers with dog on leads, and me, striding through all of them like a dusty old owl caught out in the sun. At the gateway, I throw my empty coke can into a bin.

The little park, we used to call the one back home when Lauren and I were kids. Shit. I still haven't called her back. It's always hot there too in my memories. The smell of asphalt grown sticky under foot, the peeling paint on the monkey bars, and the slide frying pan hot. You had to go down it fast, no time to wait, because your legs would stick to it if you didn't. Then you'd shoot off the end to graze your knees on the ground. One time I was at the top of the slide and Lauren was waiting at the bottom for me. She was too small for the slide, too small to be in the park just with me, really. She was playing with something she'd found, waiting for me to come down whizzing down the slide so she could look up and smile at her big sister. But I climbed down the rungs into the darkness of the hedge shade and slipped away from her. Left her there on her own.

I shake my head. What am I thinking about that for? I've got enough to deal with not without raking up old family shit too.

The park I'm in now is long and sprawling. There's the skate park, concrete 'U' shapes where young people go and smoke weed. It's empty today, apart from a couple of thirty something guys in three quarter length baggies and backwards baseball caps. I walk past them on the gravel path that loops round a scruffy copse of trees and a bench.

On the bench, it's her, it's the girl.

I veer off to the right, not sure what to do. I should, I suppose, leave everything to the professionals. But I turn back, drop my walking pace to a slow amble and stick my hands in my trouser pockets.

Her bony ankles poking out from her green leggings look snappable, her feet comically large in their bulky trainers. She has one arm across her chest, the other stretched into her lap, until she raises a finger to gnaw at a nail. Surely she must be too hot in that big hoodie?

I'm approaching her from behind. Needing a reason to stop, I bend and flick out my shoelace before slowly drawing alongside her bench and sitting on the end.

'D'you mind?' I say. She looks at me but looks away at once. I sit down, feeling like I'm in a film about some lonely frontier man who befriends a wild creature, leaving scraps of food by their log cabin, then one day daring to hold one out for the creature to take from his hand. I should have bought the cigarettes after all.

I raise my knee and hook my heel on the edge of the seat to do up the shoelace. Wanting to take as much time as I can over it, I take my shoe off and pretend like there's something in it, pulling the tongue back to look. I'm aware she's watching me as I do it, her soft, baby bird face guileless.

'You was in the shop,' she says. An observation, not a criticism.

I look at her and smile. 'Yeah, thought you looked familiar.'

I'm waiting for her to react, to blame me for PC Barnes tracking her down and her mother, or father even, balling her out afterwards. She doesn't.

'That guy's a creep,' she says, and looks back down at her finger, inspecting her nail. As she does, her cuff falls down her arm. There's a bruise on the inside of her wrist, and although her skin is a similar dusty brown shade to Martin's, the bruise makes it look bone white in comparison. I'm not sure if she's aware of me looking, but she drops her hand to her lap again and the bruise slides out of sight.

'I 'ad money.' She sniffs. 'He never got me though, too slow. Never come out from that counter, innit.'

'I suppose not,' I say. He hasn't come round then, PC Barnes. Just not got round to it yet? Busy man, PC Barnes, and I guess a foiled shoplift and a revenge racist attack, isn't top of the list.

'Fat Paki bastard,' she says. 'He's always had it in for me, because of my boyfriend.'

She says boyfriend with a little emphasis looking away from me until it's out, then glances up as if she's watching for my reaction.

'Your hair's sick,' she says.

'Thank you.

'Are they real, them?' she juts her chin toward me.

'You mean my boobs?'

'Your tattoos,' she says.

'They're real.' She nods, her brown cow eyes flick over me.

'Where d'you live?' I ask. See at once it's a mistake.

She doesn't exactly flinch, but her expression hardens, because this is an adult's question, an authority question. 'I live opposite the shop,' I say, trying to make it sound as if I actually don't care where she lives. 'I've a flat there.' God, I'm wittering now. I cross my legs the way men do, one ankle resting on the other thigh, legs wide apart and leaning back. I'm not sure why I do this, other than a desperate attempt to appear relaxed. 'You should come round for a cuppa sometime. I'm in a lot. Taking a year off work.'

She doesn't ask what I do, but she relaxes a little. I guess she hasn't got to the stage in life when you stop defining yourselves by who you are, and switch to what you do. What do jobs mean to her, if you're not a pop star or a z-grade celeb?

'I don't like tea,' she says, but she smiles, her lips twitching at the corners. How old are you? I want to ask. Are you still in school, does your mother know where you are?

'You got kids?' she asks.

Her question hits me harder than it might for being so unexpected. I suppose women get asked that sort of thing all the time when they get to my age. But not if you look like me.

'No,' I say, trying really hard to keep my voice calm and neutral.

'Why?'

Fuck. There's nothing wrong with asking that question. I've had complete strangers ask me way worse than that. I could lie, of course but as she stares at me with that almost unblinking gaze, I can't think of anything but the truth.

'I can't.' Oh. That's possibly the first time I've ever said it out loud, or even admitted it to myself. My throat tightens, as if the words pulled it closed after them. 'I have miscarriages.'

The girl frowns. 'What's that?'

Is she taking the piss? No, she's not, she really doesn't know. She's waiting for me to tell her, because why would she know? It's all part of the world she's not reached yet, and if her mother or her big sister's never gone through it, and even if they have, would they say?

'It's when,' I start, and she must know I'm crying even behind the shades, because of the way my voice cracks when I say, 'you get pregnant, but the baby dies before it's born.' I clear my throat.

'That's rank, man,' she says, putting her hand not on mine, but on the space between us on the bench. Her hand is tiny, the ends of the fingers like bitten round beads, little shells of nails painted candy pink. I want to hold her hand.

I don't.

I can't.

I look back across the park to the concrete slopes of the skate park. Blinking the tears back.

A ring tone sounds, her phone. As she moves her hand to dive into her hoodie pocket, I sit up, put my foot back on the ground, try and think of something to say that will draw her back to me. But the moment she answers her phone, she's on her feet, walking away. She glances back only the once, her gold hoop earrings swinging against her neck, the sunlight catching on the slick, black cap of her hair where its moulded to her head.

'Come for tea!' I call out, then think how stupid that sounds, how desperate, and, if I were a man, how creepy. I look back down at my shoes, and realise I've successfully managed not to get her name, again.

When I look up I can't see her. I walk the way she did, but she's gone. Melted into the crowds. I want her back, I feel the loss of her as keenly as if I'd known her for years. And how old is she? Her head looks too big for her whippet thin neck. She's like a puppy yet to grow into her feet, and those soft bitten fingers, the little buttons of nails painted party pink. She's not even fourteen is she, she might not even be a teen anything. Twelve, eleven?

I'm standing with my hand up to shade my eyes despite my sunglasses, as if that will gift me with magic powers of seeing, staring across the park as if looking out to sea. I had her, and she blindsided me and, as usual, my own fucking problems came crashing in on us. God, I'm so self-obsessed. I don't think PC Barnes has spoken to her, because I'm sure she would have said something if he had, even if it was just to accuse me of dobbing her in to him, if that's what people say nowadays. And that means that when the social services people have their meeting and note that the anonymous tipster used abusive language on the phone and so might, perhaps, not be a reliable witness, then see from the notes that they can speak to a PC Barnes, when they do, he won't know who she is at all. Maybe he only said he knows her because he's seen her about, like I have, and maybe he's keeping an eye out for her, but that's all.

There's about seven million people living in London and if less than twenty percent of them are kids her age, or ten percent, because that maths is easier, that's, like, hundreds of thousands of kids she could be. And PC Barnes may well have been thinking of one of them, but not this one, because it's not as if she's the only one, now is she?

I do a circuit of the kids play area, wondering how the hell I'd explain following the girl round if I do see her. I can't explain it, so I go home.

This time when I pass the taxi rank, one of them is outside leaning against his car. He does nothing other than look at me, and it's not even a creepy look, it's just the way someone looks at you when your bright blue hair catches their eye and they've nothing else new to look at, that's all. Only it doesn't feel like that, it feels like he is letting me know he is looking at me, like he wants me to know he knows who I am, and where I live, and that I am alone.

A look can't do all that, that's stupid, that's…that's paranoia, right there. What is wrong with me? They don't know I've been watching them, calling the social. How could they?

He's still looking at me.

In the flat I open windows and draw the curtains, telling myself this is because it's hot. Really I want to lurk behind the kitchen blind watching the street. I can't escape the thought that PC Barnes doesn't know her after all, so nobody is looking out for her. I make a cup of tea while I let this rattle around my head. When I open my fridge door for the milk, there's not a lot else in there. I should eat some salad and make myself a fruit smoothie. I should go to the supermarket and buy organic veg and chicken for a stir fry, sort myself out instead of obsessing about the girl.

I'm still thinking this, when the doorbell goes. My heart lurches. I feel stupidly scared, as if there's going to be a whole fleet of cab drivers out there, with pitch forks and burning torches and the rest. Or it's the girl. She's here she's knocking on my door because they're coming after her, the shop man, the driver, all of them.

I stride over and twist the door lock, find that I'm almost running down the stairs.

But when I open the street door, it's Martin.

CHAPTER TWENTY

Bitch

HE STEPS PAST me and up the short flight of stairs to the open door above; he's inside before I've had a chance to squash the smile that rises unbidden and say more than, 'Oh, what—'

He walks into my flat as if it's the most natural thing in the world, talking almost stream of consciousness.

'Fuck me, it's hot out there, and they've got the road up round the corner, bloody bus has been sat there for fucking ages, like being in a' oven. Never mind, panic over—hey, I was meaning to say the other day, I was talking to...'

I follow him with a confused, jaw-dropped incredulity, while he dumps his bag on the floor against the back of my armchair, and almost seems to step over it to sit down, making a great sighing noise as he does. 'Fuck that's better.' He's wearing those pinstripe trousers again, and red braces over a white t-shirt. Something about those two, vertical stripes of red against his elongated torso makes me think of the wading birds that stride through mudflats near Nan's house.

'Martin, what are you doing?' Because he should not be here, he should not be doing this. There is something very wrong with him being here and just walking in like that.

'Cooling my beans,' he says, and does a bloody hell, you just don't know what it's like out there, face. 'Couldn't get me a drink, could you darlin'? I'm spitting feathers, an' I gotta get this party started.'

'What party, what are you…?' But I can see what he's doing.

He reaches into the pocket in the high waist of those trousers and pulls out a baggie, shifts the carefully arranged coffee table books and tips out a dusting of white powder.

'Right, that's enough.' I stride over to him. 'What the fuck do you think this is?'

He pauses in mid action, looking at me as if I'd made a mild enquiry about the running of the Victoria line. 'It's Saturday, night starts here, babe.'

Babe is no better than darling. 'I mean, what the fuck are you doing here?'

'It's Saturday,' he says again, as if that should explain everything. 'We're gonna get high, paint the town, that sort of thing.' He reaches into his pocket again and pulls out an Oyster card.

'I told you I need space. I told you yesterday I need some space and this, this is not you giving me space.'

'I know,' he says, working the card over the powder on the table. 'I know what you said. You said we hardly know each other, which is true, so I figured, hey, Saturday, we go out, we get fucked and we, you know?'

'I know what?'

'Get to know each other, like you said.' Then he puts his hand on his heart, he actually does it as if he's swearing an oath. 'Nothing else, friends, that's all. I promise, keep me hands to me'self all night, unless you change your mind about that, beg me or something.' He winks.

'Martin, friends ring first, okay? Friends ring and make sure other friends don't have other plans, or want to spend a night in, and friends take, like, no for an answer.'

'Your phone was off,' he shrugs. 'I left a message.'

'Did I answer the message?'

'I was already on the bus.'

'Look,' I say, 'I don't want to go out, I don't want to get to know you better, I just want to be on my own.'

He looks neither angry or amused, just stares up at me, still half bent over the table top, Oyster card in hand. 'No you don't,' he says, then looks back down at the table.

Christ. I want to slap the back of his head to make him listen to me, clip him round the ear like that brat he's being. Only he's not a brat, is he? He's a man, albeit a very young one, and he knows he's in the wrong and yet he's here, pretending like everything is okay with that. So, which one of us is he trying to convince?

'People who say they wanna be alone, don't mean it. You're just scared your shit will bring everyone else down. But you and I are over that. I've got my shit, you've got your shit, blah, blah, blah, so what? We'll just—'

I speak over him. 'Martin, I want you to go, now. I told you yesterday, I'm not in a good place right now, and I want you to leave me alone.'

He puts the oyster card down on the table, then he reaches out to touch my cheek. I pull away, so he knows that's not cool.

'But we understand each other,' he says. 'You understand because you lost too, like I lost—'

'Martin, we're just two people, all right? And we had fun, with each other, when we needed there to be fun.'

He's nodding, as if this conversation is going to turn out well for him.

'But now it's over, and I want you to leave.'

'No you don't, you—'

'Martin…'

He looks away. His chest rising and falling rapidly, throat rippling under his skin as he swallows repeatedly. The light through the window behind casts him into shadow, the day beyond it is cloying, yellowing and clouding over. When he looks back at me, I can see the wetness of his eyes, the way they've softened. He's so not in a good place, and I'm not sure it's the sort of bad place I'm equipped to deal with. Or is this just what he does, when the girls turn him down? Is this his normal routine?

This isn't normal behaviour, is it?

'You need to go, Martin,' I say. And, oh Christ, like a ghost behind his eyes, I see the child in in his face, the one pushed out of the door and left with a stranger.

This is not the behaviour of a sane, well balanced person.

It makes no difference to how I feel.

It makes no difference to how I feel.

'I can't do this…'

'But I want you,' he says, and there's a laugh behind the words, something sad, something still a tiny bit hopeful.

I could do it, I think. I could do what he wants, what he *thinks* he wants; humour him, because he's young, because he's attractive enough to make it bearable.

Fuck, it would be so easy.

But it would be wrong.

Really really wrong—because this is not safe behaviour, for me or him.

'But I don't want you,' I say.

He stands and I get up too. When we're both standing, I'm reminded again of just how much there is of him, how he's got the thick end of a foot on me. He's scowling as he takes a step toward me, his hands gripped into fists, then he releases them, one finger pointing at me.

'Martin,' I say, and I hope to God my voice sounds cool, and firm and authoritative, and not as scared as I feel, because he's really not well, is he?

'I told you,' he says. 'I told you the truth, an', an' I meant it, I really told you it, an' you just can't—' He makes a move towards me. Is he going to push me? Grab me? Shake me? I don't know, but whatever it is, I flinch back from him, not by far, not by much but enough for it show it's all about fear. 'Get the fuck away from me!'

'No,' he says, and as he steps back his foot catches against the leg of the chair and he stumbles, and knocks the table, 'I didn't mean…I didn't—'

'Get out,' I say, and in trying not to be scared, I sound really angry. 'Get the fuck out of my flat now. I don't want to see you again, I don't want to hear from you, I don't want to—' The pile of books that he'd moved tumbles over and crashes to the floor.

He reaches for his bag, swings it up onto his shoulder and it misses me by inches. On his way out, he kicks the table by the door, which crashes over. I yelp. The brass dish where I keep my keys hits the floor, bowling away to clatter down on the kitchen tiles.

'Go fuck yourself, you fucking bitch. Go fucking fuck yourself, then.'

Before I hear the street door slam shut behind him, I've already slammed the flat door and flipped the catch down.

'Yeah?' I yell back at it, 'well, you go fuck yourself too.' I hit the flat of my hand against the wood. 'Go fuck yourself and leave me the fuck alone.'

I am so sick of people telling me what to do, what I need, what I want, what's good for me.

I am sick of not being able to do anything about anything.

Why am I crying, is it him, is it because of him?

Oh fuck, Martin, why did you have to go and like me? That's not a normal reaction, is it?

It's not all because of him. I press my forehead against the door, my hand beside my face and eyes screwed shut against the tears. He's really not well, is he?

Fuck.

I thought it was going to be her at the door, the girl. I thought it was her, coming round for tea, and I am crushed because it wasn't, I am terrified because it wasn't.

Where is she?

I didn't even get her name.

CHAPTER TWENTY-ONE
Dinner time

JUST AS I'M deciding Martin has really gone so it's safe to step away from the door and go back to watching for the girl from the kitchen window, my phone rings. Flashes Max's name up. I give in and answer it.

'Hello, babe?' he says.

'Hello Max.'

'Listen, I'm gonna be in town tonight. Can we, erm, can we talk, like?'

'We're talking now, Max.'

There's a pause. 'Can we meet up, I mean, like for dinner, or something?'

'Which, dinner or something?' I'm being a bitch, I know, but this at least makes Max laugh, only a little laugh, but hey, it's a start. Then I remember about Cassie, so I say, 'Don't you need to run it past my best friend first anyway?'

'Babe, don't be like that,' he says.

I'm tempted to ask him why, but everything that's

been going on has really taken the edge off my urge to torture him, so I let him off by asking where and when.

To fill in the time before I meet Max and stop me thinking about him and what tonight might mean, or about Martin calling me a bitch, or that he bothered to come over here to say it, or that he seemed determined to pretend nothing had happened between us in the way of an ending, I ring the social services back. I get a different person, so I have to explain everything again.

'So,' she says, pausing to digest the scree of words I've spouted at her. 'You already rang us earlier, with a report?'

'Yes.'

'And you want to add this to that report?'

'Yes.'

'Hmm…the thing is though, the report was anonymous, so I can't add this one to it, I'll have to make a new report.'

She goes into a long reason as to why this is, all of which I listen to, trying very hard not to interrupt, and not to use anything that might be construed as abusive language. After batting the problem back and forth, we come down to the nub of the matter.

'So, although you spoke to the girl, you didn't manage to get her name?'

'No, but there was this bruise on her arm.'

'You see, I can log this again, but all that's gonna happen with it, is that it's gonna go through as a new report to the Monday team meeting, and it's not gonna tell them a whole lot more than what you already did.'

'I just…' Breath out slowly. 'I just know she's in trouble, and I don't know what to do.'

'Look, you doin' the best you can by her, by sayin' something to someone. You just got to have patience, you know? We're gonna do the best we can for her.'

'But I don't think the policeman does know her, you see? I mean, I'm sure she'd have said something about him coming round, blamed the shop guy for calling him, but she didn't, and so I don't think he's ever gone to see her, and I don't think he really does know her, so when they ask him, he's not gonna—'

'Darlin'?' the woman says. 'I got all that. Let's just take it one step at a time, shall we? You done a good thing, there's nothing else you can do right now. Go an' enjoy your Saturday, an' leave it to us, alright?'

'But—'

'Alright?'

Alright.

I shower and change. I'm having the conversation with her in my head again as I do, some of it even out loud. I keep myself going all the way through getting dressed, in jeans and the nearest I get to a pretty top, and putting some make-up on and arranging my hair into a blue quiff. For once, I get it looking pretty smart. I should argue with un-seen social workers more often.

There's a voice mail on my phone when I go to put it in my leather jacket. An apology from Martin, and he tries to do a joke, then can't think what to say, then is drowned by traffic, then says he's sorry, again, and that he'll call me, and will I text him at least?

No, I won't, because you don't mean this Martin, you just think you do, I tell my phone, which I know would be more effective if I was brave enough to tell him.

By the time I reach the tube station, there are two more texts from him, another apology, and a cheerier message suggesting we still ought to get to know each other better. Just before I go underground, I read the last one again, think about replying, then don't. Don't engage, I tell myself. Then there's one from Mum too, that brings with it a stab of guilt, But I don't engage with her either.

When I emerge five stops later, my phone vibrates with more messages from Martin. They go from "*did you get my last message?*" to "*you know, I'm really worried about you*" to "*forgive me for caring, you fucking bitch*" then end up in a scree I can barely read. It's been done over by auto-correct, so hardly makes sense, but seems to roll from pleading, to demanding, to him desperate to tell me something, which means I just have to call him.

Shit.

I take a deep breath, block his number, delete all of his messages and his contact from my phone, which I realise is just like putting him on hold and solves nothing. But I can't deal with him right now. Hell, I'm not exactly issue free myself, am I?

By the time I reach the restaurant, one of those Turkish ones that's all glass mosaics and floor cushions, my phone has told me there are three notifications on my Facebook wall, all from Martin, all of the concerned variety. "*Hey, are you okay?*" then "*I'm really worried about you, can you call me?*" and finally "*I'm looking out for you, when no one else is.*" I block him from there too, as far as is possible.

I have to tell him. Max, I mean. Tell him about Martin. Even if I've blocked him, because he's not going to go away easy, is he?

The weight of it pulls on my shoulders, makes me stumble and come to a stop before I can go in and see Max again.

There, see? If anyone was thinking I was going to get away with it, the whole Martin thing, then guess what, they were wrong.

There isn't a way out of it, not one where Max and I go on, where we have any chance to try again. It's too risky. I know he doesn't know now, or at least I think he doesn't know now, but he will know soon. I am going to have to tell him, because this is what this is for, this meal, it's a reconciliation, right? This is him trying to make amends, and so I've got to as well, or it won't work. And I do want it to. I want it to be me and Max again, and our baby. My brain kicks in and I start to rehearse how I'll say it. But nothing works, nothing is going to make this any better.

I try again, straighten up, draw in a jagged, painful breath.

Max, this is going to hurt me more than it's going to hurt you....

Seriously, brain?

I can feel it again, that sense of a hand around my throat that used to wake me up from my sleep gasping for air. Grasping for all the things I've lost—Nan, the babies, and now Max? All of them my fault because I'm such a nasty girl.

Hot tears push at my eyes and I blink and blink, trying to wipe them away without smudging my mascara. I have to tell Max the truth, so this really might be it, and I have to face that.

He's inside waiting for me, and when I see him it takes everything I have, every inch of strength not to crack, not to make a run for it. He's chosen a secluded corner and is sitting rather awkwardly on a round cushion, lurking behind a low table decorated like a chess board. The background music is all sitars and eastern promise—though thinking about it, it's probably ouds and eastern promise them being Turkish, but anyway— it's dark, cool and smells as much of damp and joss sticks as it does cooking. It reminds me of a well-appointed squat, the sort owned by someone whose mummy and daddy will bail them out, should any of this shit get real.

I walk over to him, my shit getting more and more real with every step as I thread my way through low tables and floor cushions.

'You alright, babe?' Max says when he sees me.

There's a long, hanging brass lantern above our table with a suitably damaclesian spike, which he has to dodge round to get up, and this means he steps forward to greet me leaning all over to one side. I'm not sure what the etiquette is when you greet the partner you've been cheating on after he left you, so when he moves in to kiss me, I swerve away, pretending to catch the swinging lantern.

'It's so good to see you, babe,' he says, and he's grinning at me, like he's amazed I haven't hit him, and is taking this as a good sign. 'You're looking well.'

'Have I been ill?' I ask.

'No, no, I mean, you look great, you know?'

'Oh, yeah, thanks.' God, can't even manage a quip, bloody hell.

I sit, which is not comfortable on a round floor cushion when wearing skinny jeans. The waiter brings the obligatory bread and olives and puts them between us like a crash barrier. Max is talking but I'm not listening. I take a piece of the bread, all warm and floury and pull it between my fingers, and work it back and forwards as if I'm trying to shape the words I need to say from it, until it becomes grey and pudgy. Max has ordered red wine, already filled my glass and is filling his again. Then he orders small dishes of oily things, which on a normal day I'd love, but when they come almost immediately, as if the waiting staff can feel our awkward atmosphere and would really like it if we buggered off and stopped bringing the place down, I don't even want to look at them. So I drink instead, and watch Max talk. This is like some kind of reverse first date. We know all of each other's bad points already and are trying to forget them, rather than having them all yet to discover. The time I first peed on a stick, we were still really strangers to each other. I realised I was a few weeks late, one hungover morning, thinking how it was surely impossible, and surely, way too soon for all this?

I'd slung the test into my supermarket shopping basket along with a box of tampons, because of course there was no way I could be pregnant, could I? I didn't even rush home and do it then. It was a few days later, a Sunday morning searching the medicine cabinet for painkillers and coming across it and only then remembering to do it, and then sitting on the loo, really not sure what I was meant to do next.

It's how I feel now, watching Max working diligently through his taramasalata, I'm still not really sure what I want to do next, or rather, I do know, I just don't know how I'm going to tell Max about it.

'Look,' he's saying, 'I mean, shit, I've been doing a lot of thinking, yeah?' I'm going to interrupt him, then I notice something about him I would have seen earlier, if I hadn't been so in my own head, rehearsing my downfall. Max is sweating. There's a sheen of moisture across his forehead and nose, and it's not that warm in here, because to compliment the authentic Middle Eastern setting, they have installed a ferocious authentic air conditioning system.

'Okay?' I venture.

He does a bit of verbal place keeping, 'Yeah, you know, it's been, like really hard being without you, right?'

And he looks at me expecting, I imagine, me to agree. 'Right?'

'Look, you know sort of when we first met, right? In the beginning?' The he stops again, as if there's something really big he needs to tell me now, something like a confession. Christ, was he seeing someone else, when we first met? Is that it, was there someone else and now he's gone back to her? One of those friends, one of those *if we're both single when we're forty, we always said we'd get married ha-ha friends?*

Wait. Does this mean I don't have to tell him about Martin?

'I mean, Christ, Babe, I'm just all over the place here,

look at me.' He chuckles, then in a great swoop he catches hold of my hand. 'You know, you're so bloody sexy, right?'

'Oh,' is all I can manage. Because this isn't what I was expecting.

'Seriously, babe, I've…I've missed you, I've missed you so much.'

'I've missed you too, Max, it's just—'

'Fuck me, babe, I'm so…I'm so horny, just seeing you again.'

'Oh—' is all I can manage again. I guess he hasn't been seeing someone else after all.

'Seriously, I'm…' He's all flushed and sweating and telling me how horny I make him, how he's been thinking about nothing else. 'Nothing but fucking you, like when we were first together, like when…when all of this, was just about…'

Christ, the people on the next table can hear this, I'm sure they can. Him saying how he'd love to fuck me right now, right here in this restaurant. I should love it, I shouldn't give a sod what anyone thinks, because this is me, right? This is what we do, what I do. I can see myself in the past totally getting off on this, totally loving it but images of Martin not Max are flashing through my mind, Martin's body, Martin's smile, his laugh, him the salt in the wound of Max's faith in me, Max's trust in me.

'M—'

'You remember that weekend, right, the one in Amsterdam, when we first got together?'

'Yes, yeah—' I say through my fixed smile, gripping his fingers back as if this will pull his conversation onto safer ground, because I *swear* the people on the next table can hear every word he's saying.

For goodness sake, dear, my mother says in the back of my mind. *For goodness sake!*

'What I'm trying to say is, can it be like that again, just for a bit, yeah? Like Amsterdam, babe?'

'What, with canals and stuff?' I say, itching with guilt.

'I'm serious,' he says, pressing my hand. 'Do you remember how good that was? Just you and me, fucking each other, all the time? I want that again, with you, just that…fucking you—'

I look away, feel hot colour wash over my cheeks.'

'Have I embarrassed you?'

'Shut up!'

'I have, bloody hell, that's a first!' He leans into me, his voice low, intimate. 'See, I knew I could get to you, babe, knew you felt it too.'

Poor Max, I'm about to break his heart for him, and here he is, being all nostalgic for the kind of sex I've been having without him.

'You know, that weekend yeah? We were so wasted, and I was so horny, so hot for you, yeah? Christ, I even fucked you when you were passed out, because you looked so sexy just lying there, and—'

When you were passed out.

He's talking. He's going on about what it felt like to fuck me and I'm hearing the words like a shower of stones thrown at me, handfuls of them one after another.

When you were passed out.

'Sorry, Max. You just said you fucked me, while I was…unconscious?'

He blinks, like he's not sure why I'm bringing that bit up. He was all the way into 'Can't we just try being like that again, like in the beginning.' Knee deep, thigh deep, well into his stride, into the world where things were simple.

'Yeah, but—'

'You fucked me when—'

'Yeah, but not like, I mean, we were at it all that weekend, like I said, like—'

I pull my hand away from his. It comes away sweaty and hot, then chills in the aircon. A hotel in Amsterdam. Wait. A lost weekend in a hotel in Amsterdam, and us pretending we really were going to see some museums and shit like that, and not just get wasted, and instead of course us getting completely wasted and me passing out and waking up the next day in all that soft yellow light, curled up in Max's arms and feeling so happy, so fucking happy.

'So, when I was unconscious and you fucked me—'

'Not like that,' he says, defensive now, glancing at the table next to us, caring if they can hear or not now, because they are looking, because I'm not whispering now.

'When you fucked me when I was unconscious, did you use a condom?'

'Babe, please—'

There's the memory of me in the bar a couple of weeks later; me telling Cassie even before I told him, me saying *I don't know how it happened, of course we took precautions, of course we did, but do you know what? I...I don't care—I want this, I want this...*

'I'm just saying I wanted you so much, that's—'

'That was the weekend I first got pregnant, wasn't it?' My heart is hammering inside me, flooding me with cold, hard bright blue energy. Now he's stopped talking, because he can't think what the hell else to say, other than the truth.

There it is again, the tightness at my throat. The memory of Amsterdam mixes up with the earlier memory of the hotel room in the airport Holiday Inn, and the asshole, and my art work, and me saying, *I know, I know it was stupid risk, what did I think I was doing, going back to his hotel room with him anyway?* Because you can't trust them, can you? Men, men you don't hardly know, alone, in hotel rooms. I mean, whatever was I thinking, getting that off my face with a man I hardly knew? My fault, really, when you *think* about it?

'You said it was what you wanted, when you found out?' he says. 'I mean, it was okay, in the end?'

You wanted it.

'Okay…babe?'

I'm shaking. I think I can feel it again, the sensation of there being wings under my skin, the real thing under the tattoo, writhing, pushing towards the light, pressing up through bone and flesh to be free.

'Look, you're the one who always pushed it, you were always up for anything, you know you were, right?'

You wanted it, right?

I stand up, the things on the table jump and jolt as my knee crashes into it. Everyone is looking at me now, everyone in the whole place is looking at me and I don't care. They can all see right through me, right through my clothes, right through my skin, right through to the bone.

'Don't you fucking dare—' I hiss.

'You fucked me when you woke up,' he says, face all red now, expression twisting with humiliation and anger, 'soon as you woke up, you…we—'

He's such a good bloke, Max.

I should scream at him, tell him about Martin, do it now so I can really hurt him with it. Yeah, well, I've been fucking someone else, Max, someone half our age, nearly, and with a dick twice your size, doing all the freaky shit you want to do to me, and doing it better, and…and…

But I don't.

I can't say anything. Not about Martin, it doesn't seem fair. To Martin, I mean.

'It was what you wanted, in then end?' Max says.

He's gone all small and quiet, just standing opposite me with the stupid lamp hanging between us, and me not even being able to scream at him. The buzz of conversation begins to seep back round us, the sound of throats clearing, fingers going back to picking at bowls and plates, a little ripple of laughter, someone else's phone ringing.

It was what I wanted, but it's gone now, isn't it?

Maybe it never was, not really.

A little pearl, lost in an ocean of blackness inside me, a warm, midnight sea and then, and then.

I haven't really been aware of him coming up, but there is a waiter standing with us now, a little man with a wide smile under curly hair.

'Please,' he's is saying. And I'm not sure what he wants, because what is any of this to do with him? 'Please, I can help, yes?'

Help?

'I help call taxi, yes?'

Oh, right, he wants us to leave. We're making a scene in his nice restaurant, we're polluting the place with our nasty. I get it. I don't really want to be around me either right now.

I look over at Max, and all I see is the ugly of him.

'I'm going home,' I say.

'I get taxi,' the waiter says, and Max starts rooting through his pocket, gets something out, money I think, hands it to the waiter. The waiter has his hand just resting on my elbow, reaches to take the money from Max, is saying something like, 'Yes, lady, you come, lady,' all while nodding to Max, winking, doing an *allow me to take care of this mess for you, sir,* face, an *all-boys together* face, a *women, what can you do, right?* kind of a face.

'Thanks, mate,' Max says to the waiter. Then to me, 'We just need to talk. Somewhere quiet, yeah? We'll go home, yeah, and—'

'It's not your home, Max,' I say. 'Not anymore.'

I pick up the glass and drain the last of the wine.

WHEN I TOLD him the first time, when I came and sat on the bed next to the lump of him under my duvet, holding the test in hand for proof, he looked at me for a while but didn't speak. Then he took hold of my other hand.

'I want it too,' he said. 'I want this too.'

I STUMBLE AWAY from the waiter, away from Max, out through the maze of tables, cushions, hookah smoke, knickknacks and rugs onto the street. I could get the tube, that would make sense, but I don't think my legs will get me that far. I lean against the wall, far enough away from the glass door so that all the people waiting for seats won't have to stand and stare at me, but near enough that I can get there without collapsing.

I will stand here and wait for the car to come, and I will go home, because I am not sure what anything else means right now. There is a hissing in my head, a crackle and burn of static which is crackling round my eyes, so that when the yellow light on top of the car that pulls up beside me blazes through it, I move as if disconnected from the pavement, as if the door sucked me in. So it's only when we pull out, that I realise I'm in one of the cabs from over the road, that Max must have given the waiter a card, one of the ones we both have a stack of, because that's our local firm, right? It's the one taxi service that knows exactly where I live, and the driver is the one I saw with the girl and her friend, the one who got into the backseat with them both.

CHAPTER TWENTY-TWO

Taxi driver

A TSUNAMI OF anger and fear and 'fuck you' and panic and 'keep cool' all swirled up together slams into me. Presses me against the car seat as if we're taking off into outer space and the G-force has got me.

Do nothing, something inside screams at me desperately, this is not the time or the place. Go home, go to bed, keep watch, keep a record, do the right thing. You don't know what you've seen, only what you think you've seen, and you're a woman alone in a car with a man, a drunk woman. Don't be a fucking idiot.

The driver's eyes meet mine in the rear-view mirror. I imagine he does that "*snog, marry, avoid*" thing in his head, and guess I'm way up there on the avoid side. He looks again and does one of those barely-there head nods. I do one back and look out of the window.

I wish I was sober. Sober me might have known what to do, or rather, sober me would know that what I do next, is a bad idea.

'Busy night?' I ask.

It's the kind of thing you say, if you're the kind of person who finds it awkward sitting in a car with someone in silence, especially if you've recognised them. He replies, but I don't catch it exactly, something like, 'Yeah, the usual, nothing special.' Mostly conveyed by a shrug of the shoulders.

'Saturday night,' I say. I smile, and he smiles back, turns enough so I can see the white row of his teeth.

'Saturday night,' he repeats. 'You know it.'

I wish he hadn't said that. It makes me think of Martin barging into my flat, hell-bent on a Saturday night of drink and drugs and getting to know each other. It makes me think of Saturday nights all over London, of things being got ready, plans being made, because, hey, it's Saturday night, and what else is that for, but to get fucked all ways round?

It was a lost weekend, in a hotel in Amsterdam.

'You going home, not going out, eh?'

He knows her, the girl. How does he know her? He must know her name.

'No, coming home,' I say.

'Shame,' he says, and winks at me. 'It Saturday night, yeah? You should be going out, right?'

'Yeah,' I say.

He laughs to himself.

We're rolling through the traffic past Manor House

tube, turning onto Seven Sister's Road. The sky above is orange and grey, the air so thick and wet and heavy with fumes when I roll down the window, I can taste and feel it.

The driver laughs again. Why? Why is he laughing? His eyes reflected in the mirror glide over me. Is he laughing at me? Laughing at a memory, forgetting I am there and then remembering when he sees me, or what? Laughing because of what he's thinking about—snog, marry avoid—that's just the polite name for the game, right? I make myself look out of the window again, before the eye contact gets serious. Snog, fuck, murder.

You're making all this up, I tell my reflection. It's all in your messed-up head. You're just a fare, that's all. He doesn't know what you're thinking. What you think about him. You don't know what he thinks about you, you're giving yourself too much credit that he even thinks anything about you.

Can he tell?

Can he tell how I feel, can he sense it on me, how stripped I feel, how laid bare by Max and Martin, like it's burning on my skin. You wanted it, right? That's what they both said. Both think of me.

Don't think about that. He can't know, he doesn't know. But he does know her.

What if she was my child? Don't even go there because she isn't, even though she could be, even though she could probably be my fucking grandchild. But what if she was Cassie's child, because I can kind of cope with that, I can see how that would work. If she were Cassie's child, and they'd had some huge row, and she'd gone and stayed with a friend, because that happens. Turned her phone off, refused to talk, and then ended up rolling round some supermarket car park one evening, and took a lift, because they do that, kids, because they think that kind of thing is a big adventure. What if that was it, and I saw her, wouldn't I say something?

'Looking forward to the Olympics?' I say, because I need him to talk to me. I haven't decided what I'm going to do, and I might not do anything, I really might just talk to him and let him take me back home, and go back and watch out of the window, I really might do that.

'Whatever?' he says, 'I dunno.'

I don't care what he thinks about the Olympics. I'm leaning a little forward now, resting my forearm on the back of his seat, trying to focus, only my vision is really off. Like I'd drunk a whole bottle of wine and eaten nothing but a few olives and a smear of hummus, that sort of off.

'It's good for the kids, though, I guess?' I say, not quite cutting him off but not quite making sense either. He just shrugs, glances at me in his mirror.

'Sure, kids.'

I reach into my pocket and hold my phone, because if

I've got a phone, I'm okay. I can call for help, can't I, if I have a phone? I mean, nothing's going to happen, he's not going to do anything, but you know, it just feels good to have it there, to be ready. Snog, fuck, murder, you know, just in case?

You are making all this shit up, you do know that, right?

His driver's ID is hanging from the rear-view mirror. It's in a stiff plastic holder, so it doesn't jiggle about much, but I still can't read the name on it. I'm just about to say something, I start, even, 'Hey, my friend, right—' only as I do, his phone rings and he picks it up.

My stomach does a sideways lurch, a tide of adrenaline and soured red wine. We're passing through the Lee Valley Park now, not that you can see it. It's just another road at night, passing sports centres that could be industrial units or slaughterhouses, you wouldn't know by looking.

He's talking on his phone, but I can't understand what he's saying. I'm getting angry now, like he's doing it on purpose, like he knew what I was going to say and is trying to avoid me.

We go on and on along desolate concrete roads and overpasses, and part of me feels like saying, 'Hey, you do know it's illegal to talk on the phone and drive, yeah? You could lose your license for it, you know, you should get a hands-free kit?' Because he needs telling, he really needs telling, because he's talking on and on. Hell, he might even be talking about me, because I can't understand what he's saying. He looks at me again, I'm still sitting forwards; his eyebrows do an 'up' gesture, he's looking at me because I'm still sitting forwards. Too close. But if I move back, won't that look worse, look like I'm uncomfortable, like he's making me uncomfortable.

He looks again, says something, laughs in a way which almost includes me, does an eye roll. I smile at him and he grins.

The sweat is running down the inside of my jeans, sticking my pretty top to my back. Can he smell me? Why did I put on a pretty top, the sort that shows the outline of my nipples, the sort that will darken and go see through with the sweat? Can he see that too?

Snog. Fuck. Kill.

We're back onto busy streets now, get cut up by a bus, then by another bus, and he swears, slaps the steering wheel, but he's still talking on the phone. Nausea finally wins, lets me slide back under its acid pull so I can lean back against the seat. Pull my jacket closed despite the sweat.

He tosses his phone into the passenger seat, so I guess that must have been goodbye. I wet my lips, taste the sour.

'So, good for the kids, right? The Olympics?' so that he remembers where we were.

'Sure,' he says.

'Hey,' I could stop here. I should stop here. We're nearly home, I recognise the church, the bridge where the railway strides over the street, the metal flank of the viaduct christened with a tag. 'Speaking of kids, yeah?'

Did he just look in the mirror, did his eyes flick up to meet mine, or did I just imagine it?

'Thing is, I've got this friend, my best friend, and her kid, right, her daughter? She's only twelve, but she's thinks she's so grown up, you know? You know the way kids are these days, yeah?'

'Yeah,' he says, not looking at me, looking off to the right, leaning a little, as if he's trying to decide which is the best way to go round the market square.

'Yeah, so they've had this row, right, and she's sort of run away. I mean, my friend knows where she is, yeah, well, she has a good idea because the girl rings her, right, from time to time. But she won't come home.'

He's nodding. Is he just listening to me like this is another story from a drunk passenger?

'Thing is though, I'm glad I'm here really, I mean in your cab and that, because I've been meaning to say, I think I saw her the other night, getting into one of your cabs, yeah?'

He turns quickly to look at me, then he's back staring at the road, hands where I can see them now, shoulders straighter, all the easy gone out of his spine. He meets my eyes in the mirror and I feel a hot, angry oh-so-fucking sure of myself head rush that makes me go on, makes the story tumble out of me in a stupid, self-satisfied babble.

'She was with this other girl, must have been a friend of hers, but the same age, only eleven, right? And she looked a bit drunk, yeah, and the two of them got into a car and, thing is, I was just wondering where you took her?'

He's shaking his head with a *no idea* kind of an expression. We're at the top of the side road that runs down to my flat now, the little, dead-end road that went somewhere once, before the supermarket car park blocked it off.

'Because I saw you, and two other drivers, right, getting into the car with them, my friend's kid and her mate, and I just wondered—'

'What you wonder?' he says.

'Where you took them, that's all.' He's indicating right, he's going to turn for home now. I just need him to give me a clue, to say he's not seen them, or let something slip, a name for the social, for the—

There's a thunk sound. A central locking kind of sound.

'You remember, yeah?' I say, still expecting him to turn right. 'You can't have forgotten, it was only…'

He accelerates.

We're not exactly going fast, because this is London,

and the average traffic speed in London is barely ten miles an hour on a good day, and although it's after ten so not as busy, the road isn't clear. That's not the point though, the point is that we're not turning right down the slip road to where I live, we're going past it.

'Hey, that's it there,' I say, as if he's just forgotten.

'Yeah?' he says. He's laughing, like it means nothing to him, like I mean nothing to him.

'Hey, pull over, right? Pull the fuck over now.'

'What?' he says. He even lifts his hand up to his ear and does the universal sign language for *can't hear you.*

'Stop this fucking car!' I demand, but there's a space now, a stretch where the road expands into two lanes once it's free of the bus stops and the pedestrian crossing, so he speeds up and the whine of air through the window increases, the force of the acceleration like a hand on my chest, pushing me back.

'Shut up, bitch,' he says.

'Stop the car, or I'll—' I show him the phone in my hand, I would even go so far as to say that I brandish the phone in my hand, my heart thudding in the back of my throat, sweat itching over my shoulders and a stupid, girlie flutter in my voice when I say, 'Or I'll call the police. I'll—'

He grabs for my phone and hits my hand, and because he does it so fast and so hard, I flinch and let out a yelp, and the sweat slicked phone slips out of my hand

and lands on the passenger seat next to his.

'Shut the fuck up. You want to know? I fucking show you, bitch.'

'What the fuck are—'

'Keep mouth shut, bitch. Now you know.'

Lit up shops and a pub go by, and traffic lights, and a bus, and the slick black, grey, black of buildings, and an explosion of laughter from a crowd of people. We're not going as fast as I think we are, because I'm not thinking rationally at all, in my head we're already up to a hundred and more, hurtling away from anything that might be safety. A big jumble of publicly safety advertisements spool through my head, stranger danger, if it's not booked, it's just a car, one in three rapes happen when the victim is—

'Hey!' I slam the flat of my hand against the window, start hammering on the glass.

Well, you wanted it, you asked for it.

'Fucking shut it!' he demands, and swerves the car to the left, not much, but enough to throw me against the glass. 'Hey,' he turns and jabs his finger at me, face full of warning. I jerk back from him, and my right hand finds the seat belt lock. I push down on it, and the belt comes free.

He doesn't see. He's turned round again, and I feel the car begin to slow.

Slowing down, are we there yet? Where yet? To do

what?

Junction, it's a junction—big crossing, all lights on red. He's looking, eyes front, red lights, blinking amber ones, everyone going straight ahead or turning right, they're the options. Straight ahead takes us further along the high street, but right, right is down to another industrial estate, to empty-eyed warehouses and a closed down supermarket, half way through demolition.

He reaches out and click, he's indicating right.

He's going right, away from people in cars, away from people on the street, away from all of that.

Click-tick, click-tick.

Lights go amber.

I grip my hands together and bring them up in front of my face as if I'm praying.

Lights go green and we're moving, turning right, away from everything. I clench my hands, force the fingers together. So quickly I don't even think, I thrust my two clenched fists back hard to the left, then send my right elbow smacking down into the back of his head.

The car squeals, tires burn on asphalt. I'm thrown into the back of the driver's seat as he stamps on the brakes, pinned as the car's sucked into a skid. The crunch of impact shocks through me, a dead crunch, knocking the breath out of me. Gravity kicks me in the ribs, holds me, sends me slithering sideways, off the seat and down on to the floor of the car.

I love the sound of breaking glass.

Everything screams and beeps and whumps and thumps. There's the explosion of the air bags, the suck of sound, horns and screaming tyres, as whatever's behind us, manages not to hit us.

I'm reeling, I'm dazed, I'm stuck and I can't get free. Then I'm struggling, propelled up by the wave of adrenaline that hits me harder than the crash, has me screaming and gasping so that I can scream again, and scrabble and heave myself up. I remember the central locking as I force the door open, then remember in the crazy disco of flashing hazard lights, that airbags cancel door locks. When my foot scrapes on tarmac, there's already shouting, the white light of head lamps burning my eyes, the sound of car doors slamming.

'Mate, mate, you alright, mate?'

Because I'm a twenty first century girl, and hell, it costs me forty quid a month, the last thing I do before I run, is wrench open the passenger door, lunge in and snatch up my phone from the floor. I don't even think about it, it's instinct. Like I was saving my child from a burning building. As I grab it, the driver struggles against the deflating airbag. 'Bitch!' Loud enough to be heard over the electronic panic of his car, so I know the fucker is basically alright.

Then I run.

CHAPTER TWENTY-THREE

The law

THIS IS NOTHING like the recreational, just because I want to feel virtuous sort of running I usually do. This is me clawing my way up a hill of treacle and debris as if I'm on all fours, with a metal trap door slamming shut in my chest after every breath I drag into my lungs. This is running blind, this is feet slipping on pavement that is neither wet or slippery but seems slick as an oiled eel.

When I go beyond the point when I think every part of me is going to burst, I clatter into the shelter of a boarded-up doorway and press my back against it. I breathe deeply, the sound coming out somewhere between a laugh and a howl.

I'm not being followed. I can't remember passing anyone, though I'm sure I must have, but none of the people I've passed, or the driver, or the guy who must have swerved to avoid running into the back of us, have come after me. I stare at the street, at my feet, shuddering air into my lungs, building up the courage to look again.

You're so brave, babe, you're so strong.

I'm going to wet myself.

I suck in air and force my head up, positive I'm a hundred miles away from E17 and all its many delights. But I'm not that far from home, hardly round the next block. One of those side streets that runs parallel to the main street, and is a mix of half-hearted food places, ethnic shops for one community or another, and accountancy firms. It felt as if he'd driven me miles away at breakneck speed, but actually we'd hardly made the far end of the high-street, where the wholefood shops and yummy mummy cafes begin to appear.

I'm still holding my phone. Should I call 999? I thumb in my code and go to the dial screen, but then don't, because really, is this police worthy? Maybe I should just shut up and stop being so dramatic. He hardly did anything did he? Should I ring the police anyway, seeing as I'd crashed his car for him?

Fuck though—the clunk of the central locking thunks through me again, a weird, after echo and the sense of falling, or tumbling along the back seat of the car as he'd sped away from my turning, taking me away.

Bitch. Bitch! Now you goin' to know.

Had I meant any of that to happen? I feel like I've pressed a button on a fruit machine and got a pay-out on three lemons—hit man, man crashes car, run away, as if that was all part of the plan. Maybe it was?

What *exactly* was Mr Taxi Driver going to make sure I knew?

You can't just ring 999 for any old thing. I start walking. I mean, it's not really, well, a *crime*. Unless smashing up a car is a crime, which I'm kind of responsible for. I don't know what to do. Who should I call? Cassie, who I'm still not speaking too? Max—hahaha—no. What about Alan A, who sure as hell wouldn't be expecting this, after his oh-so-casual Facebook message? Who else? No one. I can hardly call Martin, can I? My circle of friends, real friends, has become a hard-edged triangle. Everyone else fallen away, kept at arm's length by me trying to get pregnant and having miscarriage after miscarriage. Because what else do you do? Explain that what you did at the weekend, was have lacklustre routine sex at a pre-arranged moment, while mainlining food supplements and peeing on sticks to confirm what your fertility app is telling you—do it, do it *now*—and waiting, and pacing, and the twist of hope and the slick of disappointment. Well, you get the picture. Besides, I'm not meant to be that person, that baby-mad clock-ticking bitch. That's not who I am.

There's Big Al I suppose, but then he's got his own issues. Or my mum, perhaps?

Hey Mum, some guy possibly just tried to kidnap and maybe rape me, but it's okay, I made him crash his car and got away, but just wondering, should I call the police?

No, I don't know he was actually going to do it, I just thought he might and…what's that? How's Max? Oh, he's great Mum, we're great. Turns out he actually did rape me, so what do you think, police or….?

Yeah, exactly.

I'm walking fast and as if my feet are a long way away from me, my bones aching and yet feeling light as a feather. And lucky, should I feel lucky? Is this another moment when everything could have been a lot worse? I need to get home, because when I am home, I will have two doors between me and the world, and I can give an actual address to someone, if I decide to ring anyone about this. That will make me seem like a better, more reliable person, a person whose word can be taken at face value, someone who will be believed.

I'm coming up on the back of the church opposite my road, so I start to run again. I'm thinking of two doors locked behind me, one, two. Thinking about it so much, that when I cross the road, I don't even consider the traffic, and have to jump back as a car screams past me. The driver yells something. My heart crashes against my ribs, and I don't even feel able to flip him the finger, I just keep going, jog over the traffic island and head to my door.

I don't let myself think about the other drivers, or that the one I was with has phoned ahead, or at least, I pretend I'm not thinking about it by keeping my head down and not looking at them. As if they were all gorgons, all Jabberwockies and Bandersnatches. I fumble in my jacket pocket for my key as the lights from the taxi rank sweep over me. Lines from one of those bloody safety awareness videos from school come back to me. *As you approach your door at night, have your keys ready in your hands, held between your fingers so you don't have to hesitate when opening the lock. Hesitation makes you vulnerable to attack, hesitation makes you a victim, makes it your fault, means you wanted it after all.*

I make the outside door, grip the handle as if I might be swept away by a tide, deaf to any noise from behind me. The key sinks home, the door opens, and I slam it behind me as I hit the stairs, blinking in the click of automated light. With the street door closed, I say, 'Fuck,' then I say it again as if it's powering me up the little flight of stairs. 'Fuck, fuck, fuck, fuck.' Until I'm safe inside. I lock the door and slide home all the bolts.

I snap on the lights then go and peer out of the kitchen window. The road outside looks as normal as it always does, no crowds with burning torches and pitchforks.

All the sickness I felt in the cab comes lurching back. My stomach turns over and doesn't right itself. 'Oh shit!'

I lunge for the bathroom, bang the door open and make the toilet just in time to be sick. I bring up pints and pints of red liquid, peppered with olives seemingly as complete as when they were on their little blue dishes at the restaurant. I'm clutching the bowl, on my knees, feet bent awkwardly in my boots, throat burning with acid. 'Oh, Jesus, no!'

I'm not scared of needles, or blood, but I hate being sick. The sound of my retching is making me gag, the thought of it so appalling I'm crying. I flush, and spit and flush again, then I'm gulping water from the tap and swilling, gasping in horror when bits are swilled out of my mouth into my basin, my lovely, clean basin. I have to clean my teeth. I brush and brush and spit, brush and spit, scrubbing at my tongue as well as my teeth, trying to eliminate the taste of vomit at the back of my nose and mouth.

I throw off my jacket. My skin itches, I'm shaking, my stomach aching. I lean against the bathroom wall, cool, white tiles at my back. I slip my hands between my thighs and press it against my crotch, cup my vagina where it sits inside my jeans, and sort of hold it.

After a while, I straighten up, sniff and wipe my nose. I get gloves, the latex disposable kind I use for work, because I have boxes of them everywhere. It's so important to be clean was the first thing Big Al taught me, it doesn't matter how uncool you think it looks, there is nothing more important than being clean. You're dealing with blood and skin and people are just great big bags of bacteria. You're cutting their skin and dipping your wick in their blood. You can kill them, if you're not clean.

I open a new packet of cleaning sponges and tell the world I will throw this one away as soon as I'm done. On my knees I scrub at the toilet bowl, bathroom trigger spray in hand. I need to do this. I need to clean, that's my priority. I could ring Cassie, but she'll just tell me I've been an idiot, which I know already. What was I thinking, what the hell's got into me? What did I think the taxi guy was going to say, even if he hadn't gone all psycho-driver on me? What if I've just made it all worse?

'I can look after myself,' I snap at the toilet. I change gloves and get a new sponge so I can tackle the seat. Clean, don't think.

I wasn't sick on the bathroom mat, but nevertheless I fold it carefully into quarters and carry it to the bin in the kitchen. It's probably for the best, it was only cheap anyway, and old, well, old-ish, so there's no point in washing it. It smells of sick, I'm sure it does. It's fine, nearly done, wouldn't know it ever happened. Just the basin, clean under the taps, and my toothbrush, which will have to go now, but if I go early, I can get a new one, and the taxi rank will be quiet so I can slip out and—

The door buzzer goes. The sound of it sends a sweep of cold sweat washing over me, prickles under my arms and across my back, so sharp it's like a cat's claws. I hold my breath, as if they might hear the slightest movement through the door and know I'm here. Do they know I'm here? Of course they bloody do, the kitchen lights are on, which means the kitchen window is a blazing rectangle of white.

It has to be the driver. Or drivers, lots of them, all come to get me. I have to know. I go swift and quiet to the wall beside the kitchen window and inch round to look. The buzzer goes again. I'll call the police. I'll get my phone and call them.

Only it is the police.

Their panda car parked next to mine. It must have been the guy in the other car who's called them, the one who was approaching when I got away, only how could he know where I lived? Shit, I really must be famous, local hero.

I'm so glad to see them I go and open the door, and run down the little flight of steps and pull open the street door all still in my gloves.

'Hey,' I say, because it's nice PC Barnes with a mate, a fellow officer, a woman he introduces as PC Lucas.

'Can we have a word, miss?' he asks. I resist the temptation to ask him which one. I wonder if he's going to ask if I'm alright, but as he doesn't, I say that of course they can have a word, and won't they come up? Then I see his gaze flick to my hand where it's resting on the door frame, and see he's looking at my latex glove.

'I was cleaning,' I say, peeling it off as they follow me upstairs. They watch me as I go to the kitchen and drop the gloves into the bin.

'There's been a report of a—'

'Look,' I say, hands out, standing in the middle of the kitchen. 'I might have overreacted, but I still think you should have a word with him, because I really thought he was, well, it felt like—'

'Do you want to sit down?' PC Lucas suggests.

That's nice of her.

'Oh, sure,' I say and we do, them on the sofa, me opposite. They look uncomfortable against the leopard print fabric, like they've been caught at a strip club. I swallow a laugh.

'We've had a report of an assault,' PC Barnes begins. I want to tell him that's an exaggeration, but for once I shut up. PC Barnes gets out a notebook, opens it and appears to read from it, but it's PC Lucas who carries on.

'Earlier this evening, a cab driver reported that he picked you up from a restaurant, is that right?'

'Yes, I was at dinner, in a place over Stoke Newington way.' The two of them glance at each other, as if I've just given them a very important piece of information.

'Mr Rizvi says that you were drunk,' PC Lucas continues, in a maternal kind of a way, in a way that seems to say she's disappointed in me, but she's sure we can work it out. 'He says that you...became abusive, when you were asked to pay, then—'

'Wait, what?' I sit up.

'He says you demanded he take you to a cash point,

then—' PC Lucas falters, clears her throat. 'He says you offered him sexual favours in place of the fare—'

'What?' I burst out laughing. 'You're fucking kidding me!'

'Miss, please,' PC Barnes says, frowning, as if he'd expected me to come clean about this, me and him being old friends n' all.

'Then he says you racially abused him, attempted to sell him drugs—'

'This is un-fucking believable—'

'Please, miss,'

'But you can't think that I'd do anything—'

'Can I ask you to remain calm?'

'Calm? He locked me in his cab, he drove past my road, this road, and…and he wouldn't stop when I asked him, when I begged him, when—'

'Are you alleging that he…he tried to…'

'Kidnap me,' I say, 'yes, that's just what I'm alleging. He went past my road, and when I tried to point out that was where I lived, and he'd gone too far, he locked the doors, with the, the,' I'm flapping my hand, trying to mime pushing down the kind of door locking mechanism that hasn't been used in cars since the 1980's. 'He did the central locking, and I screamed at him to stop, and he told me to shut up, and called me a bitch.'

'Did he threaten you?' PC Lucas asks, keeping her voice low and measured so as not to be inflammatory.

'Yes he fucking threatened me,' I snap. 'Don't you think it's fucking threatening when someone locks you in their car, and,' a memory flashes through my mind, 'and takes your phone off you, and says...' But what did he say, that I can say, without having to explain about the conversation I was trying to have with Mr Rizvi?

'What did he say?' PC Barnes prompts.

He doesn't believe me, I think. She doesn't believe me, that PC Lucas, with her crappy hair and her stupid big stab vest, she doesn't believe me either.

'He said I was going to find out where he was taking me,' I try, fingers to my forehead, because they're not listening, not hearing me. 'When I asked him what he was doing, he said I'd find out when I got there, something like that?' I expect him to write it down, but he doesn't.

'Mr Rizvi says you hit him,' PC Lucas says.

'Well...' and I'm struggling for the words, feeling pressure building in my chest as if I was running again, running from Mr Rizvi. 'Of course I did, but not like that.' I get up, because I can't stand it, because it sounds so terrible, if you say it like that, if you don't know what really happened.

'Take it easy please,' PC Barnes stands too, hands out, patting the air as if he's stroking it better. 'We're just trying to—'

'You're making it sound like I'm in the wrong here.' I'm so angry, my face is burning, I can feel it, and the words are harsh and rough in my throat—'He tried to kidnap me, alright, he tried to—'

'You really need to keep calm, miss,' PC Barnes says.

'Look,' I take a step forward and I point, and when I do, my shin hits the pile of books that Martin moved earlier and I shoved back into place, before I left for that bloody meal with Max. 'He's lying, this Mr Rissy, or whoever he is,'

'Rizvi.'

The books go thump, thump on the floor all over again.

'Whatever, look—'

'Just a moment, please.' PC Lucas darts down to the floor, right to my feet. I step back from her, and as I do, I see what it is she's noticed, set free by the tumble of the book stack. The little plastic bag of MDMA. I mean, unless it's cocaine, of course.

'That's not mine....'

CHAPTER TWENTY-FOUR
The law wins

THEY ARREST ME for assault, possession of drugs, not much, granted, but apparently my answering the door wearing surgical gloves caused PC Barnes and Lucas some issues too, as well as refusing to go quietly. Resisting arrest, if you want to be precise about it.

I try to get a word in about the girl, about what I saw, but as ever my timing is way off, and they're not in the mood to listen.

The duty sergeant, look at me with the lingo, is remarkably nice. He seems genuinely concerned that I've ended up here, though not surprised.

'I'll see about getting you some tea. Now, you're not going to give me any trouble, are you?'

When he asks me who I'd like to call, I say Big Al. That will be a first, Big Al being on that end of this equation.

I sit in the cell, which isn't too bad really. No, it's terrible, but weirdly right then, it actually feels like where

I need to be, like I'm contained for my own safety. I can't mess anything else up in here, can I?

Nan was arrested once. I went round to see Mum and Dad, because I do actually do that sort of thing, when my life isn't imploding, and let myself in and Mum was crying. She isn't a crying mum, she usually does that *oh goodness, look at the fuss I'm making* thing and takes herself off at the first sign of tears, so of course when I saw her proper weeping, with Dad standing off to the side and a little behind her, diffidently patting her shoulder, I knew things must be bad.

'Fuck, mum, what's the matter?' I threw my bag down and braced for the worst.

'Language,' Mum muttered, rooting in her pocket for a tissue.

'It's your nan,' Dad said, doing one of those smiles which are more about stretching your mouth than actually smiling.

'Nan, what—?'

'Oh, don't you worry,' Mum said, 'She's fine, of course she is. Only got herself arrested.'

'What?' The relief and surprise made it come out in a laugh.

'It's not funny,' Mum snapped. 'What on earth she thinks she's doing at her age.'

'Your mum's just worried about her,' Dad said. 'It's a lot of stress for your mum, because she's worried about your nan.'

'I'm not,' Mum sniffed. 'I'm bloody furious. And you breathe a word of this to anyone else, well...just you don't, all right?'

'Sure she won't, will you, Lydia?' Dad said, lifting onto his toes, doing that warm, blank smile which closed down any discussion as completely as a slammed door. Off you go, Lydia, don't bother your mother now. Why don't you do some drawing, eh?

So I went to find Lauren and she said, 'Oh, you know, it's the road thing. Protesting. I suppose you think it's funny.

'It's awesome. Nan's awesome,' I said.

'She's seventy-three,' Lauren said, turning to look up at me. 'She's not bloody superwoman, you know. What if next time she gets hurt and doesn't recover, breaks her hip or something?' Which I guess, thinking back, was a fair point—police brutality not being advised when you have brittle bones.

'The blessed road isn't even going near her place,' Mum said later, as we ate ham sandwiches and crisps around the kitchen island.

'It's going through ancient woodland,' I said.

'Only a bit of it,' she replied.

NAN MADE THE front page of her local paper. *Road protest pensioner charged with common assault.* When I drove down to see her the weekend after, she'd already had it framed and put up in the kitchen. I stayed with her most summers when I was a kid, from when I was eight or so. Nan had come to find me, said she thought I might like to come and stop with her for a few days, seeing as Mum was having such a lot of trouble with Lauren, and would I mind? Of course I didn't, because I was having a lot of trouble with Lauren too. I couldn't see why all three of us, Mum, Dad and me didn't just go and stay with Nan without Lauren, as she was that much of a pain. I'd tried leaving her in the playground the week before, only she'd followed me home.

'Famous, I am,' Nan said, flicking her cigarette ash into the saucer she was using as an ashtray. 'Do it again in a heartbeat, I would. Can't let the bastards think they can push you round.'

LYING ON MY side, looking at the cell wall I say to Nan, 'It's over, innit?' She always used to say to me, 'If there's anything ever the matter, you can always tell your Nan. That's the best thing about nans, we're old enough to have heard everything ever, so nothing shocks us, not like mums.'

'It's over, Nan,' I tell her, though I can't even say the words *me having a baby* out loud, not yet. 'Maybe it never was, not really.' All that madness, and Max going along with it. Why had he really? He had wanted it too. He'd stuck with me and held my hand and gone to the clinics and told me everything would be all right. One day. Everything would work one day.

The door of the cell opens in a clatter of keys and pulls me up; it's the duty sergeant, coming in all bright and cheery.

'All right,' he says, 'won't keep you hanging around anymore, wasting your time and ours.' He grins. 'Said you'd be no trouble.' He brings with him the rumble of voices and a sharp, hard clang of a slamming door.

'What?' I pull myself up from the bench I've been lying on, rubbing my arms and legs to bring them back to life.

'Come on,' he sniffs. 'We're too popular of an evening to give you a hotel.'

I had made my mind up to bang the table, demand they listen to me whatever the charges. Throw my chair, push the table over because I only did it because I was scared, alright? I was an idiot, yes, I know, but that doesn't stop me from being scared, or thinking about her, the girl, in the back of that car with them, watching the city roll past the window on her way to do what? But he's holding the door open for me, and this is a get of jail for free card, so.

'Oh, right…okay.' I swallow. 'What about…?'

'Come on,' he says.

He escorts me out along the corridor, whistling between his teeth—Tammy Wynette, if I'm not mistaken— and into a what I guess you'd call an interview room, only softer looking than I'd expected. Low sofa, side table, sad looking plant and a generic Ikea picture on the wall.

'Bit of paperwork,' he says. I'd kind of expected this would be handled back out in the reception area where I'd been booked in. This space reminds me of hospital waiting rooms.

'Have a seat,' he says. I do. Look how meek and mild I've become, when confronted by the law. Guess I am basically a nice, middle class lady underneath it all. Just like Mum, I don't want the neighbours to know. I take a deep breath, push it out between pursed lips, and take the bull by the horns.

'Look, I'm sure everyone says it, but that…stuff you found, it really isn't mine, ok…'

The sergeant looks at me. 'I didn't hear that,' he says. 'We didn't find anything at your flat. Nothing we're bothered about.'

'But—'

'I'd stop talking, if I were you.' He remains impassive, and I finally get the hint. 'We decided you're not exactly Pablo Escobar, are you, love?'

'No, I guess not,' I say.

'Now—the other thing,' he says. 'We got a call, 'bout half hour after you come in.'

There's a lilt to his accent which marks him out as not

altogether local; a bit further west than Ealing. Shropshire lad, I tell myself.

'Just put it together when I went for my tea, had a moment to myself.' He winks. 'Lovely chap, that PC Barnes, bit keen though, bit quick off the mark.'

'Is he?' I say.

The Sergeant nods, as if we've an understanding now. 'Funny place, the 'Stow', for London. Not always as cold as people think. Chap called in on the 111, you know, 999-light, as I like to call it. Anyway, said he saw a bit of a prang on the High Street, nothing unusual there, but then he said,' he clears his throat, which I guess is his way of telling me this is a direct quote, 'some bird wiv' blue hair an' tats...' He looks at me, does an eyebrow raise. '...runnin' away from the car. Said something about it didn't sit right with him.'

Well, there we go, East Seventeen—who knew it was so community minded?

'Anything you want to say about that?'

'It was...another blue-haired bird with tats?'

'Funny, that's what Mr Rizvi said. Asked him if he wanted to add to his statement from earlier, but turns out he didn't, other than to say that the woman in his taxi tonight wasn't you after all, says it was, well...' he looks at me, waiting for me to join the dots.

'Someone who looks like me?' I venture.

'That's right,' he says, folding his arms across his

barrel of a chest. 'Another blue-haired bird with tats.' The humour on his broad face dims a little. 'So, anything you want to tell me? Why was you running away, then?'

I breathe out, look at the Duty Sergeant, at the strip lights reflecting on his balding head. He's wasted on the police force; he should be a publican, sleeves rolled up and polishing a tankard behind his bar, apple-cheeked wife and a string of kids.

'There's this girl,' I say. 'She's only young, and she hangs around them, the taxi drivers. I've seen her getting into their cars, I've seen her there all hours and...' I tell him, and he listens, raising an eyebrow when I say how I've told PC Barnes all about her, and he said he knew her. 'But he hasn't done anything.'

'How do you know?' the Sergeant asks. 'How do you know what he's doing?' I go to answer, I even open my mouth, but then I close it again. I guess he has a point.

'Trouble is, London's full of girls like that. No one's forcing them to get into trouble, but they do, and we do our best. I've had 'em spit at me, kick me in the shins, won't say a word against him,' he does speech marks in the air, 'because they love him.'

'I was trying to get a name, her name,' I say, but it's pointless. He's closing down on me, I can see it, going over familiar ground. *Appreciate your concern. PC Barnes is a good chap, sure he's on it. Better leave the investigation to the professionals. If you have any further concerns.*

'It's a lifestyle choice, with a lot of them,' he says, then gives me things to sign.

'Shame you had to go through all this. Imagine the CPS would have given it short shrift, but...' He does a face. 'It's the racial element.' He leans back in his chair, tells me that they always have to jump to it when there's a hint of racist abuse, otherwise the PC brigade will be on their case. Then he shows me the tattoo he has on his shoulder, nothing special but nicely done.

'Boyfriend, is it, coming for you?'

'Boyfr—no, he's....he's just a friend.'

'You better go wait for him, then. You got our number? In case you need us?'

'Yeah,' I say. 'Cheers.'

Lifestyle choice.

I wait on one of the plastic chairs in the reception area for Big Al to come and get me. Soon he's shouldering his way into the police station as if through an invisible crowd.

'What you been getting up to, Chicky?' he asks.

'Nothing you've never done. Can you take me home?'

CHAPTER TWENTY-FIVE

Names

BIG AL PUTS me into his car and somehow I keep it together until he closes the car door, and then the tears come again, rolling over my face. He gets in, opens the glove box and gets out a box of tissues with saying anything much, and I love him for it. Right now, I think he is the only person in the world I've got left, and part of me is glad it's him.

He takes me to his flat.

'You can have the sofa bed,' he says when I protest, not hard but just enough for appearance's sake. 'Long as you promise to stay there and not take advantage.' He looks sideways at me. 'I'm a married man, for a couple of days more, anyway.' Married man or not, I almost go to kiss him, because right now, he feels like the last person in the world on my side, a big, beardy, little bit overweight platonic rock in my sea of troubles. All I manage is a tight little smile, because there are so many tears pressing in behind it, I think if I say thank—you, I'll drown him with them. I love you, Big Al, you grumpy old bastard, I tell him inside my head. The strangest of bed fellows, misery has found for me.

Big Al's flat is above the shop. When I was setting it up, when I came to him with the idea of it, knowing that he needed me way more than I needed him, he asked about the flat. Not that he might live in it, not then, but if there was already a sitting tenant, then if we should look for one, seeing as otherwise the place would be empty, and might attract squatters and such like.

'Terrible risk, that is, them getting in.' He'd sniffed. 'Mind you, tenants you got to be careful of too, don't want someone as seems alright, then starts drawing on the walls and so forth.' Then he suggested that perhaps, just temporary like, he might stay there, then the place wouldn't be empty at night. It would, he reasoned over the fry up we had in the cafe over the road after signing the paperwork on the lease, make sense, as you always have cash with a shop, and weekends being so busy like, well, would save rushing to the bank with it.

'Makes sense, me stopping there,' he'd said, and sniffed, looking out of the window, the winter light making his face harder and older and gentler all at once. 'Only temporary, like.' So I guess I'd been there for him too, when he'd needed me?

He'd done the place up quite nice. Simple, lots of those washed out colours everyone uses when they don't intend to stick around for long, black bits and pieces of furniture that show the dust unless your careful, none of it looking too bad considering.

Big Al folds out the sofa bed for me and unwraps two Asylum Tattooists size 'S' promotional t-shirts from the boxes out back.

'Nearest I can come to a change of clothes for you, chicky, seeing as you's about half my width an' fussy as 'ell. Might be able to sort you with some smalls, though.' He goes into his bedroom and brings out a red lace thong, with a sheepish grin.

'Should I ask?'

'Probably not, but don't worry, I washed 'em.'

I'm sure I won't sleep as the room is bathed in sodium orange, and Big Al has rather oversold the delights of the sofa bed, but I do. For once I pass out without a fidget or a sigh into such a deep nothing, it's almost like drowning.

When I surface, I can hear the noise of Big Al being busy in the kitchen, the kind of busy that wants me to wake up but doesn't want to be blamed for it. It's the best sleep I've had for a while, nearly as good as when I slept next to Martin, before he was Martin, of course, before he was real. He's all too real now though, isn't he? Too real and too dangerous. Too lost. Just like me.

I go for my phone to see what the time is, but its screen remains blank no matter how hard I press. Well, there we go. My phone died in police custody.

'Al? You got an iPhone five charger?'

'Not me, chicky, Nokia all the way, ain't I?' He grins at me from the kitchen door, holds up a frying pan. 'Bacon sarnie? Two lumps, or one?'

'Three.

We fold up the bed and talk shop while he makes us bacon sandwiches that drip in both grease and ketchup, and more than a little curiosity. When it gets the better of him, Al takes a swig of tea and says, 'So, what's it all about, chicky?'

I stick to the basic facts as much as possible. Don't mention the girl. I do this because there are five framed photographs on the shelf above the electric fire, which apart from some tattoo prints, are the only decoration the room boasts. They're Big Al's children. Five of them. The eldest must be mid-thirties, the youngest a toddler. Whatever else Big Al is, he's a doting father, and if I told him what I suspected, he'd no doubt round up some of his old crew and go break heads, and frankly, that's the last thing I need.

He looks as if he's prepared to believe me, until he says, 'Strange though, him changing his mind like that, didn't put up much of a fight, did he?'

'What can I say? Can't make that shit up, now can I, seeing as I'm here?'

'Suppose not,' he says. 'How much of the rest of it is you making up?'

There's a little of my tea left, which I tip down my throat before answering. 'God's own, Al, I swear.'

'None of my beeswax.' He picks up our plates. 'But you wanna watch out for you'sel. Seeing as how you won't let no one else do it for yous. When you coming back to work, then?'

He pauses in the door, plates in hand, tea towel over his shoulder in the manner of a short order cook. 'They keep askin' for you, no matter how much I tries to put 'em off. Popular girl, you is, in some quarters. People miss you.'

'Won't be long, I promise.' I smile.

I look down at my bare legs, at my feet, though I guess they're never bare. There are four names on my feet, two left, two right.

'Cherry Lancaster,' I said, Max next to me, naked and with his arm about me, me with my knee up and heel hooked over the edge of the mattress, so I could draw on my foot with a marker pen.

'What if it's a boy?' he asked.

'No idea, haven't thought. I kind of feel like it's a girl, feel it in my water, you know?' Then I'd laughed. 'Fuck, just think, when she's twenty-one, we'll be nearly sixty, we'll be so fucking old!'

'No we won't,' Max said. 'My Uncle turned sixty and fucked off to Ibiza. Got so out of his mind he ended up living in a cave.'

'Will you live in a cave with me? When I'm sixty-four?'

'I'd live with you any-fucking-where,' Max said, and rolled me back onto the bed and held me while we laughed. Two months later, I'd tattooed her name on my foot, Cherry Lancaster.

'We'll try again,' Max said.

Cherry Lancaster, Virginia Lancaster, Hermione Lancaster, Kingsley Lancaster.

'Suppose I better get going,' I say to Big Al.

'Don't rush on my account,' he says. 'Got a nice fat box set I've been saving. You could watch it with me? Got the kids on staff today, giving me'self a Sunday off for once.'

I look out of his window, at the bright, hard skyline warming toward noon, the expanse above cracked with wires and vapour trails, and think how, without my phone, no one can find me. How easily even I, might slip away, and be nothing after all, just like I never was.

Cherry.

Virginia.

Hermione.

Kingsley.

'Sure,' I say, 'make us another cup first, will you?'

What's *her* name, the girl?

CHAPTER TWENTY-SIX
Not frightened of blood

I WENT OVER the next weekend, the one after Nan was arrested, on Saturday morning. Don't remember why, sure there must have been a reason, can't remember what it was. It was weird, because Mum was crying again when I got there.

'What now,' I said, rolling my eyes knowing as I knew she couldn't see me. 'Nan been arrested again?'

Lauren spun round to look at me, her face all red and running with tears. 'Shut up,' she yelled, 'shut up—you must know, why they hell are you here else, they must have rung you, or something?'

'Who, who's rung me, what?'

'They've just rung, the hospital, Nan's dead.'

I'm standing in the doorway. Stupid, sick with embarrassment and shock, stuttering that I didn't know, I hadn't meant anything, that I'd been on the tube, so how could anyone have rung me, all the time thinking of the camera and the last picture I took. Nan, standing proudly by her framed newspaper front page, saying 'Not sure why you're taking my photo, going somewhere, am I?'

WHEN I WAKE up at Big Al's, I've been crying and I know it's because I was there again, standing in the doorway unable to go in, as if there was a glass sheet between me and them. They weren't even looking at me this time, the three of them all sat together on the sofa, saying how sorry they were, but how it was for the best, that Nan would have hated getting old, being infirm.

Probably for the best.

'I better go home,' I tell big Al.

'When you coming back to work?' he asks, handing me the tea he insists I drink before I brave the streets. I let the warmth of the steam touch my face.

'I might go down to Nan's place for a week or so, clear my head.' Then almost before I've realised that I'm saying it, 'Max and me are over, Al, like…really over. For good this time.'

I'm not sure what I expect him to say. He doesn't say anything a first, then he puffs out his lips, does a huff sound.

'Sorry about that,' he says. 'Never thought he was good enough for you, if that helps?'

'I think you're right,' I say, 'not that it makes it any better.'

'Sea might be the right thing for you,' Big Al says.

'The sea's good for tattooists, sailors on leave, kiss-me-quick hats an' that. Sailors and soldiers and police, anyone who's had a brush with death, come too close for comfort.' He looks at my bare feet against his grey carpet.

'Only for a week or so,' I say. 'Then I'll be ready to come back properly.'

'All right, Harpy gel,' he says.

I HEAD HOME. They'll be watching for me, the cab drivers. I expect they'll make a scene, shout out at me, stop me in the street, even, and I almost want them too. This time I might make enough of a fuss to be arrested again. Get the police round here to find out what they're doing with the girl. But the road to my flat, and the taxi rank and shop, all of it so drearily, wearily familiar this Sunday evening, is peaceful. There are cars, of course, but only one parked outside the taxi rank.

I speed up anyway, glancing over at the rank from behind my shades. No-one's watching. I'm still half looking that way when I slip my keys from my pocket, getting them ready for the lock on the street door, only it swings open before the key has a chance to make contact.

Cold sweat prickles over my shoulders. The lock is broken, the paint work around it splintered. A wild idea that the police have done it flashes through my mind, but why would they, I let them in for fuck's sake? A smell hits me through the two inches of open door, thrusting me into the memory of Max's paint shop, all those hard, bright colours and the roar of the air brush—spray paint.

Max?

I look round, sure someone's got to be watching me now, only they're not. My hand flinches to my phone. But it's dead. I could turn around and go back to Big Al's, make him look after me, but I've done a bit too much of that already today. So I put my hand up and push the door all the way open.

The light sensor at the bottom has been smashed. All the way up the hall the lower half of the white walls are looped with messy, red paint—great big red words. The same words over and over. Bitch, fucking bitch, fucking bitch.

It's like they're shouting at me so I run up the stairs, wanting to get in, get home, charge my phone, do something, ring someone—only a shape unfolds from my top step.

I scream, as it comes towards me and then I see it's Martin, hands out, trying to speak. The word rings in my head, the last word he said to me: *Bitch—bitch—fucking bitch!*

I'm shouting, he's shouting. There's a stink of alcohol weeping from his pores, fighting with the chemical stench of the paint. I'm telling him to get out, to get the fuck away from me, angry and scared, red beating behind my eyes. All the time he's saying something too, as if wants me to listen, as if he's trying to either calm me down so I will listen, or yell louder than me so I have to listen. His back against the wall and hands out, trying to pull back from me. Through all the shouting he doesn't try and grab me. He's almost making a big show of trying not to touch me, hands up in angry surrender, not able to look at me fully.

'I 'ave to talk to you, this ain't me, this don't matter, but I seen her, here, I—'

'Get the fuck away from me.' I make for the top step, still with my keys in hand, scrabbling in the dark for the lock, trying to be brave, scared as hell.

'You gotta listen.'

I turn the key and the door swings open. 'Fuck off, Martin.'

'You can't! You just got to I'm sorry—' Then he does lunge toward me and slams his hand into the door, pushing it hard back against the wall. I hear it crack into the paint work as both of us tumble inside.

All the strength seems to burn from my legs as I stumble backwards, the screaming I'm trying not to let out becoming wrenching sobs. 'Get away from me, get the fuck away from me!'

'I just wanna talk.'

He's hanging back from me, hands out. 'I saw her, here, she knows you, she's here, I saw her—'

I have to get away from him, put something solid

between us. Somehow I find the strength to scuttle back from him into the sitting room. I have to get control, I have to get him to listen to me—tell him anything, something—that will give me a chance to get him out. But he is so big, so damn tall. He's not coming for me though. He's crying too.

I back away and get the armchair between us 'Whatever this is,' I say, in a voice that is now calm and strong. 'Martin, whatever this is, you need to calm down, you need to back off, you need to go away. There's nothing between us, it's over, and—'

'But you know her. She was doin' the—'

'Who, Martin?' He's got his bag on his shoulder and the strap is a black diagonal across his white t-shirt, a t-shirt stained with sweat, as if he's run a long way to get to here.

'Josie,' he says. That tips him right over, comes out more sob than name, and he has to drag the back of his hand over his eyes, wiping his nose on his arm. 'Josie Bee, my Josie, she was…I come to see you and I seen—'

'What the fuck have I said, you don't get to come here anymore.' Frustration and anger blaze up inside me. 'There's no us, alright? You don't get to come here, you don't get to see me—'

'She was 'ere! It's the only… you can't…you have to let me stay, I have to stay—' But then it's all sobbing. He falls back towards the door, shambling, shaking his head from side to side—he's going to leave. I've got the key in my hand, and I'm going to lock the door soon as he's gone. I'm going to shut him out and pull the fucking sofa across it, and—

He bolts for the bathroom, two strides, three, and he's slammed the door shut behind him.

'Martin!' I'm after him in time to hear the lock click home. 'Martin, Martin? Open the door, Martin.'

'Can't go. Josie. Sorry.'

I hear him slump against the door, slide down.

'I got to stay.

So I tell him that he has to come out, that he cannot stay, that this is my bathroom, not his, and I need him to get out and go home. Then I swallow, then I make myself count to ten, and when I manage four, I say that I don't know what he wants, but if he will only open the door, we can sit and talk about it. Would he like that? Then I listen.

I hear something, perhaps the sound of his feet shifting on the floor, and then his breathing, like he's trying to stop crying, then a sharper, harder noise, something desperate in it. A cough? A muffled yelp? Then gasping, retching, almost a laugh in it, a sound that pants with pain.

'Martin?'

As I'm standing there, pressed against my bathroom door, as if only I could press hard enough, I might be able to see right through the wood, transport myself through the other side to him, that snippet from the Radio Four programme flashes into my head again. *The mentally ill are far more of a danger to themselves than others.*

'Martin! What are you doing?'

Boots scrape on the floor, the panting, sobbing sound sounds worse for growing fainter.

The lock on the door is an industrial one, because I was going through a phase when I thought industrial style fittings were cool in a domestic setting. So it's one of those *Engaged/Vacant* ones, set in a round housing. It has a large screw head on my side of the door, so it can be opened in emergencies. Like now.

I run to the kitchen and rip open the cupboard door under the sink. Kitchen spray and bleach and disinfectant spill out as I thrust my hand in and grab the toolbox. It falls open as I drag it out by the handle. The tools clatter out. I grab the flat head screwdriver and run back to the bathroom. Fuck, I wish we had a land line.

'I'm going to open the door, Martin, but you can still open it for me, yeah?' I jam the end of the screwdriver into the slot on the lock. It's handle twists in my sweaty hands, then the fucking thing slips out. I throw it on the floor and wipe my hands furiously on my jeans, grab it and try again. This time it holds, this time it crunches round, the edge of the green vacant section growing tantalisingly larger, until the door gives way and I fall into the room.

The clean, white walls are covered in red, but this time there are no words. Martin is folded against the bath. I don't know where it's come from, but the razor he's used is still clutched in his fingers, arms crossed above his head, knees drawn up. There's blood everywhere.

I snatch a towel from the rail and crouch down with him, pulling his hands away from his face. He seems almost in a trance, eyes too white and rolled back into his head, which seems too loose on his neck.

'Martin, look at me.' I wrap the towel about his arms, then I'm turning his face to make him look, as much blood on me now as him, but more of it coming, creeping, weeping, oozing through skin, fabric, sticky, dark. 'Martin—look at me.'

I see his eyes focus on me, then his face comes to life, the sob and the words he was trying to make me hear before, bubbling through his lips.

'She was 'ere, saw her, run after her, but—'

'Martin, I have to get you to hospital.' He starts to shake his head, but I say it again, 'You have to come with me, can you do that?'

'I'm not going nowhere, don't care what you say, don't care.'

'Martin, we have to get you to hospital, we're going to get up now, okay?'

'No, I wanna stay here, gonna stay here, wait for her.'

'I'll take you to her,' I say. 'We'll go in my car, yeah?' I can see him thinking about this, his brow creasing up with the effort of understanding me.

'But she was here, she was—'

'I'll take you, yeah? But you got to help me, yeah? I can't carry you, you're too heavy, so you got to help me, yeah?'

'Why?' he says, and then he kind of looks at himself, at his hands where they're sticking out from the blood-soaked towels, the razor in his fingers. He drops it, 'Oh shit, oh...... shit.'

Like he's no idea how this happened.

I get him up then, with him almost helping me, slipping and sliding and leaving red handprints on the toilet bowl, the basin; him leaning on me heavier than I can bear, but me doing it all the same. He's sobbing again, but not as violently as before, a kind of low moan, a mutter and a shake of the head.

'Come on, Martin, down the stairs?' Christ, he's so big, all those legs and arms. I have to lean him against the wall of the stairwell and let it take his weight, me one step ahead of him, while he paints it all over again, leaves a bloodied trail and bloodied footprints.

We stop in the doorway and I hold him in my arms as best I can. It's getting dark, the air sooty with evening. Anyone watching would think we were just drunk and in love, lingering in the doorway for a kiss.

I have to get him into the car. If I can do that, I can come up with a plan. I cannot ring for help and the horror of what that means almost has me falling over, dropping him. This is what it means to be alone. This really is down to me.

I click the button on the key fob and the car flashes its welcome. The driver's side is closer, so I aim Martin for the back seat, all the while he's back onto whoever she is.

'I seen her, I seen her.' Like he can't get off it, like he's not got the energy to think of something else to say.

I lean my back against the car and he falls forwards against me, and the two of us nearly slide onto the pavement before somehow I get control of the situation.

'We've got to get into the car, Martin, you've got to help me. Fucking snap out of it, yeah?' He sort of does, enough for me to flick the door catch and lever it open with my foot. He slumps into the seat, and I fold his legs in after him, over and over, his great feet slipping out, and him starting to thrash against me and try and sit up, and me shoving and slamming the door on him.

When I look up, there are two taxi guys looking at us, stood outside their office. Fuck it, I think, this is no time for grievances, and I come round the front of the car and step into the road.

'Hey, dial 999, call an ambulance!' The two of them don't move, just stay watching me. 'Call an ambulance!' There's a fair haired one, and a dark one, I recognise them both, neither are the driver from the other night. Neither of them respond. I take a step closer, I'm gesturing, pointing at the car, 'He's hurt, my friend, hurt badly, my phone's not working, please, call the… dial 999, I can't…'

They turn round and walk into their office. The fair one glance back and grins at me. Then they shut the door.

I should, I am sure, run up the road to the shop, or try and grab a passerby and get them to dial 999, but all the while I'm telling myself this, I'm getting into the car. I mirror, signal and manoeuvre, and pull out, because there isn't time for anything else.

'You're gonna be alright. You're gonna be alright.'

CHAPTER TWENTY-SEVEN
Retained material

THE THIRD TIME they suggested I retain the material for analysis. The nice nurse, Sandra, came and saw me in the little room with wooden hearts on the wall.

I'd opted for chemical management this time, speed things up, give it a kick start, as the doctor said. Sandra gave me a leaflet and bought me a bag of huge maternity pads and padded nappy knickers. 'Just in case you just want to go to sleep and not worry about it.' Then she said about retained material.

She was younger than me of course, soft looking, doughy. She said I would mostly likely pass it on the loo, and so the best way, *the best way*, was to use a sieve.

'You'll have to put these four pills inside you,' she pushed the box towards me. 'You put your fingers up-inside yourself, feel for your cervix, or just put them up, you know, far as you can. I can do it for you if you'd like, but you have to lie down for an hour afterwards, so…'

'That's alright, I can manage.'

The pain had me walking round and round, bent over, snapping at Max, shaking, crying, crouched over the toilet, the door locked and Max on his knees on the other side.

'Are you alright, Babe?'

'Fuck off.'

'Babe, please? Are you…is it?'

'Fuck off Max, please!'

'Babe, are you…?'

'Just fuck off, Max,' in barely a whisper, eyes closed, in a bubble of my own pain too thick to speak through, as the retained material slipped out of me and rattled into the sieve. I still feel it as I'm going to sleep, as I'm thrashing free of a half waking dream. I feel it when I'm stuck on a bus, as I'm plucking my eyebrows and now, as I'm driving my car with Martin bleeding in the back, I feel it again. The sensation of something slipping away, something I can't hold onto no matter how hard I try.

CHAPTER TWENTY-EIGHT

Nothing hurts like
the first time

A FEW MINUTES into my mercy dash, my hands sticky
with blood on the wheel, Martin throws his arm over the
back of the passenger seat and tries to pull himself up. He
partially dislodges the towel that has glued to his wounds.

'Lie down,' I snap, but he's trying to apologise, trying
to get hold of my shoulder to say he's sorry. Then he sees
his arms as if for the first time, and starts to gulp, to suck
in air until its rising into a sob.

'Just hold on, all right?' He slumps back out of sight,
and now it must be really hurting, because he's gasping,
crying, hiccupping with it.

I don't know how I get to the hospital. I don't know
how I remember where it is, seeing as every time I've been
there, I've never driven, but then it's rearing up in front of
me, all white lights and no parking signs. Ignoring all of
these, I pull up in the "Ambulance Only" zone so fast I

manage a tyre squeal. Martin is lying down, bloodied arms held up in front of his face, moaning now, as if the effort of screaming has become all too much for him. Christ, is he going to pass out now?

There's no way I'm going to get him out of the car. As I run for the door which slides obligingly open for me, I hear the voice of my GP rolling through my memory. 'Best way to jump the queue at A&E, be covered in blood or fake a fit, works every time.'

It's Sunday, but it's a London A&E, so there's one hell of a queue for me to jump. Ignoring the dirty looks that flick into 'o's of surprise when they register what I'm covered in, I push to the head and grip the edge of the counter.

'I need help,' I demand. 'He's in the car.'

Even the receptionist, who let's face it must have seen some scary shit, says, 'Oh my God, are you alright?'

'There's a friend in my car, he's bleeding really bad. I need help now.'

An orderly in blue comes running, leaping out from somewhere in the admin area behind her. I run with him, 'Where?' he asks me.

'Out front, blue Vauxhall.'

He barks instructions over his shoulder, and more people scatter and go do stuff behind us.

Back at the car I pull the back door open, and the paramedic or whatever he is, catches Martin's head as it flops out.

'Alright mate,' he says, crouching down and holding Martin's head so he can look at him.

'What's his name?'

'Martin.'

'Martin what?'

'I don't know.'

He gives me an *ask no questions*, look.

'Alright, Martin? Martin, can you hear me?' He opens Martin's eyes, squints into them, 'Martin? Martin? How long ago did he do this?'

'Not long, fifteen tops, I had to get him downstairs.'

'You didn't dial 999?'

'Phone's dead.'

'Hey, are you injured?'

'No, nothing, this is all his,' I say, as a rattle and crash behind me heralds three more people in scrubs, running with a gurney. The first paramedic begins to demand things of them, to ask for loads of shit I barely hear. They're trying to get Martin out of the car, but now he's woken up again and he's thrashing out at them. They fall back a step, so I push forwards and yell at him. 'For fuck's sake, Martin, they're trying to help you—let them!'

And he hears me and relaxes into sobbing again.

I run round to the other side of the car and open the driver's side rear door. A great spool of Martin's legs flop out, like one of those saw-the-lady in half tricks, where you can't quite work out where everything needs to go to make it work. I push him, get both his feet and shove at them, then, as the Paramedics lift together and get the top half of him safe, I dive my hand into his pocket and grab his wallet and phone as he's lifted clear of my car.

I run back round to the gurney, because he's woken up again and is trying to get off. He calls out for me, grabs hold of one of the paramedics to ask where I am.

'Here,' I yell and lean over him. He relaxes back enough for them to start pushing him along, me running beside him. His eyes close.

'Has he done this before?' One of them asks me.

'Not this bad,' I say, all those little angry lines along his arm, none of them ever as deep as he's cut this time. Sticky fingered, I get a card from his wallet. 'Fallow, his name's Martin Fallow.'

The paramedic nods.

'Martin, Martin Fallow?' Martin looks, focuses, then his eyes roll back and he thuds down, lips and face whiter than they were ever meant to be.

'Martin!' I yell, but they're pulling him away from me.

'You have to stay here,' one of them says, and looks like he wants to apologise, but then he's gone, the four of them running with Martin, and a door slams in my face.

I stand there, his phone and wallet still in my hands, hands bloody as Lady Macbeth's. I reach out to steady myself, leave a red smudge on the wall, then sit down hard on a plastic chair.

THIS IS WHAT you do, when it's the first time. When it starts, you tell yourself it's nothing but nerves, hypersensitivity, because you read that stupid article in the paper about it, and now you're aware of every twinge—an anxious sailor reading clouds scudding across a blue sky. You carry on as normal and when you go to bed, the feeling is so slight you sleep soundly, not listening to the shipping forecast.

This is what you do when you wake up. You do everything as you always have, remembering to take your vitamins. Then you go to the bathroom.

Then you're crying, the world spinning on its axis without you. Shocked. Disbelieving. Because this is the first time. You phone Max, and then you stand staring at your phone. Who do you call now? Are you allowed to call 999, or is that overreacting? You should ring your doctor's, but you're terrified of talking to the woman on the desk, the woman that always has a way of making you feel like you're seriously wasting her time. You ring her anyway.

When Max comes home, you tell him you're going to the doctor's, but they can't see you for an hour. You watch TV, not talking about it, not saying what you're both thinking, then you leave. In the surgery, every second sends spurts of panic coursing through you, though you're outwardly calm. Max is furious with the wait, but then the doctor is positive, gives you a fifty-fifty chance and encouraging words. You take the words home and hold onto them.

This is what you do when it gets worse. Max drives you to the hospital, the two of you not saying what you're both thinking, listening to your favourite radio show, unable to bear a silence. This is the way you thought you would drive one day, six months in the future, and you're doing the breathing exercises. Only it's all too soon.

You get lost in the hospital while Max is parking the car, the corridors are half-lit and the signs are written in a language you seem unable read, until a smiling man in a Christmas jumper shows you the way, chats to you, turns out to be a consultant, who opens doors for you, bobbing away and leaving his smile as the storm hits.

You wait in the waiting room until the nurse comes to ask you questions you don't understand the relevance of, but you answer them anyway, sure it's nothing more than a way of giving the doctor a tea break. They ask for a urine test, but when you go to the toilet, something you thought was safely caught in the net of your body, slips back to sea. Your hands are red, and this time it's your blood, all yours, and it won't stop, thick and oily and pouring out of you in a hospital toilet. You call for help, but there's no one there to hear you, and so you must walk back to the reception desk with your jeans wet, holding the tray they gave you to piss in, which is now full of your blood.

When they take you to a side room, like the one they just took Martin to, you lie down so the doctor can examine you, and you ask him what's happened. He won't tell you while you're on your own, you ask him again, but he tells you to get dressed. You tell him it's not important, him watching you put your socks on, not after where he's been fishing, but he's had his training. Max comes, and he explains to you both, and perhaps this is the first time that you realise it really is Max's baby too, because this is the first time you've ever seen him cry. He says the neck of your cervix is two centimetres open, and there's no way back after that. He asks if you want him to stop, but you say no. You ask if you can go home now, but you have to stay.

'Well,' the doctor says as he gets out a canula. 'I guess you're not afraid of needles.' He tries to get it in three times, then you both agree that perhaps you don't need one for now. 'I bet you're wishing you hadn't said yes to this,' he says, as he straps up the mess he's made of your hand.

'It's not the worst thing that's happened tonight,' you say, because you don't feel like being kind.

When they put you in the bed on the ward, you keep apologising to everyone, telling them that, on a scale of one to ten, your pain is one, sometimes a half, not because it is, but because if you say it is, maybe it will be okay after all, like that's still possible. You don't like fuss. You don't sleep, until a doctor wakes you up to ask if she can put a needle in your arm again, and you tell her she can't, and she scuttles away. Then you don't sleep again.

In the morning, they ask if you'd like to speak to some religious people, because they're "*usually wandering around somewhere*", as if the hospital is plagued with monks. You say no, you have no religion. The look offended, and say some of them are quite nice, anyway. You wonder about the ones who aren't. Do you want to see a counsellor? No, you don't, because you don't believe in them either.

A new doctor comes to see you in the morning, probably your age. He tells you this is what happens in one out of five pregnancies, that anyone has as much chance of losing a pregnancy as you, and there's no reason why next time, it won't be fine. He asks if it was planned and if you're with the father of the child. The word child catches against the bones in your chest. Yes, you say, it was planned, very planned and wanted, and everything you'd wished for, because even though it wasn't at all, now, now you know that it was. He nods. He says normally they'd advise a six month wait before trying again, but in my case, two months should be fine.

'Is that because I'm old?' you ask.

'I didn't say that,' the doctor says, blushing to the roots of his hair.

While I'm sitting as Max must have sat so many times, waiting to find out if Martin lives or dies, I remember I've got his phone in my pocket.

CHAPTER TWENTY-NINE

4 4 4 4

LOOKING AT THE phone in my hand, at the implacable black rectangle of it, it comes back to me. The two of us together the first time, soft and warm, intimate strangers in the refuge of my bed. Him wanting to show me something, something he'd made, and fetching his phone. His fingers with their bitten nails pressing the touch screen, and me seeing the code, and remarking on it.

I wipe my hand over my face and look up. Everything's calm now, just the drone of the TV fixed to the wall, the walking wounded, the staff. Martin's phone lights up, and I press the number four, four times. It opens without protest and shows me his world. I resist the temptation to scroll though his pictures, mostly in case I find one of me asleep or some creepy shit like that, and go for the phone book. I type in Mum and up it comes, just like that.

The phone rings somewhere. I imagine the sound of it cutting through a Sunday evening, echoing in a house, because it's a landline number, because she's a mum, and mums always have landlines. Then it's answered.

'Hello?'

'Hi, erm…' I close my eyes, because I have to say this right, and not fuck it up. 'Is this Martin Fallow's mother?'

'Yes,' the voice says, deep, lit with a West Indian accent. 'Who is this, please?'

'I'm…my name is Lydia, and I'm at the hospital with Martin. He's had an accident.'

A male nurse comes out from the doors that sucked Martin in, catches my eye and smiles at me. He's not one of the ones from before, and for a second I wonder how he manages to pick me out of the crowd, then I remember the blood, tattoos and blue hair, and all.

'Hey, do you want to come through?'

'Is he alright?'

'He's gonna be, but he's lucky. Come through, and we'll talk.' He smiles, waits for me to get up. His face is crumpled, tired but sort of warm looking under his widow's peak.

'So,' he says, as we sit in an empty cubical, me on a plastic chair again and him on the edge of a crisply made bed. 'I'd just like to check a few details with you, if you don't mind.'

'He is going to be alright, though?'

He does a kind of head tilt. 'We're going to need to keep him in, and then he's probably,' he pauses, 'are you his next of… I mean, you're his mum, right?'

'And there I was beginning to like you.'

He slaps his hands to his eyes. 'Oh, shit, it's been a long shift, I'm sorry. Are you his…?' He peers out between his fingers then lets his hand drop.

'You might say we dated, only that would be a massive exaggeration.' And we laugh.

He gets me to run through what happened, makes a few notes. I tell him I've phoned his actual mum, which makes him smirk again.

'Would you like to see him? Before you go home and…' he kind of waves his hand at me.

'Sure,' I say. Hours ago I was convinced I had to tell the world about us, to suffer the consequences in order to win another shot at my future. I look down at my fingers, where there is still blood collected around my nails, Martin's blood. No one needs to know anything about him, about us, after tonight.

Funny thing, the future. Slippery, hard to grasp.

They haven't managed to find a bed quite long enough for him. His feet are hanging off the end, though they've propped his shins up on pillows to make it more comfortable. There's a nurse with him, wearing a royal blue hijab that matches her uniform but for the gold work edging.

She smiles up at me when she sees me approach with the doctor. 'You can't have long he's got to sleep. Five minutes, okay?'

'Sure,' I say.

Martin's arms are outside of the sheets, mummy wrapped in muslin. There's a blood line going in and all manner of things that go plink-plink around him. He turns his head to look at me, and smiles, his movements sleepy, eyes taking a while to focus.

'Sorry,' he says, then tries to sit up, only the blue nurse presses her hand gently on his shoulder. He doesn't fight, they must have him more comfortably numb than even his usual poisons might manage. I take his hand.

'But I saw her, I did. I know I weren't meant to come over no more.'

'No, you weren't.'

'I had to, though, 'cause you blocked my calls, innit?'

'Never mind that now, you really ought to—'

'But she was there,' he says, and he's trying to sit up again, and the blue nurse frowns up from what she's doing with his clipboard of notes.

'Who was there, Martin, who did you see?' I say in the calmest voice I can manage, which makes him relax again. The nurse watches but says nothing.

'My sister,' he says, in a sad, lost voice, in his little boy's voice. 'She's missing, yeah? It was my fault. I was trying to tell you, because I knew, I knew you had to know, because you know her, don't you?'

'When did you see her?'

'I was fourteen, and she were eight, five years back, but it were my fault she got took,' an—' He has to swallow, I think he's getting agitated again, but he's not, he's fighting whatever sedatives they're pumping into him. 'Saw her, doin' your stairs an' that,' he smiles now, his eyes are closing. 'Ran away, an' I lost her again. Hurt too much, hurt, so...' his hand goes limp in mine.

'I think he's gone to sleep?' the nurse says. She smiles, her eyes dark and luscious, the shape of candied almonds. I let go of Martin's hand and place it back on the bed.

'He's a silly boy,' she says.

We both hear the squeak of approaching feet and look round to see who's coming.

I know without being told that this is Martin's mother. She looks like she sounded on the phone, and under better circumstances, you'd have no option but to describe her as a jolly West Indian woman.

'I'm his mother,' she says, and though there's a hard edge under her words, an edge that comes from trying to stay in control, her tone remains light and calm.

'He's all right,' the nurse says. 'We're taking good care of him. He's lost a lot of blood, but he's getting more, and he's sleeping.'

I want to go. I want to creep away under the pale green curtains, snake off like all those wires trailing away from us, but Martin's mother has that sixth sense you must get when you become a mum, because she holds up her finger to me. Without a word, she tells me to wait while she gets a full run down of Martin's medical report.

Then she looks at me. 'And you're Lydia?'

'Yes,' I tell her.

'Are you a…friend of his?' she asks, with the slightest raise of her eyebrow.

'From college,' I mutter, because I can't think of anything else to tell her right now.

'Of course,' she says, and her expression softens, and she touches the cross she wears at her neck. 'God bless you, for what you done here, Lydia, God bless you.'

I feel my face burn with the guilt of just how I do know her son. 'No, really,' I mutter, but she holds up the finger again.

'You save his life, an' I imagine he a deal of trouble for you, to boot.' She looks down at him, and sighs. 'My poor boy,' she says. 'I had him since he were five, bless him.'

So his story is true, that part anyway, and I say, 'Oh, you're his foster mum, he said about—'

'He told you?' she says, a little sharply, then shakes her head. 'You must be a good friend, then. He never talk about it much.'

Huh. Only to all those girls at parties.

Then she's looking at me. 'If you don't mind my saying, you're in one hell of a mess.'

'You're right, I should get going.'

'There's a washroom at the end,' blue nurse chimes in helpfully.

'Thanks, but … I need to make some calls, and my phone's dead, so I should head off really…' I hold my phone up, as if to demonstrate its deadness.

'There's a charger at the nurse's station,' blue nurse says, beaming. 'I'll plug it in for you, if you want to wash up, yes?' Slamming the door on my retreat.

'There you are, then,' Martin's mum says, and settles her mouth into what I imagine is a well-worn line of victory. 'Come on, I've wet wipes in my purse, we'll go and do what we can.'

'Oh, there's no need, for you to—'

'Come on, girl,' she says. 'You look like mince steak.'

CHAPTER THIRTY

Washroom

MARTIN'S MOTHER, MARGARET, puts the plug in the basin and fills it halfway with water from the hot tap, then the cold, as the hot is two degrees below boiling.

'You better take off your shirt, you can wear your jacket to cover your modesty once we're through. Don't trouble on my account, I've seen pretty much everything on God's green earth.'

'Least I wore a bra,' I say and do as she asks. I fill my hands with liquid soap and begin to rub and, while the water blushes from pink to red, Margret gets a handful of paper towels and works them over my back.

'Amazing where you got his blood,' she says, and smiles, only for sadness to quickly chase it away. She dabs at the back of my neck. 'Can't see what's blood or picture, girl,' she says.

'Has he done this before?' I ask.

But instead of answering, Margaret says, 'Why'd you go and do a thing like that, eh? Draw all over your lovely skin, you bad as my boy, there.'

'Oh,' Christ, I think I'm actually blushing, 'it's for my work, you know?'

'What line o'work you in, hmm? You a circus performer or something?'

'No, I'm a tattooist.'

'You are? Well, that explain it, I suppose.' She squeezes out her paper towels and pauses before putting them into the bin. 'He done this before, not as bad though. I feel it coming, he's been bad these last weeks, getting worse again. He goes through…he has good and bad times, you know? He don't live with me no more, seein' as he's all grown up now, but he come round all the time. I know when he's going to be bad, though, because I see him less, and when I do, he's all bright and loud, all, I'm gonna do this, mum, an', it's gonna be like that, you know? Pete say he get all mouth an' trousers.'

Which is a pretty accurate description of him.

She dumps the towels in the bin. I rinse my forearm again, and as I do, a little trickle of mathematics goes off in my head. This sister, the one he's been on about, he said she went missing five years ago, and five years ago, he was fourteen. I feel my scalp creep and find I have to clear my throat because it's dawning on me that no, Martin is not twenty-seven, or twenty-five, because he's not even twenty, is he?

'You alright, darlin'?' Margaret asks.

'Just a tickle,' I say. Nineteen. Oh fuck. So, not self-conscious posturing and Jack-the-lad irony, then. My God, he really is a kid…the Boy, is a boy. I catch myself in the mirror, half naked and chilled in the white space of the room. Thin and scribbled on. The weirdest thing is that it's not that he made me feel young, but he was like an echo from when I was young and at college and meeting Cassie, from when all of this, Max, the miscarriages, wasn't a thing yet. Taking me away from it all back to when life was simple. Still me as I am now, but a different me, one without all the losses and bleeding and wanting, a me who might have been happier with who she was. Only that's not fair, is it, to use him to make me feel better. Boys and girls, they're not made for that, are they, their bodies aren't time machines for our egos? I put the back of my hand to my forehead, lean over the basin. *I didn't know, they lied about their age, it wasn't my fault, they wanted it too.* Isn't that what we all say?

'You feelin' all right, dear?'

'Yeah, just a bit sick, you know?'

She hands me some dry towels and, as the pink water spirals away, begins to wipe over the basin with more hand soap, like it's an automatic response. One I can appreciate.

'D'you mind if I ask you what happen?' she says while I'm dabbing at the back of my neck. 'How come you found him, where were he? Doctor says as how if you hadn't been there…' She shrugs, because we know what the doctor meant.

I bite my lip and tell her what I imagine a brief would have advise me to say, had we time to confer beforehand. 'We were sort of dating.'

And bless her, she doesn't give me one of those maternal glares.

'But then I realised how young he was, and told him it was over.' Which at least, I suppose, makes me look a little better than the cradle-snatching old whore I feel I am. 'He…well, he kind of kept coming round, though, and I had to ask him to leave.' I wince, because it now sounds as if I'm appallingly arrogant, 'I mean, I should be so lucky, right?' I try and laugh.

'He do that,' Margaret says. 'Always been one for the ladies. I don't mean nothing by this, dear, but he'll get fixed on a girl from time to time, go on to me about her, about how she's all that, then it's over and he's all broken up, until the next one.'

'So I'm nothing special, then?' I grin, and she grins too.

'That's not what I meant, now. But…' and she picks up my leather jacket and starts to wipe it over, spreading it out over the basin and scrubbing at it with hand soap.

I resist mentioning that it cost five hundred pounds, and tell myself that hand soap will be fine, because skin is skin, preserved or otherwise.

'But he was still coming round?'

As I speak, it all works itself out in my head. 'Someone trashed the entrance to my flat. Look, don't get me wrong, but I kind of thought it was Martin, only....only now I don't think it was. Can I ask you, does Martin have a sister?' I say 'have', because I'm not sure how she's going to take this, or just what eggshells I'm stepping on. 'Josie?'

Margaret scrubs at my jacket, then straightens up. 'He told you he was fostered, yes? And about the man who threw him out when his birth mother died, because he weren't wanted?'

We both do that momentary shake of the head, *the how could they?* shimmy.

Margaret folds her arms across her chest, damp paper towel still in hand. The yellow light of the bathroom brushes shadows under her eyes, and makes her look tired but strong, like she's weathered so many storms. 'Bout three year after we got him, Pete an' me, they ask if we could take a little girl, Josie. Pete's white, you see, so when they got mixed race kids, they like to put them with a mixed family if they can, you know? Someone like them. Martin were about eight or so, and she were only small, just over one. Far as we knew, her mother had up an' gone, and her daddy was inside. There was a grandmother, and for a long time we thought as how she might take her, only it never quite happen. So, they were like brother an' sister after too long. Josie dote on that boy, she always runnin' after him, "Martin, Martin, do this, have that, play with me", you know?' Her face warms with the memory of it.

'Martin said to me...' I'm not sure how to go on, because she looks at me sharply. 'Something about her...did she go back to her birth family?'

'When they grew up, they went to school, of course, and when Martin went to big school, Josie went to her little one. They were round the corner from each other. You got to her school first, and there was this big car park to the side of it. By then we'd moved out of London, because Pete wanted more space.'

I want to ask why I need to know this, and Margaret must sense it, because she raises her finger again.

'It important you see how it were. The carpark joined onto Josie's school, but it weren't part of the school. People park in it all the time, it always got someone there, and there was a side gate into the school. It weren't the main school gate, you see? The car park entrance were at the corner furthest away from the side gate, and there was another path to the left of that, and that went all the way down to Martin's school.'

I've lost track, but I nod, because I can see it matters.

'The way we did things in the morning, the way we did things for two years after we move there, was that I drop Martin and Josie off at the big roundabout on the way to my work, an' he were supposed to walk her through the carpark to the side gate, and see her inside.'

'Okay,' I say, tensing.

Margaret's quiet for a moment, her mouth pulling into a tight smile, and I can feel the pain of it, what she has to say next, as if it were a thread caught in her throat that she has to pull free.

'He were just a boy, Martin, and you know what boys are. Always running off to be with his friends, always after the girls, an' little Joise runnin' after him. What big brother got time for his little sister?' She touches the side of her eye, an unconscious movement, no tears, but for the sake of tears past. 'It came out, that he would just say goodbye to her at the carpark entrance, and she'd walk across it alone to her school, because he met his friends there, so they could walk down the footpath the other way to their school together. I found out, because one day, Josie's school had one of those days, inset days? Where the teachers are all there, but no kids, only it were just her school, and I never got the note, I never knew.'

She pauses, swallows. 'It were my fault too, you see? Always rush in the morning, got to get to work, got to get the kids to school.'

I know what she's going to tell me. I lean back against the cool wall of the washroom, and I can see what must have happened. Martin, a younger, although not by much, shorter Martin, his mates waiting for him, bag over shoulder, high fives at the top of a footpath. I bet they were a right bunch, I bet they were all back chat and scratching their names into the desks. And Martin, anxious to get going, to talk over whatever scheme they were hatching, or catch up with some girl. Martin hardly giving his sister a backwards glance as he let her walk through the carpark alone, like he did every day. Only there was no school and the side-gate was locked. So then what?

Margaret exhales a long breath. 'I used to go fetch her, because that suited my hours better. So nobody knew she were gone until I pull into the carpark, and there were no one there.'

'Oh, fuck,' this time I do swear and neither of us care. 'But the police, did they?'

'Oh, they were very good, the police. Came in moments, all over the news, too.'

'Did they ever…?'

Margaret's shaking her head. 'They are pretty sure, no, they are sure, her father took her.' For a second, I've forgotten the father, then it comes back to me, the father who'd been in jail when her mother had left her. 'Came out that he'd been making enquiries, been trying to track her down. They think he must have been watching, waiting for a chance like that. It's even possible,' she shrugs, and the way she says it makes me think this is something she's decided upon, to make it easier to bear, 'that he'd already spoken to her, got her alone before, so she weren't scared to go with him, you know?'

I know that she wants this to be the truth.

She dabs my jacket a few more times with a dry paper towel, then holds it out for me.

'Martin blame himself, of course,' she says as I take it. 'He couldn't go to school, couldn't sleep. That was when he start to...' She doesn't want to say it.

'Cut himself,' I say for her.

She nods. 'I don't know why, but he say it helped. I told him, Lydia, I told him over an' over, the man were watchin' her, he were waitin' to take her, he's the villain in all this, not you. I don't think he ever believe me.' She looks at me, head a little on one side. 'He get like this, about girls, time to time, ones he think need him, ones he think...he can save.'

'Why do you think he's done this, now?' I ask, because I can't let myself think about what might qualify me as one of Martin's distressed damsels. Jesus, "lonely and desperate" must have been burning off me like a flame.

'Wrong time of year,' she says.

I guess this must mean that Josie had been taken in the summer.

'He's been...better, it's like that with him, but like I say, this been gnawing at him over the last few months. He's been workin' too hard at college, hardly coming round, and when he do, can't sit still a moment, but ... I don't know what push him so far this time.'

Thing is, as she says this, I kind of have an idea about what that might have been. I don't say anything to Margaret, because it seems all too nebulous to put into words, and because now I'm thinking back to my flat, and the busted in door, and the red painted walls, and then something else smacks me in the face.

'Oh shit,' I say. 'My car!'

CHAPTER THIRTY-ONE

Call your mother

OF COURSE MY car has been towed. My status as voluntary paramedic has no bearing on the case, I will have to fill out the required forms, produce the required ID and pay the two hundred and fifty pounds fine within the specified time slot, or incur further penalties.

'Pete an' I will pay for it all,' Margaret says, and when I protest, I get the raised finger again. 'No, you don't worry about a thing, Lydia. We'll sort it.'

She asks for my phone number, which I give her, and we say goodbye, me remembering to give her Martin's phone and wallet.

'Now, how will you get home, hmmm?' she asks, as if I'm an eight-year-old.

'It's okay, really, I can get the bus.'

Much as I like her, I need to be alone now.

IT'S A STICKY night, so walking in just jeans and my leather jacket zipped up over my bra, isn't the least bit cold. It's odd, even though I know no one can tell I'm just in my bra, I feel as if they can, as if everyone I see is getting a shock when they look at me.

I get on a bus that is going sort of the right way, and when it turns off on its own route, bid it goodbye and walk. What's that about not walking alone at night? Oh shut up, I won't think about that. Just put my head down and keep going.

There's something about walking that gives your thoughts enough of a gentle shake up to make sense of them, like when you sift stones and the big ones come up to the surface, and the little ones kind of fall into place below, or so Nan used to say.

It's nearly too late to ring Mum, but after a good half mile of thought sifting, I do.

'Are you walking?' She asks after the hello bit, and the, *I'm-not-going-to-be-cross-because-you're-forty-one-but-why-haven't-you-called-this-week?* bit.

'Yeah, just coming home. There's a…problem with the bus, you know, diversion thing, so I thought I'd walk it.'

I tell her how busy the streets are, what with all the Olympic stuff, and how bright and continental it all is, which is shorthand for safe, and a lie. I'm almost alone, apart from the spill of light from Sunday pubs, and a few hunch-shouldered night workers.

'Well, look I've been trying to ring you for a while,

because there's something I need to tell you, all right?'

'Sorry, I've been…' I look at my other hand, though it's hard to say in this light, I may still have some of Martin's blood under my nails. 'A bit busy, you know?'

'Yes, well, I have been calling quite a lot,' she says.

'Yeah, look sorry about that. So what is it, you and Dad aren't splitting up, are you?'

'Don't be daft, why on earth would we do that?'

I'm walking round the park now. While I'm waiting for her to go on, I stretch out my right hand and let my fingertips run along the railings, so they vibrate, and feel the rattle of it down my arm.

'Look, I said I'd tell you, just get it over and done with. It's your sister. It's Lauren.'

'I know her name,' I say, and then I stop, my fingers caught against the railing, waiting to launch onto the next one. In the moment between knowing and not knowing.

'Your sister's pregnant. We didn't know how to tell you.'

There are buses up ahead, wallowing into orbit around the tube station. I'll be home soon.

'This seems to have worked, in the whole telling me stakes.' The rear lights of the buses burst into red stars as I blink. Then I smile. 'How far is she?'

'Fourteen weeks. We wanted to be sure, well, as sure as we can be, because…'

'That's wonderful,' I say, and I blink again, and the

stars are gone. 'Really, wonderful news.'

'I really wanted to tell you face-to-face,' Mum says. 'I've been ringing and ringing, but—'

'You know me, Mum, busy lady.' I take the pedestrian crossing, walk past the Tesco Metro, then stand at the corner by The Goose and wait for the lights.

'I know it might be hard for you to hear,' Mum says. 'I mean, what with everything. Lauren didn't want you to, you know, get funny with her, so—'

'Do you think I'm some kind of monster?' I say. The lights have changed, but I haven't crossed. I let them go red again. 'What did you think I'd do?'

'Well...'

'Mum, it's not like I'm going to, I dunno, steal the baby or something.'

'Well of course not,' Mum says. 'Don't be silly, of course we didn't think that.'

What do I feel? Like I knew, the moment she'd started talking. Of course this was going to happen—but actually, I am fine with it because...because the world is full of babies which aren't mine. I get that, right?

'Look, I know you've been through a tough time, but there's no reason it won't work for you too, is there? I mean, I was only reading the other day that if you want to get pregnant, the best...best thing to do is be round a pregnant person, because the...the hormones sort of—'

'Max and I have split up,' I say, because I really don't

want to hear yet another home spun 'cure' for my condition.

'Oh, what on earth happened? Is that why you haven't been answering your phone? Oh for goodness sake, why didn't you tell me?'

Yes, indeed, why didn't I?

'He's such a lovely man, really good for you as well. What did you do?'

'You assume it's something I did?' I start to cross the road, lights or no light, self-preservation and anger lengthening my stride.

'You have to admit, Lydia, you're not always the easiest person to live with, and Max had put up with a lot these last few years, he really has. I know you have too, but…but another man might have walked away already.'

I stand still, close my eyes and listen to her voice as it rolls around my head, trying not to let it settle. It's a long-practiced defence, something I've done for years. Almost as if I turn her words into ball bearings and let them roll away to the far corner of my mind, where they slowly add to the pile that's growing there.

'Is it just a temporary thing? I mean, your Dad and I have had tough times, especially when you were little. Both of you, you were both very difficult babies, and it's not easy for a man sometimes, being with a woman going through, well, that.'

I bite my lip, because I know what's coming next.

'I mean, you know I nearly died giving birth to you—'

'I know, Mum.'

'And your father, he was so sure I was going to die, so sure you were going to die, that he was going to lose the both of us that—'

Max raped me, I want to scream at her. *I know the story about how you nearly died giving birth to me, and that Dad was so sure it was over, he went down to Waterloo Bridge—but Max raped me, Mum, that's why we broke up, in the end. That's why.*

'…only because this man came along—'

'Mum,' I say. I open my eyes. 'It was Max, Mum. He did something really bad.' Even saying that to her is making me feel sick and dirty and wrong, like why am I bringing her my nasty?

'Did he?' Mum says. She pauses afterwards, waiting for me to say more.

I could tell her, I really could, but somehow, for some reason, I don't. Maybe because as she says it, the way she says it, makes me start to question myself. I mean, come on, was it rape, really? I mean, it wasn't real rape, was it? I mean, they were just pictures, right, drawings? You can do more drawings, you've done more drawings—so it's not really, really, real, right? Aren't you just making a fuss over nothing, *really?*

'Look, Mum. Max and me it's…it's not for the best or anything, but it doesn't matter now, yeah? And I am happy, really fucking glad about Lauren, yeah?'

'Do you have to swear?' Mum says.

'Fuck no.' I bite my lip, then let myself smile as I hear her tut at me. 'Tell Lauren I'll pop round soon, yeah?'

'And us? You'll manage to come and see us too?'

'Sure. Bye Mum.'

She slips away from me as the line goes dead, and I feel like I've messed up again, let her go. Perhaps if I'd pushed it, said it, maybe she'd have been different, maybe she'd have listened? I mean, if I can't even tell my mum, maybe none of it is real after all.

WHEN I FOCUS on where I am again, I'm nearly at the cut-through, a little gap between shops that hardly qualifies as a road, and which is now blocked off by a set of old-style cast-iron bollards. The girl is leaning on one of them.

Soon as she sees me, she stops biting the side of her finger and straightens up. She takes a step away, turning as if she might run, then twists round towards me, one arm still across her chest, as if holding an unseen wound. Her other hand swings free by her side, until she points a finger at me.

'What's your fuckin' problem, yeah?' she demands. Backlit by the streetlamp, I can't read her expression in the dark. She could be any age now, angry, aggressive, carrying a knife for all I know.

'You tell me,' I say. I stop where I am, out of reach but facing her.

'Sticking your fucking nose in,' she says, but she's already losing the strength of her bravado, flinching back from me even though I haven't moved. 'It's none of your business, yeah? And you can tell that fuckin' weirdo, tell him to fuckin' leave me alone.'

'Which one?' I ask.

'What?'

'Which weirdo? I know quite a few.'

She's a little more turned into the streetlight now, and I can see her trying to work out what I mean, anger dissipated by confusion. I know who she means, because I've a pretty good idea now what happened earlier. Someone, maybe even her, broke the lock off my street door, and went to work with the spray can. I'm guessing, even if someone opened it for her, she was alone when she sprayed the walls, because I think she'd have to have been. Alone when Martin turned up uninvited and unexpected to see her doing it. If someone else had been with her, and by someone else I mean a man of course, I think he'd have driven Martin off, picked a fight, you know how boys are. But if she was alone, he'd have seen a little light-skinned mixed-race girl, about the age his sister Josie would be now, in the stairwell of my flat. I guess it never occurred to him to ask why she was there, and why she was trashing my wall, if we were friends and all, because he was already too lost in his own particular nightmare to think straight. After all, he was coming round to see me after I'd thrown him out and blocked his calls, he wasn't exactly doing the right thing, was he, five years after his sister had been taken?

The confusion on the girl's face right now makes me even more sure that at least some of it is right, she doesn't know what to say next. If she tells me that yes, the weirdo is the great tall bloke who caught her spraying up my stairs, and scared her off, ran after her even, well, she's kind of sticking her hand up to it, isn't she?

In the end, she tries to front it out. 'He come round when I was doin' your stairs. Started gettin' all…I dunno, acting fucking weird, an' shit.'

'Why did you do my stairs?'

She sticks her chin out a bit further, folds her arms and juts her hip to one side, pubescent gangster style. 'My boyfriend says you smacked up his mate's car, made trouble for him, and they stick together, innit? Wanted to teach you what you get—'

'But they made you do it, though?'

'What?' her arms unfold.

'They wanted to teach me a lesson, yeah, these two great big men, so they make you go and spray up my hall?'

'So…yeah?'

'Well, that's big of them, innit? Making you get your

hands dirty.'

Hands which she now puts in her trouser pockets.

'I had too, that's all.' She sniffs.

I take a breath and move closer to her. She watches me with big alley cat eyes, but she doesn't run. I stop at the other bollard and lean on it, my hands in my pockets too.

'What else does he make you do, this boyfriend?'

'Nothing,' she says, not looking at me. 'Boyfriend stuff,' she tells her shoes.

Oh shit, what the hell does that mean?

'I've just broken up with my boyfriend,' I say.

'So?'

'Well, he could be a right cunt sometimes,' and she looks at me then, which is why I say it of course, so that she would. 'I mean, he used to sulk like you wouldn't believe, and he kind of lied to me and shit, which was harsh. But he'd never make me fight his battles.'

I don't get an answer to that, just a shrug. I don't want to push it, because I get the feeling if I do, she's going to get all defensive on me.

'It's not like that,' she says, but she's still looking at her shoes.

'My best friend's good like that, though,' I say. 'She wouldn't let me take shit from anyone, you know? She's always like, look after yourself, and though it pisses me off a lot, she's right. We've had a bust up, and we're not speaking right now, but I'm going to ring her tomorrow and we'll be cool. You got someone like that?'

She shrugs.

'What about your mum?'

'Ain't got one, have I?' she snaps. 'Live in Marsden House.'

I've no idea what that is, but I can guess. Martin's phrase drifts into the space between us, looked after kid, ain't I?

Then I ask what her name is. In the moment before she answers me, when she looks up and the yellow-orange light scribbles a sheen on her hair, where it's pulled tight against her scalp, I think of the what ifs. I think of Martin at school, which must have been about when I was buying my flat, when I didn't have Max to think about, or a baby, and Cassie was the one who came with me to look at it. I think about buying that flat, while Martin was saying goodbye to his sister at the carpark, hardly giving her a second glance, because some friend of his, some mate, wanted him to come, or because there was a girl waiting for him, and he wanted to go, hardly looking back as his little sister, bag on shoulder, padded coat, hair pulled back into a pony tail, turns and walks away, alone. I think of how the stairwell of the flat looked when I first saw it, all new painted white and clean, waiting for bitch to be sprayed on it. What if Martin had walked his sister all the way to the school, or noticed the car park was too empty? And then there's my what ifs—what if it had worked that first time, or the second, or the third? What if Max hadn't been a fucking arsehole?

'So, what's your name, then?'

'Chloe,' she says. Then, when she sees me smile, 'What's funny about that?'

'Nothing, it's a beautiful name. Lovely. Suits you.'

What did I expect? That she would turn out to be Martin's stolen sister? That I was going to tell her that she still has a family, of sorts, and that the crazy weirdo who chased after her was her brother, all grown up? I reach into my jacket, take out my wallet and hold out one of my business cards.

'What's that?' she steps back, eyes narrowing.

'My number,' I say. 'I don't give these to anyone, you know, only people I actually want to call me.' She glances down the alleyway. 'Take it, you know where I live. You ever want to come round and talk or something, seeing as you don't have a mum or nothing, well, you can. This is so you can phone first.'

'Ain't got no credit,' she says.

'Then don't call, just come round.' I hold the card out to her again.

She looks at me, and then takes the card and folds it away into her hoodie pocket like it's contraband.

'Whatever,' she says. She turns away and starts walking off. Then she turns back, just as I'm straightening up, preparing to walk away.

'Sorry,' she says, 'about your stairs.'

CHAPTER THIRTY-TWO

You all right?

WHEN I GET home, I clean the flat. All the while thinking about sharks. How they can sense blood in the water from miles away. Only one drop is needed to send them into a frenzy. The water in the white washing up bowl I drag across the floor with me goes from clear to pink to red. The sharks will be knocking at the door any moment; bet they're already circling outside. Blood will have blood, as they say.

I ring the hospital and ask them about Martin, and they say there's nothing else they can tell me. Then I leave it until I imagine they have a shift change, which is based on nothing more than a wild guess from watching too many hospital dramas, so of course is shit, and so of course when I do ring back, I get the same voice on the phone, with the same patient tone, saying the same thing.

Why am I ringing anyway? Is it because I am worried about him—which I am—but is it also to kind of make sure he's still there? I mean, because he's safe there, right?

He's safe and tidied away and out of harms ways; they are containing him for me. He is retained material.

I go to bed and watch the inside of my eyelids for long enough for it to count as sleep. But all the while I was just turning it all over and over and over in my mind. Martin's so angry, so hurt, so desperate, he'd rather die than go on being him. I get it, I think. I get how that feels.

When I get up, I've decided. I mean, I've got to get my life back on track, right? Everything I thought I wanted, everything I do want, has been blown out of the water, not by me (well, yes by me, but not officially by me) by Max, by what he said. Christ, all the things that made me are broken into pieces. But I can rebuild them all, right? I mean, look at this way, I'm the good guy, again, far as anyone knows, right? I can go and tell Mum about what Max said, go and tell Cassie, have all their sympathy and empathy and not have to say anything about Martin ever again.

I could call Max, in a day or two. Say I'm prepared to talk, ask him round and he will be…contrite, he will be sorry. He will agree to anything, won't he? I mean, he owes me, right? He owes me one last shot at being a mother, at getting me pregnant, at this time it finally working. He can sell his fucking bike and pay for a private clinic, one of those ones which practically promise you a baby. I mean, that's okay, right?

Shit. This is not me getting my life back on track, is it?

VISITING HOURS ARE from two PM on the ward Martin's been moved to. It's not a completely secure ward, but they ask me a lot of questions when I get there.

'He was in my flat last night,' I tell the receptionist. 'He cut himself and then I brought him in. We're friends, and obviously I'm really worried about him.'

'Of course you are,' she asks me to sign the book and then buzzes me in.

The ward only has four beds in it, and the other three are empty. He doesn't see me at first, so I get to stand to one side of the doorway and look at him. He's sitting up in bed, looks like he's watching the TV or something. Hell, he looks fine, great, doing really well, so maybe I better not disturb him. Then he sees me. He doesn't smile, he doesn't wave, so I kind of do, in a half-hearted way, and then I have to go in.

The room has a different smell to the usual hospital one, as if they use nicer cleaning fluids in this bit. Maybe they do, maybe it's a special one for suicide risks? Which of course I am only thinking about, because it stops me thinking about how he looks.

He looks like a child, like a big, long, lean child; a boy that I fucked, because I thought that might stop me hurting. But that never stopped him being a boy, did it? A boy with a shit load of his own hurt.

'Hey,' I say, throat all dry, heart hard and tight in my chest, banging and banging to get out.

'Hey-'

He's just looking me, not mean, not sad, not anything, just looking at me because I am new in his field of vision, and the TV has no sound on it, so he wasn't really looking at that either, just flicking, flicking, and now he looks as if he's going to flick through me too, as if I am nothing more than another silent ghost on the screen of his world.

What have they done to him?

'Hey,' he says again. The edge of his mouth curls, then a tiny grin pulls itself across his face, a stupid, sad, slit of a grin. 'You all right?'

I go and sit on the blue plastic chair at the side of the bed, because I need to sit down, because my legs feel weak and stupid, and he starts to talk to me. I don't understand it because it's just a tumble of sentences, as if we were already in the middle of a conversation and he's just picking off where we left off.

'...it's just, yeah, like there's always been this thing, like, I've always known it would happen yeah?'

Only nothing he says is really words, it's just phrases going round and round.

'...sweet...nah what I mean, yeah?....Always said, like, sweet...mate...yeah?'

And all the time I'm thinking how he's just a boy, he's just a kid.

'So, you'll tell her, yeah?' He reaches for my hand which feels weird, because he's hardly moved since I've been here, has just been a talking head, and it almost startles me that he can move.

'Don't, not if it hurts.'

'It's cool, babe, it don't hurt. I can't feel a thing, can't feel anything,' he says. He chuckles, closes his eyes and then something pulls him back to me. 'But yeah, when you see her? You'll tell her I'm sorry, yeah?'

He's taking about the girl, about Chloe, who isn't his sister.

'Martin, I saw your mum last night. She told me about Josie, what happened.'

'You've seen her?' he asks, though I don't know if he means his mum or the girl. I put my other hand on top of his, making a hand sandwich of our fingers because he's rambling again, asking me to speak to her, to talk to her.

'Martin. It's not your fault, right? What happened to you could have happened anytime, to anyone. Her Dad took her, he was always going to take her, okay?'

Is he hearing this? He's looking at me and his lips are moving, like he's trying to copy what I'm saying to try and understand it. Should I be saying this? I don't know, but at least he's listening, or trying to.

'What happened, wasn't your fault. You don't need to

keep…hurting yourself.'

'Okay,' he says. Just like that.

Then I see it.

If I was a man, and this was a film, he'd be like one of those girls. One of the bad ones, ones of the naughty ones, who tries to help the hero, even though they're bad—like a bad Bond girl. Or one of those girls in films and books who are in the wrong place at the wrong time, and the sole reason they are there, is so that they can get hurt or killed or cut up really bad, like he is, because then it gives the hero something to learn? The whore who dies leaving their child to the hero, so he can redeem himself through fatherhood; the mad wife who has to die in order for Mr Rochester to be released, her madness absolving him of being a git. They are nothing more than a chance for the hero to see themselves reflected through the girl's pain, and go hmmm, that's an interesting insight into the darkness in my soul, I'm going to brood on that for a bit, then I'm going to be a better person because of their sacrifice. But they're still going to be left behind, the dead one, the mad one, the lost one.

I squeeze his hand.

I am probably not going to be a better person.

But I could be a more honest person.

Not least because I am a shit liar.

'That girl, the one you saw at my place? She isn't your sister. She's a girl called Chloe, and she's in danger, or I think she is.'

His face twitches, he frowns.

'She's not your sister. But that wasn't your fault, that—'

'What you saying?' he pulls his hand away.

'Her name is Chloe, and she isn't your sister.'

'No, she is, she—'

'No, Martin, she isn't. None of this happened because you are a bad person, it just…happened.'

Because you're a mushroom too.

It's no good though, not now. For a moment I think he's understood me, but then the grin slides back across his face and the strength leaves him. I'm trying to tell him it all again, but he sags against the pillows, his eyelids fluttering to a close.

'I'll come and see you, yeah?' he's saying. 'Next week, when I get out, when I…' and then he's quiet, asleep, sucked under a chemical haze and taken far away from me.

'No,' I tell him. 'I'll come and see you, next week. In a day or so, yeah? I will come and see you, I promise.'

YOU KNOW THAT thing about, if you save someone's life, you are responsible for them forever? You know it's bollocks, right? People say it's an ancient Chinese proverb or something, but it's not—it comes from a 1975 episode of the TV series 'Kung Fu', which in turn may have stolen the idea from radio shows, where anything mystic had to be "oriental" to give it some heft. It's shameless orientalism, cultural appropriation. But as I walk away from the Boy, it's going round and round in my head because, even if it's a bullshit saying, I did save his life. But it's not over yet is it, the saving of his life? I can't leave him now, and I'm not going to.

I text Cassie when I'm outside; I'm expecting her to ignore me, but she doesn't, there's an answer right away.

I text back, 'I'll head over now.'

HER OFFICE IS part of an old foundry warehouse, which has been gentrified so far away from its roots that you wouldn't know if there wasn't a handy blue plaque to tell you. She's pretty high up now, enough to have an office with a secretary, who recognises me and tells me she's expecting me with a bright, professional smile.

If I was worrying about Cassie's reaction to me, which I must have been because I'm all stiff and awkward when I go in, then I guess she was too. We both stand there, arms by ours sides and not quite knowing what to say.

'Oh, fuck it,' she pushes past the visitor's chair in the room and throws herself at me, and I catch her and we stand there for a long time in each other's arms, just saying how sorry we both are.

'No,' she pulls back from me and scrubs eye makeup all over her cheeks with the back of her hand. 'No, it's me, I should say sorry.' She breathes out, all shaky and goes for the tissues on the desk, takes one and hands me the box.

I sit in the chair opposite her and she retreats back behind her desk. It's good, we can talk, we need to talk, but there's still something between us, more than a desk and a pencil pot. Something I've got to tell her.

'Have you spoken to him?' she asks.

For a moment I think she means Martin.

But then she adds, 'I haven't, I promise.'

Max.

She bites her lip. 'He did ring me, but I didn't pick up.' She glances up at me.

'It's all right,' I say. 'We had dinner together, well, we looked at some food together. Look, do you want to go for a drink over the road. I've…I've got some stuff I really need to talk to you about, like, really need to talk to you about.'

CHAPTER THIRTY-THREE
Only bad girls get their wings

WE BUY A bottle of wine to share, but we hardly drink any of it, have hardly touched our glasses when they're bringing over artisan beef burgers with little flags in, like they've just been conquered.

'I've had to deal with some stuff too,' Cassie's saying as the burgers are set before us. She looks at hers as she speaks, and for a second I get this weird idea that she's going to make some joke about the food, only then she looks at me and there are tears at the edge of her eyes. 'I've always been, well, not jealous, but you've always had this thing I've never had, your art.'

'Oh, that,' I say, feeling self-conscious like we're trained to whenever someone says anything nice about us.

'Yes, that.' She puts her hand over mine. 'I'm not proud of myself, and I've had to face some stuff about me which isn't that nice. You're right, I was…weirded out when you were pregnant the first time, because I did always think it would be us forever. And like, that would mean you had something else as well as the art. And, I know that's a shitty thing to think and please, I never wanted you to…to go through what you did, but part of me…'

'Part of you kind of hoped I'd stop trying?'

'Sort of,' she says, in a small, upset voice.

I wait to feel angry at her, I wait to get the rush of energy which might proceed my standing up, hurling a chair, calling her a bitch, but it doesn't come. It's that bloody honesty thing again. Saying what you really feel. That shit's powerful stuff.

'I don't think I did anything, like, that evil, I mean, I really think you and Max probably do…did need a bit of a break.' She manages a small smile, which I return. 'But I think I just sort of hoped that you'd decide the way we were, you and me, our life, was, you know, enough for you after all?'

'You are enough for me,' I say, and then how weird that sounds hits us both and we start laughing.

'Fuck me though, if I'd have known that about Max. What a fucking dick!'

'His fucking dick's the problem,' I say.

'Space, for fuck's sake, what the hell was I thinking? If I'd have known, I'd have told him he needs the space made by a 22-calibre bullet between his eyes!'

'I love you, Cassie.'

And this time when we kiss and hug each other, over

the Artisan burgers waving their little flags, nobody in the place says a damn thing.

We talk for a while, and while it's not the same as it ever was, neither is it like we're circling each other, treading on eggshells. It feels weirdly like we don't know each other at all, like we've met through a mutual friend and really got on, staying late at a party after everyone else has gone to bed, laughing on a sofa about nothing until we've forged an unbreakable connection. Like our shared past is a mutual friend that introduced us, and now we've got a chance to be friends in our own right.

I'M FEELING GOOD, getting off the tube. The sky is still lit up with a hint of the day, but the streets are quiet and the pubs are full. Because the Olympics have started and everyone else, or so it feels, is watching it. As I pass The Goose, a huge cheer goes up, a rolling wave of positive noise that even brings a smile to my cynical old face. There are things out there, other things, good thing. Things which will be, you know, okay.

The mood keeps me going down the cut through where I saw Chloe yesterday, past the row of squeezed together town houses, and out onto the main road again. I cross the road without even looking, as it's almost indecently empty of traffic, take a luxurious diagonal to the other side just because I can, which takes me to the top of the little road leading to my flat.

The lights hit me first. Car head lamps by the taxi rank; full beaming right in my face. They seem stronger and brighter than they've any right to be. Enough to make me stop and shade my eyes. The blaze of them is snapped off as the car turns away, half mounts the scrap of pavement. I don't move, because there's something not right about this, not right about the way the engine is revving, sounding like the car's out of gear and burning the clutch. As the engine stutters to a stop, I hear catcalling, whooping, clapping, like a different race is being run here, a different spectator sport.

One I don't think I am invited to either.

There's a group of men outside the taxi office. Three of them watching the back of the car. They're gripped by whatever it is they're seeing. One clapping his hands, the other two with arms thrown about each other's shoulders. They can't see me because all their attention is focused on the car.

The back door of the car falls open; the inside light snaps on and I can see a tangle of figures inside; a shadow play of arms and legs.

Sharks in the water.

It's her. I know it's her.

A sick cold fear beats through me; a rush of adrenaline which makes me want to run away. Turn on my heels and get the hell out of here. But then I hear her scream over all the noise of their voices and the thundering in my head. She screams as she tumbles out of the car, or is pushed out, or dragged out, because then there are two men with her coming out of the car too, their white trainers shining bright in the darkening night. Chloe is on the ground between them, kicking at them, her high-pitched scream of panic a red line of sound over the jeer and snarl of their voices.

The one who's pulled her out drags her then drops her. I will her to get up and run so I can collect her up in my arms. But he takes a step back and then kicks her in the side, and the ones watching give a weird hiss and cheer of noise, rolling about and clutching their sides, laughing and clapping at what he's doing.

They are laughing at her.

Laughing at her sprawled on the road being beaten. Thinking nobody is here. Thinking nobody sees them.

I reach for my phone from my pocket, fighting against the fabric, the lining.

He kicks her again.

The phone is stuck.

I hear her sob, I hear it down the bones in the back of my skull, in the skin of my back, in the wings I imagine hide there, the echo of my tattoo. I feel them buck as if they are real. I feel anger rip through me as if the wings have ripped through my skin and burst out into the air above my back.

Hello anger, my old friend.

I scream.

My hand closes round one of the rusty steel stakes holding up the red warning tape strung round a hole in the ground. I tear and twist it free. The red tape spills out behind me as I run. I spin the steel rod in my hand, so that the forged knot at the end, still threaded with the last scrap of tape, becomes the end of my weapon, clangs and smashes against the concrete beneath my feet.

'Hey—you fuckers!' I am burning hot red now, my body electric and pulsing with all of the anger, all the hate, all the fucking frustration with all of the shit that's gone on.

'You fuckers.' I spit. They're all looking at me, all staring because what is this coming towards them? This harpy, this banshee, this bitch from hell—out of the dark and screaming at them. They are staring at me and I will her to notice, to take her chance. 'Chloe,' I scream. 'Run, run Chloe.'

The sound of her name snaps her back into herself. She gets it. The man kicking her is frozen off balance because he'd gathered himself to kick her again and she is up, she is running.

She barges into the man who kicked her, and catches him hard enough and at the right angle to send him staggering against the opposite curb and falling to the ground. The rest of them still don't quite seem to get what is happening, because one of them starts to clap his fall, does a big 'way-hay' of a laugh, like this was all part of the show. Chloe is running towards me, reaching her skinny white arms out to me, her mouth a black 'O' of crying.

They've got it now. They're all shouting—*crazy bitch, fucking crazy bitch, that fucking bitch*—and starting to come after her. The door to my flat is between me and her, I need her to stop running towards me and turn to the refuge it offers. But they're coming, they're coming.

I dart forwards and with all the strength I have left hurl the metal rod towards the car. As it flies, I turn and run, grab Chloe and pull her with me towards my flat.

The metal rod hits the car windscreen. It shatters and sprays glittering shards over the bonnet, the men, the road. It's enough to make them turn.

Enough to give us the moment we need.

We smash through the street door, which swings straight open as the lock is broken. I kick it shut never-the-less, blacking out the street with a hollow clang, take the steps three at a time dragging Chloe up behind me, stab my keys home into the lock, without realising I'd even got them out of my pocket.

'He's coming,' Chloe is all tears and shaking, the side of her face puffy where the bastard must have hit her. 'He'll come after me, he will.'

I can hear it already, the street door banging open again, voices coming up the stairs, as I slam the flat door behind us.

'Chair!' I yell at her, but she just stares at me. 'Arm-chair!' I run to it and start tugging it towards the door. She gets it then and grabs it too, even though she's limping, and we shove the huge, leopard spotted chair against the door. The key tray on its stand goes over as the flat door resounds with the impact of fists on wood and shouting. Chloe's backs away against the wall and slides down, curling her arms about herself, sobbing.

I leap up onto the chair and hammer the flat of my hand against it, yelling back at them 'Go on, you fuckers, I'm calling the police.' And I am, swearing and spitting at them, ripping the phone up, fingers clumsy, and then the thing lighting up and the call going through.

'I'm calling them now. I'm calling them.'

There is a wave of cheering, a rise and fall of it and I know what they're doing, because I can smell it, even through the door. One of them is pissing on my door, but I don't care.

'Hello—police, I need the fucking police right now!'

I HEAR THEM go, maybe even hurrying a little because they heard me calling the police for real, maybe they believe me. I run to the kitchen window and lift the edge of the blind, still on the phone to the man who answered, who's reassuring me that the police are on their way, who asking me if I am hurt.

'No,' I say, though all of me is shaking, though my arm is throbbing with the effort of my throw. The car is still outside, the men milling around it but they're going. One of them gets in, starts the engine.

'The police will be with you soon,' the phone man says again.

'Well tell them to hurry up,' I snap, because the car is reversing, the hole in its windscreen a black, put out eye. And then I hear the sirens and the drivers hear them too.

The milling becomes running. 'Ha!' I shout. 'You think I didn't mean it, you think I didn't. Yeah, you better run, you fuckers, you fucking cunts!'

'I take it they're there?' the man on the phone says, because of course I have bellowed all of this at him. But he hangs up before I can apologise.

In the second after I've heard it, the street flickers with blue lights lighting up running figures. Yes! Yes! The drivers are scattering, the broken car reversing, then jolting forwards, then. Then I remember Chloe.

'It's all right, the police are here, they've got them.' Which I don't know for sure, but it sounds good.

I kneel down next to her and put my hand on her arm, wanting to get hold of her and hug her, but she gets up with a sniff and stalks away from me. Right, so I was perhaps expecting something like a thank you, but I let her go because she moves like a wild thing and I know at once that if I push her, she'll panic, beating against the window like a trapped bird.

She strides side to side, goes to wrap herself in her own arms but then winces.

'You're hurt. You need to—'

'I don't want the police,' she says. 'What the fuck you call them for?'

'Did you not just see that?' I point round at the door, 'Those fuckers were beating you, they were...' I stop, because she's crying, because the police are not her friends, are they?

They are not sanctuary for her.

'It's all right, they'll be fine this time,' I say, making myself lower my voice, controlling myself. 'They're on your side, they'll be fine, yeah?'

She looks at me, weighing up whether to trust me I imagine. There is noise from outside, shouting, door slamming, because there's a little war going on outside, right? One I started.

'Tea,' Chloe says. 'You said I could have a cup of tea?'

I blink at her. Of course, when we'd spoken last night, I'd said it then. I glance over at the door. I guess the police will get round to us, but the first lot kind of have their hands full right now, judging by the crashing sounds from outside.

'Sure,' I say. 'Tea.'

I check outside while the kettle rolls to a boil. I can see the white bonnet of the police car first, then see that the cab I smashed up has crashed into it, just enough to shatter one of the headlamps, but enough to really piss off the Met. The road is still flashing blue, and an officer is standing by the door to the taxi office, talking on his walkie-talkie. The kettle clicks off, pulling me back into the flat.

Chloe is fidgeting around the place, touching things, picking things up. Her face seems softer, her curiosity making her the child she is again. I want to hold her and tell her to be more careful.

When I take the tea over to the table, my hands are shaking. What I just did finally hits me. The thought of what might have been makes me gasp and Chloe looks up at me.

'Here,' I say. 'Mug was hot.'

She sniffs, watches the mugs as I sit down and put them on the table between us. I'm torn between bursting into tears and laughing at what I just did. And I have a weird sense of victory in getting her through the door, as I've finally won. I've rescued her. What's happened with Martin makes me stop that thought right there though. This is not all about me. I make myself look at her to make her seem more real. She's wearing the same clothes I've seen her in before. One of her gold hoop earrings is missing. The hems of her leggings are dirty, an inch or two of grey like rising damp, and now I can smell her; unwashed, unloved. She's zipped her hoodie up tight under her neck and the hood is up, the bulge of her hair in its ponytail at the back. She sniffs again, reaches out to the sugar skull box on the table where I keep my business cards, more of the one I have her last night, and turns it about in her fingers.

'Look, the police will probably knock on the door soon.'

She glances up at it, at where the armchair is pulled over it.

'Don't worry, I won't let anyone in until I know who they are, you don't need—'

'What's this?' she asks. She's holding out my card, one dirty finger pointing to where it says *cover ups.*

'Oh, you know, it's like when people are young and they get shit tattoos, and when they get a bit older and wiser, they ask me to design something that makes it look better, you know? Like, when I started it was all girls wanting dolphins, but now they're all faded, so—'

'Anything, right? You can do anything, yeah?'

She begins to roll up her sleeve, the left one, and I can see that it hurts her to do it, that it makes her wince. The inside of her wrist is yellow white, the same colour as Martin's, and when she turns it over to show me, she says, 'Can you cover this?'

It's a word. I reach out, look at her for her to nod that it's okay, then take hold of her wrist so I can turn her arm into the light. There's a mark, a narrow red stripe and then the word. It's been burned into her; her skin's blistered, the letters inflamed. It's fresh. Whoever did it, maybe with something like a straightened-out paper clip heated up with a lighter, has written D – I – R – T – Y – S – L – U on her. She must have finally pulled from his grasp. There are bruises on her wrist and on her arm, just below the elbow.

Now I'm crying. All the pain of the miscarriages and what Max did to me, and the pain of losing my drawings. A cold, terrible sense of loss. She loved him, the man who did this to her. She loved him and this is what that love made her go through.

'Yes, sure,' I say, when I can speak. I can do that.'

I get up, fetch my latex gloves, cotton gauze and antiseptic. I clean the word and put muslin over it.

'I'll make it better,' I promise her. 'Got to let it heal first, okay?' I glance up, she ought to be crying too, I think, because this must hurt her, but she's not, she's just watching me tend to her. 'What do you want, rainbow unicorn, or…or Pokémon, or something?'

'Anything?' she says, and there's a spark in her eyes I haven't seen before, maybe a smile touching the edge of her hard little pout, only then the doorbell chimes and she pulls back from me, pushing her sleeve back down over her arm even though it must be agony to do it.

'Hello, can you come to the door please?' A voice barks from outside, then goes on to introduce themselves as the police. I don't really hear their names, because Chloe is up and shouting.

'Don't let them in, I don't want them, I won't go, I won't go with them.' All while she's backing away from me and the door. I'm trying to get her to calm down, saying how they're on her side, our side.

'Miss, are you all right in there?'

Chloe's gone into bathroom, slamming the door behind her.

'I ain't going!' she screams through the door.

I breath out.

'I'm just coming,' I tell the police.

CHAPTER THIRTY-FOUR
No one else wants her

THE TWO MALE police at my door, ring for back-up; which I work out from the shorthand passing between them, must mean send us some female officers.

'Is there anything she can hurt herself with in there?' one of them asks me.

I say there isn't, although recent history might argue against this. While we're waiting for the back up, they take an initial statement from me and ask if Chloe or I need an ambulance.

'I ain't going anywhere,' Chloe yells from inside the bathroom.

'You don't have go anywhere,' I tell her. 'But I think you should let a paramedic or someone to take a look at you, yeah?'

'You did it,' she retorts. I judge from where her voice seems to be coming from, that she's sitting on the floor against the door, so I sit down on my side.

'I'm not a doctor,' I say. 'I know bits, but not everything.'

'Is she injured?' the larger of the policemen asks.

'Yes,' I say.

They call an ambulance then the paramedics, female police officers and two social workers all arrive at once, queuing momentarily up my stairs to be checked in, like my flat is the number one place to be. I give my statement again, still sitting on the floor. I say that she is hiding in my bathroom because she is scared of the police, and that I can't get the door open from the outside, which is the best lie I've managed in days.

After a lot of gentle talking against the backdrop of crackly shortwave radio communications and stab vests, Chloe agrees that the two paramedics, a pair of stocky women who remind me of Shetland ponies, can come into the bathroom and look at her, as long as I'm there.

When the door clicks open, I go in first. Chloe is backed into the space between the bath and the loo, arms wrapped about herself.

'Hi,' I say. 'So, this is…' I look at the Paramedics in turn, who introduce themselves as 'Babs' and 'Luci, with an 'i',' like this is some weird job interview scenario. I tell Chloe that they are just going to look her over, make sure that she's all right, and that she won't have to go any-where she doesn't want to.

I sit on the loo. Chloe sits on the edge of the bath and without being asked, pulls off her hoodie and t-shirt, like she's pulling off a plaster. The gauze on her arm doesn't come free, but she winces, though I'm not sure if it's from her sleeve pulling on the burn, or the mass of purple bruising blooming up her side. Somehow I manage to keep my expression neutral, gripping my hands into fists. I should have smashed that iron rod into the bastard's face.

'Ooh,' Luci is saying, all ready with plastic gloves on her hands and leaning into the bruises. 'That looks nasty, love, can you...can you turn into the light a bit more?'

'Here, look, let me put the one on over the basin,' I say and I reach up to do it. When I look back, Luci has bent to look at Chloe's side.

'Is the baby all right?' Chloe asks.

I don't think I've heard her right at first, her voice is small and dry now she's not having to shout through a door. Then it slices through me, cold and heavy in my guts. Luci with an i looks over at me for confirmation, like I should know, me being her friend and all. Chloe is looking at me like it's me she's asking.

So I say, 'What's the pain like?' I put my hand on my abdomen. 'Is it here?' My heart is thudding inside me, over and over, the sound of it crashing in my ears. 'Or here? Does it feel like a period pain, a sort of burning inside feeling?'

Chloe puts her hand to the bruise, then to the place on her I'm indicating on myself. 'No, just the bruise hurts.'

'How far are you?' Babs asks her.

Chloe narrows her eyes. She doesn't understand, does she? I doubt she's had an appointment with a midwife, or her GP, or sat there counting on a calendar and guessing what size it is now—a seed, a grape, a plum—a fruit bowl's worth of anticipation and dread. I sit back down on the loo and put my hand on hers, where she's gripping the edge of the bath.

'When did you tell him?' I ask.

She blinks, shrugs, looks away from me. Her free hand slides over the bruising again, then comes to rest over her stomach, still nothing but a fold against her jeans, though maybe, now you come to look, now you know, you can see it.

'Last week,' she said. 'He said…couldn't be his because…' Her gaze flicks up to Luci for an instant, then she looks back to me. 'But it is, yeah?' she lowers her voice. 'He never uses nothing, because that's special, between us. That's our thing, so it has to be him, not the others, yeah?'

From the floor, Babs clears her throat, loud enough to make me look up and see her turn back to the bag on the floor, not to look for anything, just to wipe her hand over her eyes. I look up at Luci, who gives a slow head shake, mouth set in a hard, thin line.

'We need to get a doctor to look at you, at inside

you,' I tell her, somehow keeping my voice cool and calm and gentle, when all I want to do is turn and smash my hand through the bathroom mirror.

'How?' she asks, her wide, high forehead crinkling.

'It's okay,' I say quickly, realising how that must sound to the uninitiated. 'They use a...a sort of camera, but one which can see through your skin, it kind of...hears the baby, hears how it's doing, hears its heart beating.'

A little pearl, lost in the grey darkness.

'Does it hurt?' she asks.

'No, it's just a bit cold feeling, but it doesn't hurt at all. We should go now, with Luci and Babs.' Chloe's hand shifts under mine, grips it tightly. 'I'll come with you, all the way.'

'He wanted me to go to the doctor,' she says, her voice growing louder again. 'He said the doctor would get rid of it, I ain't doin' that, yeah, I ain't gonna kill it.'

'No one can make you do that,' I say, squeezing her hand back. 'No one's going to do that, I promise. We just need to make sure it's all right, after what he did, that's all. I'll come with you all the way, every bit of the way, okay?'

'Will you?' she asks, as if she doesn't believe me.

'Yes,' I say. 'I promise.'

'On your fucking life?'

'On my fucking life.'

IN THE AMBULANCE, with Luci driving and Babs sitting with us as we roll and bound through the streets followed by an entourage of police and social workers, Chloe makes me promise again that they won't do anything to her baby.

'I'll deck them if they try,' I say, which makes her smile. 'Nobody gets to do what they like to your body, no one, no matter what they say.' Not anymore.

Babs puts a blanket round her shoulders and, braces herself against the gurney with her sensible shoes as we turn into the hospital ground. She's scrolling through her phone as she does, and then she leans over to me and holds the screen out for me to see. I can't really focus on it as I'm already feeling sick, but then she says, 'Guardianship,' to me.

'What?'

'When they ask,' she says, 'you want to apply for legal guardianship of her, right? They're like dogs, social workers an' that, not in a bad way, like a good way, but they response to the right command, yeah? You say that's what you want to do, and they'll make a fuss but they'll go for it, if they know what's good for them.' She glances at Chloe. 'Seeing as they've dropped the ball on this one.'

'Will they let me?' I say, and when I say it, the weird thing is how emotional I feel, how the rush of it makes me want to cry, to take hold of Bab's hand and kind of make a deal with her, to say *you'll put the word in for me, yeah*?

'I mean,' I stutter, 'I mean with the…my?' I touch my neck. For the first time ever in my life I touch the tattoo at my neck as if I want to apologise for it, for what I've grown into.

'Course they bloody will,' Babs says, breaking into a grin. 'Bite your hand off, if they've got any sense.' Then to Chloe, 'All right, lovely, we're here now. You just stick with this one, and you'll be fine,'

I could kiss them both.

CHAPTER THIRTY-FIVE

Visiting time

THE PLACE MARTIN is in, is all right, as it goes. It's a mix of hospital, school and dormitory with a sprinkle of prison, but like they've at least tried to use all the best bits. It's out to the North of London, in one of the posher, greener bits, so that's nice. It reminds me of going to the clinic, but I let it off.

There's the signing in bit, and the waiting to be buzzed through by a smiley nurse, who peers through the safety glass panel in the door. She takes me down soft grey corridors, which are cool despite the heat, to a room with too many sofas in it, a mismatched herd of gold and pink and floral patterns, which I imagine must have been kindly donated from the surrounding comfortable suburbs. They make me think of old people, shut away and waiting for the grandchildren to visit. At least Nan never ended up like that, at least she went out fighting.

'Here she is, Martin love.'

I look round from the window, at the nurse and Martin coming in.

'Hey,' I say, 'how are you doing?'

Does he look well? He looks even younger again, and like he's put on weight. His face is softer than even a week ago, puffy looking, though when he smiles at me, it's Martin alright, his grin like an anchor for his real self, or do I mean old self? They call it that when the pattern in the wallpaper stubbornly shows through the layers of paint you've tried covering it with—grinning through, they say. Martin's like paisley wallpaper painted magnolia.

The nurse says that she'll be back in a little while. Martin sits in one of the armchairs by the window, 'Sweet,' he says, 'sweet, babes.' Sniffs, wipes the back of his hand under his nose.

'She's nice,' he says when she's gone. 'All right, you know?'

'It's good to see you,' I tell him, and for a little while we just talk and it is good to see him. He tells me about the food, about his room, about the man next door to him who's going to teach him how to cheat at dominoes. 'My Dad used to play dominoes,' he says, 'in the pub on a Sunday.' Then he says, as if the memory of one thing has sparked the other, 'Have you seen her?'

I guess who he means, see it in the way his face becomes eager.

'You know she's not your sister,' I tell him, not sure how to make it any gentler than that. 'She's not Josie.'

He nods, looks out at the garden and the light touches the wetness of his eyes. I lean forwards put my hand on his knee. 'But she was lost too, in a way, this girl. Her name is Chloe, and she's…she's the same age as your sister, well, sort of. She's had a…shit time of it, been through some bad stuff, so she's staying with me for a bit, yeah.'

He sniffs and looks back at me. There's a sag in his shoulders now, he's slumping against the chair.

'I didn't mean to scare her,' he says.

'You didn't,' I tell him. 'I mean, not really. You're the least of her problems.'

'I didn't mean to,' he says.

I want to say that she reminds me of him, but that's just because of her story, of the bits of it she's told me. Maybe it's just familiar because how else would it have been, how else would she have ended up where she did? Not as lucky as him in some ways; staying with her mother till she was older, the two them moving between towns, between houses, until there'd come a day when her mother just wasn't there anymore.

'Have you seen her, though? Have you seen Josie?'

So I guess he's not ready to hear any of it yet. The nurse comes back then, appearing at the door, fidgeting to catch my eye before she comes over.

'How are you doing, Martin love?' she asks him.

'Sweet,' he says.

'I'll see you next week,' I tell him.

I'M MEANT TO be going to see Mum and Dad, and I'm going to, only I go to Lauren's house first, Lauren and Michael's house. I don't ring first, because I know she'll be in, because Lauren has worked at the same haulage firm for the last three years, with an early start and an early finish, almost the exact opposite of my working life. Big Al never opens before twelve, he always says it's a point of principal, 'Early birds might get worms,' he says, 'but who the fuck wants worms?'

Lauren lives a mile away from Mum and Dad so the route to both is pretty much identical. This makes me feel like I'm trying to conceal my motives, like I'm pretending to the world I really am going round to Mum and Dad's, only to veer off at the last possible moment for Lauren's as if trying to shake off someone tailing me. Then it strikes me as weird that I even feel that, that I am guilty about going to see my own sister. Then I realise I can't actually remember when I did do that without clearing it with Mum first, keeping her informed.

'Thought I'd call in on Lauren next week, you know, see how she is.'

'Really, when? I'm going over too. Shall we go together?'

I park up opposite her house, pulling into the layby that means that houses on this side of the road command an extra ten thousand pound when it comes to resale value. Something Michael explained to me at some length the last time I was here.

'No, Mum,' I say. 'Let's not go together. Not this time.'

PEOPLE SAY THAT we don't look alike, Lauren and me. Well, that's what neck tattoos and blue hair will do I guess. But the thing is, I actually think we do look alike, when you get past all of that surface crap, which of course most people don't. When she opens the door, I really see how much we're alike, but it's different somehow. I used to think that she looked like a sort of clean version of me, in my bitchier moments a boring version of me, but she doesn't, she looks like a naked version of me.

'Hey, look, don't call the cops or nothing, but it's your big bad sister come to say hi, and—'

Lauren bursts into tears.

'Oh, shit.' I'm genuinely stuck for what to say or do. 'Christ, I was only kidding Lauren.'

'No, it's all right,' she says, 'Come in, bloody hell, come in.' She reaches out and pulls me into the house so she can get the door closed.

The house smells of her, of course it does, but I don't mean that in a bad way; she and it smell nice and clean, that sort of warm, flannelette sheet scent, fresh laundry and tidy beds.

'Gosh, look at you,' she says and gives me a hug.

I'm so mean saying she smells like that.

'Goodness, what's the matter with me?'

'I guess it's the whole baby thing,' I say.

She looks at me, eyes big and bright. 'Oh, no. She told you, then?'

'Yeah, few days ago. Look, there's been so much going on, like, so much I've got to tell you, it's fine, it's.'

'I did ring,' she says. 'I really wanted to tell you myself, you know? Before anyone else, because anyone else doing would just make it weird—did she make it weird? I rang, I really did—did she make it weird?'

'Not really,' I say, as I sit on one of the cream armchairs in her cream sitting room. They won't last, with a baby then a toddler after that. Lauren sits on the sofa, lifts her feet off the floor and draws her knees up to her chest.

'She did though, didn't she? I tried not to tell her for so long, not till we'd had the twelve-week scan and all that, but she got it out of me, and I knew that was it. I tried getting there first, but...' She sniffs.

'It's okay, you should have told her first, really.'

'No!' Lauren says. 'No, I didn't want to tell her first, I wanted it to be mine for as long as possible, not hers, not her taking over. And now look, I go and get all teary at dinner last week and out it all comes, and she does just what I knew she would do—takes over everything.' She slumps forwards and puts her chin on her knees, a gesture so reminiscent of her as a child, it makes me smile. 'Just like the wedding,' she says.

'I thought you wanted all that?'

Lauren shrugs. 'That...I don't want to go over all that again,' she says. 'Look, I wanted to tell you about the baby because I know you'd never be weird about it, but everyone else seems to think you would be, so if I told you, then everybody would have to stop fussing.' She drops her knees, puts her feet on the floor. 'I'm so hopeless around her, like she sees right through me.'

'Oh, she does that to us both,' I say. 'Maybe it's a mum thing?'

'Don't say that,' Lauren sits up straighter. 'It's our mum, it's....don't you ever think about it, the way she always somehow sort of comes between us.' And she starts talking about when Mum wouldn't let me take her round her friend's house on the tube, or in my car when I learnt drive, and all the time she's talking, the hot cold heavy dread sensation I've felt so much recently creeps out from the base of my spine and seeps through me again, until I can't stand it. Because surely she's only saying this, because she doesn't know, doesn't remember.

'Look, it's not her fault, all right?' I say. I cut across Lauren to say it, probably more loudly than it really warrants. I mean, unless you're inside my head and get it that I have to say this now, or I never will.

'It's me right? When I was...you were about two, and

I was, well, six or seven, I took you down the park, the little park, the one back home.'

'Lydia what?' Lauren says, but I carry on, because if I don't say it now, I never will, and I need to say it now because, well, isn't it obvious? Because of Martin, because of what he's done to himself, and how lucky I am because I can say it, to her, my sister, who is still here.

'I took you to the park, and…and I told you to watch me on the slide, to wait for me, and you were looking up at me, laughing.' At me, her big sister—her big, exciting sister—always running after me on her chubby little legs, always wanting to be with me, and me never wanting her, complaining 'Mum, do I have to? Do I have to?'

'And I did it again, I said watch me Lauren, watch me, Lauren, but instead of sliding down, I climbed back down the ladder. Quietly so you wouldn't notice and I went off and just left you there.' I force myself not to look at her, because if I do, I won't finish. 'I don't know what I thought was going to happen, I guess part of me thought that you'd…just find another family and that would be that. I didn't even come up with an excuse for Mum, I just walked home and told her she didn't have to worry anymore, because you were gone.'

Now I look at her.

I'm not sure what I'm expecting, but Lauren has her hand over her mouth. I think at first she's trying to hold back anger, like she's going to swear at me, yell at me, but she's not. She's trying not to laugh.

'I'm sorry, is this some kind of joke to you?'

'Oh, no, I'm not laughing, I mean…'

'I tried to leave you in the park,' I say, 'I tried to get you lost, shit, do you know how dangerous that was, how—'

'Bollocks!' Lauren never swears, and I'm amazed at how shocked I am to hear her do it—me, of all fucking people! 'Michael's brothers locked him in the cupboard under the stairs overnight one time, and he and Alfie pushed Dwaine off the roof through the attic window and he broke his leg. Kids do stupid stuff, so what?'

'But it wasn't just that,' I say, desperately, as if I need above all else to prove what a monster I am before I can change, really change for good. Be a good person. 'Mum said I…she left you on the bed, fuck, I can see it now that horrible candlewick bedspread thing they had for years, she left you on it, and when she came back—'

'You'd shut me in the chest of drawers,' Lauren says. 'I know, Lydia, Mum told me.' She puts her feet back on the floor, comes over and kneels in front of me, takes hold of my hands.

'Bloody hell,' she says—swearing again—'you think…you're still worrying about that stupid kids' stuff?'

'But that's why, isn't it?' I say. 'Why Mum's always been so protective over you, I was a bloody nightmare and that's why she sent me to Nan's every summer after that because I was dangerous, I wasn't safe for you to be around.'

'But you loved going to Nan's?' Lauren has hold of my hands, and all of this, her in front of me on the floor it's a bit weird.

I want to make a joke about it, something about her looking like she's going to propose, something about how she better not tell Michael. Only I don't, I let her hold my hands and I look at her, and I say,' I did love it, I loved Nan and I miss her so much, so much, but ... I knew she was making it up to me all the time. Because Mum never wanted me around, did she?' I sniff, because I seem to be crying.

'Oh, Lydia,' Lauren says.

'It doesn't matter how stupid it is,' I say, because now I have to say all this, because otherwise I never will, 'I don't know how I let it happen, but I just could never let myself be near you, because I was sure I was a bad person. I told myself all the time I didn't need you, that I was going to be my own person and do my own thing, and I did, and that was good, but also I wanted her to forgive me, to be proud of me. University—' I can't get the words out now, I have to breath, to swallow the burning lump in my throat. 'I know she never understood, she said I could be an art teacher, and I never wanted to be, but I said yes, I could, but then…then I messed all that up because I wasn't any good, I wasn't—'

'Stop it,' Lauren says. She reaches out to grab me, all clumsy, and I slump forwards into her arms. We sit on the floor and cry together. Somehow, in the middle of it all, I say something close to her ear, words which feel like a long shard of glass being pulled from a wound. That really fucking hurts but then feels amazing afterwards, as your flesh comes back together.

'I lost my babies because I wasn't good enough.'

CHAPTER THIRTY-SIX

Kit-Kat

LAUREN MAKES TEA as we really need a break from all the catharsis. She has mugs with jolly pictures on them, funny cartoons; a Garfield tin to keep tea bags in; and a Sponge Bob Square Pants biscuit tin. I am going to be late for Mum and Dad, and Michael will be home in a half hour, so I know that I am leaving soon wherever I go next, but as Lauren says, there's always time for a quick tea.

'You know,' I say, second digestive down because I am suddenly really bloody hungry. 'I just thought that's how sisters were, you know, you and me?'

'I know,' Lauren says.

It still feels weird this, her agreeing with me; like Lauren's betraying mum, or we are together; like this is a plot we're in up to our necks no one told me about before.

'It's like when I saw how other people were, it felt...over the top, you know? Like they were being ridiculous by actually having conversations and the actually telling each other things. Oh blimey, you realise you've still not told me why you haven't been answering my calls. What's been happening?'

'Oh shit, right—well, here's the thing—'

Then I tell her it all. About Chloe and Max, and Cassie, and even about Martin, though I play that down quite a lot, because there's so much to get through and suddenly there seems to be so little time, as if the clock on the cooker is counting down to lights out.

Lauren collects our cups together and puts them in the dishwasher.

'I don't really know what to say,' she says. 'But I promise I'm not going to say that stupid thing everyone else says, you know, everything happens for a reason, because I know that's rubbish.'

'Good,' I say, 'because I really would have lost it if you had.'

'Yeah, well, I'm not going to, but look all the stuff you've been through, I mean, good and bad, like... I know about college, but you've got a business now, and you're cool as anything.'

'Thanks, sis, I'm blushing!'

'Oh, shut up. But look, the bad stuff too, all that stuff with what Max said, and losing the babies.'

This pulls me up, as she's the only person who's ever said it like that, not pregnancies but babies, like she understands they were real. They were all my babies.

Gone.

'All of that, meant that you were there when she needed you, that poor little girl. And I don't mean just because of the babies, I mean because of you, because you're the only adult who's ever been there for her, at least the only one she's let be there for her, right? I expect she's always been surrounded by social workers and all the rest, but they've never got her to do anything, have they? But she wants to be with you, in a good way, not like with whatever that horrible man's called.'

'Now I am blushing,' I say.

'No, look, you're amazing, you are,' she says, with a hint of what I might even call genuine awe in her tone. 'I don't think I can take it all in, not yet, everything you've done. And this girl, Chloe, how old is she?'

'Fourteen,' I say, then I know we both silently do the math, because the way Lauren looks at me means we realise at the same time that Chloe must have got pregnant—though the word 'got' seems deeply euphemistic when applied to her—at about the same time as Lauren.

'That poor kid. I mean, I'm terrified about it, I don't know how she can…'

'Wait, you're terrified? Nothing scares you,' I say.

Lauren pulls her 'oh, really?' face. 'What do you know about how I feel? I'm terrified, Lydia, of everything, of the whole birth thing, the…going into labour bit, and the baby. The thought of having a baby, of being a mum. That's…I just don't know how I'll do it.'

'You'll be fine,' I say, as if I suddenly had some hold on the future, one which has eluded me pretty well up to now. 'You've got Mum, she'll…ah….'

'Yeah, about that. She is driving me mad already. If she's not telling me for the hundredth bloody time how she nearly died giving birth to me, and—'

'Wait, what?'

'You know?' Lauren frowns at me, her face a pantomime of confusion now her story's been interrupted. 'She nearly died giving birth to me, and I nearly died being born, and Dad was going to jump off the bridge, only this man came along and—'

'No, that was me. That was when I was born.'

'No, no, that was me. She always said how that was me, and how…how—I mean, isn't that all part of it? She nearly lost me and so she was always, like, worried she'd lose me again and…'

'Come on,' I say, and somewhere in the back of my mind as I am saying this, I am aware of the sound of keys in the door a little way down the hall from the kitchen, which must mean Michael is coming in, returning home to his family nest, in time to hear me saying, 'Look, if any baby was going to fuck her up, out of the two of us, don't you think it's more likely to be me, than you?'

Lauren has her hand to her mouth, and for a second I

think it's me, I've done it again, and I imagine Michael thinks the same thing, because as he comes in he's already saying, 'Is everything all right, Law-law?' looking daggers at me.

'Hush,' Lauren hisses at him, and I get it seconds after she's got it.

'Oh, do you think it was even either of us?'

'I don't know, but she said it was me, and she told you it was you.'

'Just the other bloody night,' I say, pointing at the window as if through it I could see the image of myself, walking through Walthamstow late at night, with the crowd in The Goose cheering on Mo Farah, and my mother telling me yet again how she nearly died giving birth to me, how I nearly killed her. How I am a bad, bad person. 'Just the other bloody night.'

'Am I missing something?' Michael asks.

'Yes,' Lauren says. 'But then, so are we.'

I DON'T GO and see mum. I don't ring her. I don't send her a text. I go home. The word home keeps flitting about in my head as I pull up outside my flat and look across at the blacked-out window of the taxi office. It's been silent since the night of the police. The only people drawn to it the shop guys, who have come and poked at it and muttered over its bones, and the trickle of bemused passengers. Will it open up again? Will the fat man behind the desk be the same fat man, or a different fat man? Will the drivers who come and hang out outside it be the same drivers, or their friends, or a whole new batch? Will they still know what they did, the old lot?

There were other girls. Chloe has talked about some of them with me, both when we've been alone and when we've been in more official circumstances. There were what she calls parties, where if she drank enough vodka and took enough of the pills he gave her, it made it more distant, as if the things that were being done to her were down the far end of a telescope. It makes me think about *Alice Through the Looking Glass*. That drawing when Alice has drunk the potion, and she's stretching further and further away from her feet.

When I open the flat door the room is dim, just the TV lighting it up. Max's taste in electronic hardware has already impressed Chloe; she sits in front of it the way people use those blue lights in the winter. Tonight she's on the pink sofa wrapped in the leopard spot throw, which has become her spot, just as the leopard armchair with the pink throw, is mine. Her head looks tiny against the bulk of the fabric, a pin in a pincushion. When she hears me come in, she inches round to see who it is, then looks back at the screen.

'Right?' she says.

'Yeah, you want tea?'

'Okay.

I don't think she makes tea when I'm not in. There are never cups left about the flat, unless I leave them, or half eaten sandwiches, or toast, which is her main food of choice. When I go out I leave things ready for her, but she doesn't eat them until I come back.

'Do you want a Kit-Kat?' I ask as I pour the tea.

'Okay.

She's watching one of those daytime TV shows where the audience bates some working class people with bad teeth to the point of fighting, and some be-suited middle-aged white man lords it over them, part bouncer, part conductor.

'Did you see your mum?' she asks when there's an advert break, which promises us that we'll get to meet Tracy's cheating husband in a few short minutes.

'No,' I say. I slip my Kit-Kat out of its red wrapper and run my nail down the crease in the silver foil, a moment of pleasure only to be rivalled if I find a fabled solid finger of chocolate with no wafer—did once, around about 1986, might have been one of the highlight's of my life.

'Saw my sister instead. She's having a baby too.' It feels a bit like taking the first step off the side of a pool into the water, making myself feel the fear and do it anyway. I glance over at her, waiting for a reaction.

Her face remains impassive, the light of the screen bright on her eyes.

'Think she's due about the same time as you,' I say.

Chloe shifts under the blanket, the leopard spots undulating as she refolds her arms.

I've been asked to do this by one of her social workers, a new one, as her old ones have been reassigned, tactfully or otherwise. This new one, who's quite nice, has asked me to mention her pregnancy in a non-crisis, normal way whenever I can, so long as it comes up naturally in our conversation, to help her normalise her experience and take ownership of it.

'That's nice,' Chloe says. 'They'll be like, related then, won't they?' Her eyes swivel over to look at me.

I've wondered how that man convinced Chloe he loved her, got her to do what he wanted and even believe that she was enjoying it, that she wanted it. Now I know. This is why. When you are so lost and lonely in the world, you will cling on to anything. To a man old enough to be your father, to a woman more fucked up than you are, to a man with an American accent, who says he believes in you and offers you the world.

She is waiting for a response; I know she is. I bite into my Kit-Kat, the taste of it shockingly sweet and metallic against my teeth.

'Yeah,' I say. 'Sort of.'

'Yeah,' she echoes, her eyes flicking right to me again. 'I mean, yeah, sort of.' There is a brief flash of a smile between us, and my heart crushes in my chest.

CHAPTER THIRTY-SEVEN

The deeds

MUM RINGS THE next day. I ignore the call. She rings again and I ignore it again. I get a weird thrill when I do. A sense of lightness, of wanting to laugh.

Chloe is in a sulk, refusing to get out of the leopard spot blanket and not talking to me, because we have to go to a meeting and she does not want to go to the meeting. It's not a police one, which is good because they are horrible despite their sympathetically designed interview rooms and compassionately trained interviewing officers. Today it's the social work team and I'm trying to persuade her that she does need to come with me, because we are going to talk about her and she needs to stick up for herself. But she's tired, it's Thursday, there's something she really wants to watch on TV.

She's in the spare room, which in a matter of days has morphed firmly into her room. We are talking through the door.

I need to prove who I am, that I am not a criminal,

and that I own my flat, because the social workers are trying to rush through the paperwork to upgrade my status to private foster carer, and make me out to be a responsible adult, ha-ha. Of course, the deeds to the flat are at Mum and Dad's, because Dad pointed out that if there was a fire, the first thing I would need would be them for the insurance claim, and life would be so much more complicated if they too had been destroyed in the fire. My phone lights up for a third time; this time I pick up.

'Hi Mum,' I say, speaking as if someone is listening in, not in a sneaky way, but to keep me safe when I talk to her. 'Look, I can't talk right now, but I have a lot of things to tell you, will you be in later?'

'Later?' she says. She's not used to this, this bright and breezy me. I've confused her.

'I've a meeting first, so....let's say five, okay? I'll see you then, okay Mum?' This is normal, this is what normal people do. They make arrangements.

'Okay?'

'I suppose it will have to be,' Mum says. 'Lydia, what's going on, have you—?'

'Bye Mum!'

WE ARE TEN minutes late for the meeting, though nobody seems surprised by this. When it's over, I don't feel that anything has been materially decided, but everyone there has made a date for us to meet again next week, and I have a load more stuff to get from Mum and Dad's.

'I'll drop you off first, yeah?' I tell Chloe when we're back in the car.

'I've got a doctor's,' she says.

'What?'

'Two-ten, I've got a doctor's.'

'A doctor's, or a Midwife appointment?' I tap the steering wheel as I wait to pull out, trying not to ask why she hadn't told me this morning, because it's already after one, and returning to the early pregnancy unit where she's being seen, will mean a hefty detour.

'Doctor's,' Chloe says, then roots in her pocket and holds out a crumpled slip of paper.

'Fine, that's fine.'

'I don't have to go, yeah?' She's tapping too, one arm extended onto the dash in front of her, drumming her fingers as we pull out, sitting with one heel up on the edge of the car seat, the seat belt pulled over her knee, rendering it useless.

'Put your foot down,' I say. 'If we have a smack, you'll go through the windscreen.'

'So?'

'I can't afford to get it fixed this week.'

She darts a look at me, says nothing but her foot thuds down onto the floor. Before we get to the doctors, she has tuned the radio to KISS FM, and made us stop for chips.

IT'S ALREADY THREE-THIRTY when I install her back on the sofa, with a new prescription for antibiotics to continue treating one of the other things "he" left her with. Next week we have another interview with the legal team from the CPS, which will be a big one, as she'll be giving more of her statement. He's been denied bail and was charged last week with rape of a minor, GBH, ABH, assault on a police officer and damage to police property. Chloe didn't say anything much about it, then later that night she was crying in her room. When I went in she threw the new phone I'd got for her at me and screamed that he wasn't texting her, and it wasn't fair, and all she was doing was saying sorry to him, so why didn't he answer?

'You'll be okay?' I ask as I put on my jacket. August is sliding into September, the lazy days starting to hint that there's a change coming, a sharpening in the air.

'Yeah,' she says.

I want to ask if she's going to text him again, if she will march about the flat when I'm out breaking things, if she will cry that she knows he still loves her, if she will shake with fear that it's him at the door.

'Right,' I say. 'I won't be late, we'll ring for pizza when I get back, yeah?'

'Okay.'

THE JOURNEY GIVES me time to plan, lets the niggling demons of my thoughts start to cluster. I don't know what I'm going to say, how I'm going to start. Just be normal at first, talk to her about Chloe. '*So, Mum, you know Lauren told you about what's been going on?*' I'd asked her too, in our new capacity as allies and plotters, because I wanted Mum to know how it feels, the two of us talking behind her back for a change. '*Well, the man was charged, right, and we've been talking to the social work team*' but before I know it, I've tumbled into accusation, visions of me standing over her, my wings unfurled shouting, '*You lied, Mum, you lied to us both with that bloody story, that how I nearly killed you when you gave birth to me story. You told Lauren that was her—so why did you do that?*' Then I'm talking to Dad, because in my head he steps up, gets between us, and I'm shouting at him, '*Dad, what about you, huh? You must have known she was making this shit up, you must have known you didn't try and kill yourself when we were both born, right? Do you know how that made me feel, how bad I've felt all my life?*'

I'm already here, I'm home.

No, not home. I'm at my parent's house, which is definitely not the same thing.

I PARK ON the street because when I was seventeen and had just passed my test, I knocked into the wooden post at the side of the path and damaged it. So I'm not allowed to park on the drive. Still. I was only here a month or so ago but I'm expecting it to look different, for something here to have changed as much as I have. Disappointingly there's nothing much to see.

Dad is in the front garden, moving about the lawn, picking at the flower beds. He's wearing a white sun hat and seeing the hesitance as he bends, the way he catches himself, pauses hand against his knee, he looks old, older than before. It's odd to see him like this, not gardening as such, though I don't remember him ever really doing that much in the garden, but doing it alone without Mum, without her issuing instructions, without her being there.

As soon as the car door opens and I get out, he looks up and comes to the front of the drive. He's grinning at me as I approach, taking off his gardening gloves and putting them both into his left hand. But he's uneasy.

'Hello, Lydia-O-,' he says. 'Mum said you were coming round, said earlier.' He glances back over his shoulder at the house, looks back at me, looks at the house. 'Said you were coming round,' he says again.

'Well, here I am,' I say.

He doesn't ask how I am, doesn't ask how I'm feeling.

'Bit tired, I think she is,' he's saying. 'Not been herself, not really, worried I think, about something.' He puts his hands on his hips, elbows out and leaning back a little from his waist, a wide grin on his face. 'Bit tired,' he says again.

'I'm not stopping long, but hey, nice to see you too.'

'Lydia,' he says, but I'm walking towards the front door, the front door which is open. 'Lydia?'

Then we both see Mum through the door, coming down the corridor.

'Kevin, are you still here? Oh, Lydia. Kevin, why didn't you say she was here?'

'Hi Mum,' I say.

'Well, you better come in,' she says. 'And you better go, Kevin, the butchers will be shut soon if you don't.'

Dad pauses, goes to say something.

'Well?' Mum says.

'Go on, Dad,' I say. 'You don't want to miss the butchers.'

I KNOW WHERE the deeds to the flat are, say I'll go and get them while she makes the tea.

'I don't know what you want them for,' she says to the kettle.

'Lauren didn't say anything, then?' Mum looks round at me.

'Lauren?'

'Yeah, you know, my sister?' Then I go into the sitting room, go over the bureau and crouch down to open the bottom drawer. Mum comes into the room after me, stops just inside the door.

'I don't understand what you're here for,' she says.

'The deeds of the flat,' I say. They're in the blue folder she put them in five years ago. I can see it under two other folders and a brown envelope of stuff.

'Well, let me get them,' Mum says, 'I don't want you rooting around in there.'

'They're just here,' I say.

But she comes over any way so I get up and let her get at the drawer. As she bustles past me, I want to laugh.

'I don't want you going through all this stuff,' she says. When she bends down, I can see the roots of her hair, where the auburn is giving way to salt and pepper.

'I'll make the tea,' I say.

'Well, I won't be a moment, just let me get to—'

'It's okay, Mum, I can make the tea.'

SHE COMES IN and puts the blue folder on the table. Her kitchen is melamine bright and sparkling clean, of course. She gave us both the gift of that, of scrubbing instead of talking.

'Here,' she says. 'Shall I do the tea?'

'It's fine, I've got it.' I squeeze the bag in her cup against the side of the mug.

'What do you want these for, anyway?' she asks again, slapping the folder where it lies on the table. 'Green milk, please, not blue, dear.'

I go to the fridge, my hand pausing over the blue milk in a moment of rebellion. 'I need to prove I own the flat.

Because I'm applying to foster a girl I've met.'

Mum frowns, juts her chin forwards, two lines scored deep from the side of her nose to her mouth. Nan's face used to do the same thing, and I guess mine will too, is already starting to fold that way.

'She's called Chloe, and she's in care, and now she's going to stay with me.'

'I don't understand. Is this why Max left you?'

'What? No Mum, Jesus, this has nothing to do with Max.'

'Well who is she, this girl?'

'She's a kid, that's all, fourteen. She was in trouble, and now…' I put her mug down on the table beside her.

'Don't be ridiculous,' Mum says. 'You can't have some girl live with you, some girl you don't know.'

'Why?'

'Well,' but she falters.

'Chloe is staying with me, I don't know how long for, we don't talk about it. Maybe until she's had the baby, maybe after—'

'What baby?' Mum puts her hand on the table, leans forwards with her weight on it. 'You said she was fourteen?'

'She is, Mum, and she's having a baby. Look, there's…' I put my hand to my forehead, it really isn't easy to explain. Because I feel like I'm betraying a trust Chloe has put in me, as I know Mum will say something harsh, judge her, and I don't want her to—I want to protect Chloe from my mother. 'The man, the father, he's been arrested, there's going to be a court case, and—'

'Oh, is there,' She folds her arms. 'I see what you're doing. Really, Lydia, I know you've been through a terrible time, but this isn't going to work.'

'What?' Then I realise what she means even as she's saying it; start shaking my head.

'You can't just take on this girl's baby and pretend like it's yours.'

'I'm not doing that, Mum.' But she isn't listening to me.

She's still talking, telling me that I've really gone too far this time, that this isn't like one of my other fads. I mean, it's not as if I can really take care of myself, can I? Not after everything thing else, and now what do I think, that this girl is just going to solve all my problems by—

'No, she isn't,' I say.

Mum jumps, scowls at me. 'The fact that you feel the need to be defensive about it, would suggest to me that—'

'Lauren understands,' I say. 'I told her all about it, the other day. When I went round there.'

'You went round there?' Mum says.

'Yeah, crazy I know, you'd think we were sisters, or something.'

'If you're just going to be silly like that, then, well, then there's no talking to you, is there?'

'Lauren was talking about the baby, her baby.' Mum goes to speak but I don't let her. I take a step closer and talk over her. 'She was saying, Mum, how she's worried about it, you know, worried about the whole having a baby thing, because of the story, you know?'

Mum's gone all still, watchful, but she's not trying to stop me. I've said something, a magic word to stop her from speaking. As if she's scared of me. That's it. It hits me as I'm looking at her and she's looking at me, her eyes wet glazed in the light filtered through the pulled down blind. She's scared of me.

'You know the story, Mum? The one about how you nearly died giving birth to me, how I nearly died being born, and how it was all too much for Dad, so he was going to kill himself because he thought he'd lost us both. Do you remember? I mean, you must remember, because you were there, right?'

'I don't know why you're bringing this up now,' Mum tries but she's shaking, I can see the tremble in her face, around her mouth.

'It's just we were talking about it, the other day, me and Lauren, and she said how when she was born—'

'I've really had enough of this. I don't know what's got into you, Lydia, you...you come here making God knows what accusations at me, going on about some girl and her baby, some—'

'Which one was it, Mum?' I say. 'Because the thing is,

Lauren said that was what you told her about her birth, so we were just wondering, you know, which one of us it really was?'

In the space which comes after my question, I hear the clock in the top of the gas cooker ticking, then the shuffle of footsteps. Dad coming back from the butchers. Mum hears it too, and when she registers what it is, she relaxes, a flash of victory lights up her face.

'There's your father. I don't know what he's going to say about all this, really I don't.'

'Then let's ask him, shall we?' I say it low and hard, I'm biting down on my teeth as I say it, forcing the words out slowly rather than screaming them at her. All her confidence ebbs away as it dawns on her that she's boxed herself into a corner.

'Lydia.' It's a warning at first, but then a plea. 'Lydia, please.' She reaches for the table, pulls out a chair as Dad comes in, a plastic bag bumping against his knees.

'Hello?' he says, alert to the atmosphere between us.

'Hi Dad,'

Mum's not looking at me, she sits down and reaches her hand out for Dad, only it's a half-hearted gesture.

'Gail?' Dad says as Mum tucks her hand back in her lap. He puts the bag down on the counter and goes over to her as she covers her face in her hands. 'Lydia, what's the matter with her?'

I look at them as he pats her shoulder, like a man

trying to guess what's wrong with the car engine he knows nothing about, but really feels he ought to. Dad. Always driving me down to meet Nan halfway to the cottage each summer, then to pick me up in the autumn, telling me how they'd pop down for a weekend when the weather was nice, and then never quite managing it. Dad, picking things up, fetching things, carrying things. Anything for a quiet life.

Max. Listening to me rage and scream at him, driving me to the hospital, to the clinic. Anything for a quiet life.

'I'm going to be a foster carer,' I say. 'There's this young girl staying with me, Chloe. She's been abused Dad, and now she's pregnant, so she's going to stay with me for a while, so I can look after her. Mum was just worried that it's a lot for me to take on.'

Mum blinks up at me from behind her hand.

'She's just worried about me coping, but I'm going to be fine, Dad. I'm going to be fine.'

Mum clears her throat, reaches for the cup of tea I made her and takes a sip.

'Goodness,' Dad says, 'there a turn up.'

'Please don't fuss, Kevin,' Mum says. 'Lydia will be fine, perfectly fine. She's really very capable.' She glances sideways at me, just the once. When we lock eyes just for an instant, I see her and she sees me.

I see her when I was a child, standing at the edge of her bedroom. Lauren is on the bed, her little legs kicking in the air, a tiny, pink thing on all that pink bedspread. Mum is crying, has been crying all morning. She's sitting on the floor of the bedroom, and there's nothing I can do to make her better, to make her smile. Lauren starts crying too, bucking against the bed, fists punching the air. The sound is a thin, pulled tight wail of panic, of fear, of anger. The sound cuts at me, a cheese grater of noise, and Mum is on the floor, hands over her eyes. Then she looks at me, and I see her and she sees me. I go and take Lauren from the bed. She seems to grow bigger as I gather her up, she wriggles and thrashes in my arms so I can hardly hold her, hardly move with her.

'Well, you've got what you came for?' Mum says. She's blotting her eyes with a rolled-up ball of kitchen paper, gives a sniff and tucks the ball into her sleeve. She takes Lauren from me, slips her into the bottom drawer of the bedroom cabinet and closes it. The sound of crying is muffled, and when it goes quiet, it's me who goes over and opens the drawer again, me who takes Lauren out and holds her until Daddy comes home, and the room has gone dark, and my back and arms ache from holding her.

CHAPTER THIRTY-EIGHT
The sea

CHLOE IS BLOODY hell to live with. She's untidy and ungracious and refuses to eat anything much beyond toast or chips, and watches every TV show I hate, and never cleans up. When she's in the mood, which is most of the time, she'll say anything she thinks will get a rise out of me. She slams doors, and breaks things, all of that shit. I've counted to ten more times that I can remember.

Worse than that, there are days when she says she wants to go back to him and I never know if she says it to hurt me, or if she really means it. Even though he's been arrested, denied bail, even though three of the others have already coughed to it, and five other girls have come forward, he's still refusing to admit it so we're going to trial. Even after the scar on her arm that she covers with a plaster or gloves or bracelets, or draws on with felt tip pen, even after all that, she still says she wants him back. I've learned that I have to let her say it, then wait for the wave of her anger to break over me, until it becomes crying.

'She's been a bloody nightmare,' I tell Martin, in the mental health unit's sitting room. 'But I'm hoping the move will help, getting her out of the same space as all of the bad memories.'

'Yeah,' he says. They've reduced his meds again, so he's twitchy, gnawing at the side of his finger, but he knows me better, understands who Chloe is. 'You have fun, yeah, down at the sea. Without me.'

'Don't do that. Your mum's got the address, it's one bloody train ride out of King's Cross.'

'I don't do country.' He's all hunched up in the chair, one leg crossed over the other and not looking at me. 'The only good thing about the country, is it stops all the towns getting stuck together in one big lump, innit?'

'Okay, whatever, but this isn't the country, it's the sea, there's a difference.'

'Yeah?' he says.

'I LIKE IT out here,' Nan said to me. 'With the sea at your back, feels like you can keep an eye on the rest of the buggers, without them being able to sneak up from behind.'

'What about the Vikings?' I asked.

'What about them?' Nan said. 'In my experience, make them a cup of tea and they're just pussy cats. Now gel, who's for an ice-cream?'

I GET BAD dreams. I'm walking, wading as if my legs are stuck in the mud out on the flats along the coast, and my mouth is full of tar and feathers. Chloe's ahead of me, heading out to sea, and I'm trying to call out to her, to catch hold of her because I know the ground is treacherous. But I can't run, and I can't shout and she's always walking away from me, never looking back, oblivious to the danger. When I wake I'm drowning in guilt, my skin prickling with knowing what she went through, what they did to her, made her do. When I'm being logical, when it is not three in the morning, I know I am already doing more than anyone might have expected me to do, only the voice is there in the night telling me I'm not. Telling me I could have done more, should have seen her not like everyone else did, a problem, but a victim. Then it makes me question my motives for even going this far, asks me what the fuck I'm doing. What is Chloe to me really, my consolation prize for never quite managing to be a proper mother, with my crapped-out womb and all? My "*never mind babe, let's see what you could have won*" moment? Because I can't be doing this because I'm nice, can I? Because I'm not nice, am I?

Then I'm scared someone will find out and take her away from me. Almost every week I wake up sure this is the day they'll decide against me. Sure there's nothing I can do to stop the inevitable slip of my retained material. Only this time, it sticks.

Maybe because we're united in the face of authority. We can scream at each other, but when I remember we have a social worker due, or a police liaison officer, or a child psychologist, we'll snap into team mode in an instant. We have a game plan, we do our research, we scroll through pages and pages of online info and message boards, and ask questions, all to make our case. And, in forming a united front against the rest of the world, slowly, inch by inch, as Chloe swells and yet somehow remains tiny, our unity grows. Because where we both were before was still worse, way worse, than where we are now, together.

'THE TRIAL WILL be hard as hell,' the police liaison officer says. We're in a corridor, with a red and grey carpet tiled floor, and cream paint work. We're waiting for Chloe to finish talking to another evaluator of some sort, drinking the tea. The Liaison has fair hair cut short and is wearing a self-consciously jolly jumper, no doubt not to appear threatening to Chloe, who whispered to me, 'What the fuck does she think she's wearing?' behind her hand, then couldn't stop laughing.

'I know it will be, but she's strong. I can't imagine how hard this has been for her, what she's gone through to even get this far. I can't believe that fucker is putting her through all this, I mean, we'll be able to do a paternity test, so whatever, that's a crime, right?'

'Yeah,' the liaison says, and blows on her tea. 'But I meant for you, actually. Having to watch her go through it. I bet it really hurts.'

'Yes, you're right. It really hurts.'

SOMETIMES CHLOE COMES downstairs and gets into bed with me. I don't ask what's wrong, because I know. She has a dream when he comes back for her and she screams herself awake, though she doesn't ever want me to go to her. I made that mistake once. But if she comes to me, I let her get into bed and lie with her back to me, curled in a knot about her belly with me curled around her. All three of us breathing together. She's always gone when I wake up again, and I'll lay there listening to her eating cereal in front of the TV and smell a ghost of cigarette smoke.

We're living in Gran's house now. I will have to stop calling it that. The sale of my flat is under way, which I will do quite well out of, and when the mortgage is paid off, should leave me with enough not to have to set up a new business for a year or two. Although I do have my eye on an old hairdresser on the corner of Red Lion Lane, which is only about a quarter of an hour's walk from the cottage, and which looks as if it's not doing so well. Soon as the closed sign goes up, I'm in there. The next town along to us has grown even bigger since Gran died, some artist or other came and opened a gallery. Nothing like the battered caravans full of dreary water colours we used to love, and so now it suddenly has an "old quarter" full of gastro pubs, retro vintage coffee shops and baby boutiques. The village where the cottage is, is still mostly the windswept caravan park and the Admiral Nelson and the little shop, but we're close enough to the new "old" town, to go and snigger at the hipsters and the yummy mummies braving the North Sea wind.

CHAPTER THIRTY-NINE
Angelina Mylie

ANGELINA MYLIE WESTBROOK is born two weeks early, at the very end of February. She comes screaming into the world, her skin crimson brown, and with a mass of black hair curled twenties style to her scalp.

I am Angelina's legal guardian, which means Chloe is still her mum, well, she'll always be her mum, but later, if Chloe wants to, I can apply to adopt Angelina. Chloe was sure this would be what she'd want, so she could get back on with her life but now I'm not so sure this will happen. Seeing them together, I can't imagine them ever being parted, and I don't want them to be, and they don't need to be. I don't want to take Chloe's baby from her, because I'm still not a crazy baby snatcher, whatever else I am.

I am also an Auntie, to Michael Junior, because yes, however much more I get on with Lauren now, she still can be boring as hell sometimes. Michael Junior? Seriously?

Moving a hundred miles away from Mum and Dad

has improved our relationship no end; it's not as if we have resolved anything, but I am literally able to keep them at arm's length and for now, that's all I have time for.

Sometimes it's not about answers, it's about finding a holding pattern, I think. Like we're all waiting for a chance to land. Be fine, as long as we don't run out of fuel first.

Then when I'm not really thinking about any of them, Dad rings me. He has a mobile, which he says he never uses, but he rings me on it and I'm so surprised when I see Dad flash up on the screen, I answer, almost expecting it to be some kind of elaborate hoax. There's a tremulous quality in my, 'Hello?'

'Hello, Lydia-O, it's me, Dad,' he says.

'Okay?' I say, like I'm still not convinced.

'Got something for you, might say it's a surprise,' he says, then pauses long enough for me to have to say, 'Okay?' again.

Then he speaks over me, then stops then we laugh and he says 'Next time your down, pop in, perhaps? Not, you know, a big thing, just, well, a little surprise, that's all. For you. I mean, only when you're—'

'Thursday,' I say, making the decision there and then. 'I'm coming down on Thursday.'

'Eleven,' he says, and rings off, and I'm left looking at the phone, marvelling at our longest phone conversation ever.

WHEN HE OPENS the door to me he says, 'Lydia-O. *She's* got caught up at the doctor's, will be sorry she missed you.'

'Okay.' Should I ask if *she's* going to be back soon, only his smile and the way he's ushering me over the threshold, makes me think she will be, and he wants to get something done before she is.

'Might be a while yet,' he says, glancing at the street before closing the door. 'Will be a shame...'

'Alright, Dad. Suspense is killing me.'

'Yes,' he walks away from me,' won't take long, just in here, that's all.'

I have to break into a run to catch up with him as he strides through the dining room into the conservatory.

'There,' he says.

There's something among the wicker chairs and tables, draped in an old, pink blanket. With a flourish he pulls off the blanket and stands there, beaming at me.

It's a cot—it's my cot, or our cot—the one me and Lauren went through. There used to be nightmarish giant yellow Tweetie-pie sticker on the head end, which had been scratched through, the eyes picked blank by one or other of us—we both hated that damn bird—and rows of teeth marks along the bars. But all of that's gone. He must have done it. Sanded it right back to the wood, getting round all those spoke and corners until it was clean and new. He's waxed it, at a guess, and done of one those sort of paint finishes which makes it look vintage in a considered, designer way. Shabby gone to shabby-chic.

'Dad!' I can't say anything else, because my throat's tightened and there are tears pushing behind my eyes.

'For the little one,' he says.

'Don't think it will still fit me,' I manage, and we both laugh. 'Don't you want Lauren to have it, for Michael?

He doesn't answer at first; his smile becomes sad, becomes real.

'She was very sick, you know,' he says, and I know he's talking about Mum, about when we were little.

He talks to the cot, not looking at me, speaking not fast but earnestly, as if the words have been worked on for a while, as sanded and pared back then polished as the cot.

'It was her, it was your Nan, I mean. She had a bad time with Gail. It was different then, it was different when you were born. It's never easy, but it was your grandad, thought they weren't going to make it, your nan and Gail. He went to Waterloo Bridge, meant to jump, only someone came along, saved him, and they were all right, in the end. Margaret, your nan, told me once, all about it, and I pretended I didn't know, because I don't think she knew what your Mum said, that she said it about you, about your sister. I don't know why she did it.' His eyes flick towards me for a moment as he reaches out and puts a hand on the cot, stokes his fingertips along its edge. 'She was vulnerable, after you were born, after Lauren.' He flashes me another look.

An apology, maybe?

'People didn't, you know, talk about it then.' He glances down, at my feet, at my belly, at the cot, not able to say it even now. I don't correct him; I don't say it either.

'It was my job,' he finally says, after a pause long enough for the sound of a bumble bee crashing against the glass to intrude. 'To look after her, to protect her,' now he looks at me, 'to protect you. I didn't do a very good one, did I?'

The bee hits the glass one more time, finds the gap in the invisible wall and it's off, a speck disappeared into infinity.

'It's all right, Dad.' There's too much rising inside me to say anything more. Too much love and hate and anger and understanding, and sadness and joy, until all of it rolls into a kind of relief.

'That girl, Chloe?' he says. 'You just…just do what you're doing, Lydia-O. Just be you, okay?'

I hug him then and he holds me and he smells like home, and summer, and all good things.

IT'S TUESDAY, SO I'm driving Chloe to the young mum's group at the children's centre, which is twelve miles away and has gone from being "full of fucking losers" to the best thing ever.

'I thought everyone would be, like, older than me, but they're not.'

She's due to have her six week's check there, which is being done by special arrangement, though Chloe doesn't know this, because of her situation and the safeguarding issues around her. Then, they're having an introduction to baby massage, then they get lunch, and then I think they're having some talk about baby milestones, all of which she's dead excited about.

'You can see she's, like, really advanced already, innit?' she says, twisting round in her seat to look at Angelina in her baby chair, strapped in and wrapped up. 'I mean she's like, well clever already.'

'Don't poke at her, she's nearly asleep. For God's sake, don't wake her up again.'

'What you moaning for? It's me as has to feed her, because you won't let me give her a bottle.'

'It's her that won't take one. Trust me, I'm all for it, if it might mean a whole night's sleep.'

'Fuck off,' Chloe says. 'You know breast is fucking best, and she's gonna get the best, alright?'

'You should get a job for the World Health Organisation. If you wrote their slogans, everyone would be breast feeding. No question.'

I watch her go into the centre, a grey, non-descript building with a flat roof sitting in a windswept car park. She looks tiny again, struggling with the throne like child seat, bent sideways with the weight of it and yet not broken, not bowed.

MARTIN IS NOT hard to spot getting off the train, stooping out of the carriage with that grin. I feel the blood flush in my cheeks, and something lurches inside me, though I'm not going so far as to call it my heart.

He did ring first. True, he used Margaret's phone so I thought it was her. Margaret and I have been speaking from time to time about the whole fostering thing; she offered to write some stuff for me, though she couldn't do much as she hadn't known me long enough. She'd told me he'd been discharged under a community care order and was living back with her.

'It's not Mum, it's me. Don't hang up.'

'Did you think I would?'

There was a pause, which I guess meant that yes, he thought I would.

'Thought I might come down and see you,' he said. 'Down there in the sticks.'

'I think technically it's up here in the sticks.'

'Whatever. Look, I got something to tell you.'

'I think I've had enough of surprises. Can you tell me

now?'

'No. Better in person.'

So here I am, meeting him at the station, in person.

We walk down the front and go to the Lighthouse café. The sky is blown grey and white outside the window, and as we talk the glass vibrates with the force of the wind, shuddering in its frame.

'Bit bracing, innit?' he says. He's wearing a blue great coat which might have survived the cold war by the cut of it. 'Pity the bugger who wore it first because it fits me perfect. He'd have got his head shot off when everyone else in the trenches was kneeling down.'

I don't bother to challenge his grasp of history.

We eat fish and chips because we are at the sea, and drink tea.

'I want to say sorry, like,' he says. 'I was well nuts; you didn't need all that shit. Sorry and thank, you know, for still coming to see me.'

'You don't need to apologise. How are you doing? Still nuts?'

'Still on—' and he uses some brand name as if I should know what it is. 'But that's all. No longer a high risk, you'll be pleased to hear.' He doesn't want to talk about it, or rather I can see he wants to talk about the other thing more, but he does ask about Chloe and Angelina.

'Can't believe you're a fucking granny,' he says, with a

grin so sly it almost slips off his face.

'Fuck you, I'm not a granny,' I snap as he sniggers into his tea. 'I'm fostering a girl who's had a baby, that does not make me a grandmother. Just get on with it.'

'With what?'

'With what you're here to tell me, you've been jiggling your foot for the last five minutes, and when you do, the whole bloody table judders.'

He gets out his phone and shows me a picture 'What do you think it is?'

I look but can't make it into anything more significant than a blurred crowd shot, taken in a cafe or a bar, somewhere hot and sunny. The person who might be the focus of the picture, has raised their hand to cover part of their face, as if it's a paparazzi snap.

'I don't know. What is it?'

He takes the phone back and sets it between us. He doesn't want to say yet, there's a story to be told first and he's full of the telling of it. The window thrums with the wind, and spots of rain rattle against the glass.

'When it happened, yeah, when Josie got … took,' he says as if he's reaching for the right word, one that makes it less his fault, 'there were loads of people wanting to help, yeah? Her school friend's dads and that, my friends, they were all well up for getting whoever done it, before the police said as they thought it were her Dad after all.'

'You do know that's the truth, right?' I say. 'That he'd

have taken her eventually, whatever you—'

'Yeah, yeah, look,' he taps the phone again. 'She had this friend, right, at school? Alice, 'bout the same age, and she were well cut up. I mean, we all was, but they were best friends, you know? Anyway, we moved away in the end, year or so after, back to London, so I didn't see her again, this Alice. But she got in touch, when I was, you know, bad. Well, her Dad did first any-road, looked up Mum and asked to come round.'

The waitress comes over and asks if we're done, and if everything was alright, and if we'd like to see the dessert menu.

'Big lad like you's gonna want feedin' up,' she says, and gives me a mother-to-mother kind of wink. Martin grins down at her and orders an ice-cream sundae. When she's cleared our plates, he puts his hands out on the table fingers placed as if he were about to play the piano.

'So, her and her Dad come round to see Mum, say it's important. Mum said they'd been away to one of them Greek islands for the summer, because her Dad has this place out there. Kefalonia, yeah?'

'Right?' I say.

He drops his piano stance and points at the phone again. 'Long story, Alice only goes and sees her there.'

I frown at him, 'What, she sees…?'

'Josie Bee!' he says. He's bursting with it now, scrabbling to get to the picture on his phone again. 'Of course at first she weren't sure. She told her Dad, and he said well, if it is Josie, didn't she recognise you? And this Alice says she wasn't sure, but she thought she might have, but acted like she was trying not to. So her Dad, he said to see if she could talk to her, and so when she sees her again, she did. This girl, she had a bit of an accent, but Alice didn't ask her name or nothing, she played it fucking cool yeah, an' the girl said her name was Josie, just like that.' He holds up the photo again. It could be a girl, the person with their hand up, and they could possibly have dark hair. The skin of their hand is rendered white by the flash, and their face? If it was taken in Kefalonia, she could just be a tanned Greek girl, or a girl on holiday, or…

'I never knew her,' I say, not wanting to hurt him, not wanting to encourage him. I look at the hand that holds the phone, at the wrist that's been exposed by his shirt cuff now his great coat is slung on the back of the chair. Criss-cross, criss-cross, all those little white lines. He put the phone down again.

'Thing is,' he says, 'she got a bit funny then, this girl. Alice said she asked her about London, if this Josie was from there, had she ever been, and this girl goes all quiet and says she has to go. Alice asked if she could take her picture, but the girl put her hand up because she didn't want her to, see?'

He thinks this is significant. His eyes are bright with it, and I can almost see the story he's made for himself.

Josie Bee, living on an island with her ex-con Dad, smuggled out through contacts he had from the bad old days. Josie, growing up being told that if someone came asking about her, someone from London, then she was to let him know right away because it would mean trouble. Not trouble for her, but for him, some old enemy with a score to settle. I can see it all, how Martin wants it to be, that she's in danger and he has to go and save her.

'What you going to do?' I ask.

'You think it could be her, right?' He looks so bright, so eager. I wonder if he's turned twenty yet.

'Martin, I just don't know. It could be, and it couldn't, and either way I've no idea, and my telling you I did would be a lie, wouldn't it?'

He nods, his expression serious. 'Yeah, you're right, I know. But it's a chance, innit?'

'Did you tell the police?' I ask, in the hope that he has and that they've been kind to him.

'Yeah, Mum did already. They took it serious, made a report and that. Said they'd contact the police on the island, but they didn't have a record of anyone like her there, or her Dad.'

Which clearly hasn't been enough to dissuade him. What would be? What would be enough to stop him trying again?

'I'm going out there,' he says when we're outside again, and I've paid the bill, seeing as he had to borrow the money for the train from his mum. 'Not now, because, you know, but when I'm one hundred percent. This summer, I'm going out there, get a job or something, see what I can find. You're not going to stop me, then, going to find her?'

'Do you want me to?' I ask.

'Not sure. Don't even think you could.'

'Well then. That told me.'

'Anyway, what you gonna do?'

'This, what I'm doing now. Chloe's going to school after the summer, the council are supporting her back into education, as they put it, so I'm going to be on childcare for them both, along with nurseries and that, for a year or so at least. That's the plan anyway. We'll be okay, I've got the income from my share of Asylum back in London, and I'm gonna set up here.'

'Lot of call for tattoos round here, is there?' he asks. We've reached the road that leads up to the station, standing together in the shelter of a deserted bus stop, wind snatching at us from around the glass walls.

'You'd be surprised. It's knee deep in hipsters when the sun comes out. Like I say, the sea's always been good for tattoos. It's like people see it, and need to make a mark in the sand, just to prove they're alive, in the face of all that eternity.'

'That's bollocks, it's because of sailors.' He takes my hand then, which he has to stoop a little to do, then stoops a little further to kiss me on the cheek.

'I've got a couple of hours before my train goes. Where's your place from here, then?'

'Erm…I don't think that's a good idea, do you?'

He shakes his head. 'Yes, I do. I think it's a blinding idea, since you ask.'

'Martin, haven't we kind of been here before?'

He takes hold of my other hand. 'Look, I've been on fucking kick-ass meds for ages, and I ain't even got it up for months, not till last week.'

'Oh, I see, so that's why you come all the way down here, then?'

'No, I came all the way down here to tell you about Josie Bee, innit?' He shrugs. 'The fucking you part is just a bonus.'

'And after we fuck, then what do we do?'

'Look, it's been a while, one's probably all I've got in me.'

'No.' I pull my hands free and slap him on the arm. 'I've spent months being assessed and deemed a fit and proper person and talking down the caution for possession you landed me with. I'm not that person anymore, and I can't fuck you ever again, Martin. Not now I've met your mum.'

Martin laughs his Sid James laugh, *waugh-waugh-waugh,* and the seagulls overhead screech along, as if they get the joke too. I catch sight of us in the glass of the bus stop, our mismatched reflections rippling over the surface of an advertisement.

'Worth an ask,' he says.

I wait with him at the station, neither of us saying much. When his train comes in, he kisses me once more and twirls away from me into the carriage. I start walking away almost at once, though I do look back as the train pulls away and for a split second, we see each other and I see the width of his grin, wide as the London horizon glimpsed from a balcony on a lost Sunday morning. Then he's gone and I am gone too, walking away downhill towards the sea, to my home, the wings on my back stretching out wide to catch the wind and get me there faster.

ACKNOWLEDGMENTS

Thanks to Andy, Ben and all my friends for their continued support and patience, and to Amanda Saint for believing in me.

Read more from Retreat West Books.

WHAT WAS LEFT, VARIOUS
20 winning and shortlisted stories from the 2016 Retreat West Short Story and Flash Fiction Prizes. A past that comes back to haunt a woman when she feels she has no future. A man with no mind of his own living a life of clichés. A teenage girl band that maybe never was. A dying millionaire's bizarre tasks for the family hoping to get his money. A granddaughter losing the grandfather she loves.

AS IF I WERE A RIVER, AMANDA SAINT
Kate's life is falling apart. Her husband has vanished without a trace—just like her mother did. Laura's about to do something that will change her family's lives forever—but she can't stop herself. Una's been keeping secrets—but for how much longer?

NOTHING IS AS IT WAS, VARIOUS
A charity anthology of climate-fiction stories raising funds for the Earth Day Network. A schoolboy inspired by a conservation hero to do his bit; a mother trying to save her family and her farm from drought; a world that

doesn't get dark anymore; and a city that lives in a tower slowly being taken over by the sea.

SEPARATED FROM THE SEA, AMANDA HUGGINS

Separated From the Sea is the debut short story collection from award-winning author, Amanda Huggins. Crossing oceans from Japan to New York and from England to Havana, these stories are filled with a sense of yearning, of loss, of not quite belonging, of not being sure that things are what you thought they were. They are stories imbued with pathos and irony, humour and hope.

IMPERMANENT FACTS, VARIOUS

20 winning stories from the 2017 Retreat West Short Story and Flash Fiction Prizes. A woman ventures out into a marsh at night seeking answers about herself that she cannot find; a man enjoys the solitude when his wife goes away for a few days; and a father longs for the daughter.

THIS IS (NOT ABOUT) DAVID BOWIE, FJ MORRIS

Every day we dress up in other people's expectations. We button on opinions of who we should be, we Instagram impossible ideals, tweet to follow, and comment to judge. But what if we could just let it all go? What if we took off our capes and halos, threw away our uniforms, let go of the future? What if we became who we were always supposed to be? Human.

This is (not about) David Bowie. It's about you. This Is (Not About) David Bowie is the debut flash fiction collection from F.J. Morris. Surreal, strange and beautiful it shines a light on the modern day from the view of the outsider. From lost souls, to missing sisters, and dying lovers to superheroes, it shows what it really is to be human in a world that's always expecting you to be something else.

REMEMBER TOMORROW, AMANDA SAINT

England, 2073. The UK has been cut off from the rest of the world and ravaged by environmental disasters. Small pockets of survivors live in isolated communities with no electricity, communications or transportation, eating only what they can hunt and grow.

Evie is a herbalist, living in a future that's more like the past, and she's fighting for her life. The young people of this post-apocalyptic world have cobbled together a new religion, based on medieval superstitions, and they are convinced she's a witch. Their leader? Evie's own grandson.

Weaving between Evie's current world and her activist past, her tumultuous relationships and the terrifying events that led to the demise of civilised life, Remember

Tomorrow is a beautifully written, disturbing and deeply moving portrait of an all-too-possible dystopian world, with a chilling warning at its heart.

RESURRECTION TRUST, VARIOUS

A collection of funny, dark, mad, bad, upbeat, downbeat and fantastical short stories about living sustainably from the University of Southampton's Green Stories writing competition.

From eco communities to singing buildings, and sharing economies to resetting the earth back to prehistoric times, these stories showcase a myriad of different ideas about how humans can live more harmoniously with nature, and each other.

SOUL ETCHINGS, SANDRA ARNOLD

Death, motherhood, the nature of reality, and the gender expectations of cultural conditioning are woven through these biting little stories in Sandra Arnold's debut flash fiction collection. Sometimes sad, surreal and sinister, they're also shot through with love and a deep understanding of humanity.

In gorgeous, spare prose that paints a vivid picture, Sandra Arnold gives voice to characters that are often unheard. From Daisy in Fireworks Night, willing to do whatever it takes to protect her little sister; to Martha in

The Girl With Green Hair who has her body in the world we live in and her mind in the one that not many people see; and Ruby in Don't Mess With Vikings who finds strength in a diagnosis of illness to stand up to bullies. With the stories in this collection, Sandra Arnold etches marks on your soul that will last.

http://retreatwestbooks.com

Lightning Source UK Ltd.
Milton Keynes UK
UKHW021259061119
353004UK00011B/611/P

9 781916 069305